HANAH'S SHEEP AND CATTLE

A Yiddish Book Center Translation

A volume in the NIU Series in
SLAVIC, EAST EUROPEAN, AND EURASIAN STUDIES
Edited by Christine D. Worobec

For a list of books in the series, visit our website at cornellpress.cornell.edu.

Hanah's Sheep and Cattle

A Novel

Shira Gorshman

Translated and edited, with an
Afterword, by Edith Otchin McCrea

Foreword by David Shulman

Northern Illinois University Press
an imprint of
Cornell University Press
Ithaca and London

A Yiddish Book Center Translation

Copyright © 2025 by Cornell University

First published 2025 by Cornell University Press

Librarians: A CIP catalog record for this book is available from the Library of Congress.

ISBN 9781501783517 (paperback)
ISBN 9781501783531 (pdf)
ISBN 9781501783524 (epub)

GPSR EU contact: Sam Thornton, Mare Nostrum Group B.V., Mauritskade 21D, 1091 GC, Amsterdam, NL, gpsr@mare-nostrum.co.uk.

CONTENTS

FOREWORD

Shira Gorshman lived one emblematic trajectory of Jewish life in the twentieth century. In some senses, it was heroic. Born into an Orthodox family in a village in Kovno province (today Kaunas), Lithuania, in 1906, she was educated in Hebrew by her grandfather; she left home at fourteen, married at fifteen, had a daughter at sixteen. Shortly thereafter, she and her husband moved to Mandatory Palestine, where they joined the famous pioneer movement known as the Work Brigade, Gdud Haavodah. It was hard work—paving roads, quarrying stones, building houses, and so on. Like so many in her generation, Shira was firmly situated within the inherently fissiparous continuum of the socialist-to-communist left. In 1926 the movement split in two—the radical communist faction, a minority, and the moderate Zionist socialists. Shira, gifted with a fiery temperament, stayed with the former; her husband sided with the latter. (Note that neither group even noticed the very existence of Palestinian Arabs.) Shira followed the charismatic dominant leader Mendel Elkind to Russia, where for several years she worked in an agricultural and cowherding commune in the Crimea until Stalin dissolved it, arrested many of its members, and sent Elkind to his death.

Shira survived, largely thanks to her second husband, Mendel Gorshman, a gentle artist, who took her and the children to Moscow. There she struggled through the hardships and terror of the 1930s and then the war years—documented in telling detail in her lightly veiled (actually, entirely transparent) autobiographical novel. During the war she was evacuated to the Volga region. She was already an accomplished writer in Yiddish, though Yiddish writing was unpublishable in postwar Stalinist Russia. Her husband died in 1974. In 1990 she came (back, or maybe even "home," from her own perspective) to Israel. Despite the conventional distaste for Yiddish on the part of the new generations of native Hebrew speakers, she found an eager audience for her works. She died in 2001.

She chose to write in her mother tongue, though she could easily have written in Russian. The choice merits our attention. In a sense, Shira can be situated in the eastern periphery of the secular Yiddish renaissance of the 1920s and 1930s in Warsaw, Odessa, and Moscow (and later, New York). Today only specialists and aficionados of modern Yiddish honor the vast literary production of those decades, with its particular version of European humanism at its best and its endless, resonant corpus of Jewish intertexts, mostly in Hebrew. Shira knew that corpus from her childhood, and she must have read and internalized the classical Yiddish canon of the nineteenth and early twentieth centuries. She also tells us that she avidly read Chekhov, Tolstoy, Dickens, and Cervantes. But her novel is clearly, above all, an attempt to record not merely her own wildly adventurous life but also her unusual, rich innerness—her dreams, her endless cumulation of sharp psychic pain, her one enduring love, her profound conflicts, her stubbornness—in a world of imposed ideological orthodoxy and continuous danger. She witnessed, though she only rarely hints at, the disintegration of the Russian communist utopia to which she had, early on, committed herself. In that sense, she belongs also with the great Russian writers of the mid-twentieth century, the surpassing artists such as Pasternak, Mandelshtam, Akhmatova, and Platonov as well as many lesser lights. Reading her novel, one can actually hear, or overhear, the debates among the Russian intellectuals and artists of that period. In fact, much of the novel is taken up with her reconstruction of those often tormented conversations, almost as if we were reading a play that could never be staged.

This book articulates and records, indirectly, an innerness confronting a world where hope and belief in human beings are continually eroded by despair and almost unthinkable privation. And although the novel has relatively little to say about her formative years in Palestine, and nothing to say about her final years in Israel, there is something moving about reading her life now, at a time when the State of Israel is also overwhelmed by despair and self-generated moral decay. I suppose the adjective "heroic" which I used at the outset must mean the uncanny ability to survive, physically and spiritually, in conditions of recurrent adversity. In the videos that we are fortunate to have of Shira Gorshman in her last decade, we see at once how tough she was, even in her eighties and nineties, and also how compassionate and full of life she could be—how wise in the wisdom of a survivor who has forgotten nothing.

David Shulman

TRANSLATOR'S NOTE

Rather than employing the YIVO orthographic system of Yiddish transliteration, I have used my own system for spelling names and other Yiddish words in this book. In so doing, I hope to make the translation as accessible as possible to the general public, even if this means occasionally sacrificing some authenticity of sound.

First and foremost, I have chosen to transliterate the name "Hanah" in a way that will look relatively familiar to English readers. In the YIVO system, the name is rendered "Khane." That initial "Kh" represents a guttural that does not exist in English. (It is often likened to the final sound in the German surname "Bach.") In most names that begin with this sound, I have used "H" (Hanah, Hayaleh, Hayim). (One exception is the Yiddish poet Izi Kharik, whose surname is usually spelled with a "Kh" in the field of Yiddish studies.) Where the guttural appears in the middle or at the end of a name or word, I have used either an "h" (as in the name Nehemyah) or a "ch" (as in the name Borech).

I have rendered the English "ch" sound (as in "cheese") as "tch" in Yiddish nicknames (Hanatchke, Hayatchke, etc.) to differentiate it from the guttural "ch." In Russian male patronymics, however, I have transliterated this sound simply as "ch" (for example, in Nikolai Nikolaevich and Fyodor Petrovich).

More generally, I have spelled Russian and Ukrainian names and words using the most common form of transliteration of these languages into English (Chekhov, Chuvashia, Kharkov, *khudozhnik*, Mikhail, etc.), although this orthography is different from the one I use for Yiddish words.

The YIVO system transliterates the English "j" sound (as in "jump") with three letters: "dzh." I have chosen simply to use a "j" instead (for example, in the place-names Jabahi and Jankoy). I do, however, follow the YIVO system of rendering the "French j" sound as "zh" (as in the place-name Zhmerynka).

I have rendered the last vowel sound in Hebrew-derived names that end with a *hey* (such as Hanah and Nehemyah) as "ah" (although in Yiddish it is pronounced like a short "e"). In nicknames that end with an *ayin,* I have used a standalone "e" wherever possible (as in Shimke or Rivke). In cases where a final "e" might be misconstrued as silent, I have added an "h" after it (as in Hanakeh, Hayaleh, Pereleh, Shifraleh, etc.).

In Yiddish, the placement of an "l" at the end of a name or word is a way of creating a diminutive. In such words, I have added an "e" before the "l" (thus Mendel, not Mendl).

Gorshman uses Yiddish versions of many place-names (such as Moskve). If there is a well-known English name for a place (such as Moscow), I usually use it; otherwise, I generally spell the place-name as it is most commonly spelled today, so that the reader will be able to locate it easily on a map. More information about many places named in the text is provided in the glossary.

For some Yiddish words that have been adopted into English, I have used a common English spelling and have not used italics (challah, chuppah, mensch, schlimazel). I have put less familiar Yiddish words, as well as untranslated Russian words, in italics.

One important aspect of the YIVO orthographic system which I have retained is the rendering of diphthongs. Thus, in Yiddish names and words in the novel, "ay" rhymes with "pie," and "ey" rhymes with "they."

Shira Gorshman produced three different versions of *Hanah's Sheep and Cattle.* The first was a novella published in a Soviet collection of her work in 1974. The second was a much longer version published in another Soviet collection in 1984. The third version was a standalone novel published in Israel in 1993. While the Israeli edition is very similar to the 1984 Soviet version in most respects, there are a few notable changes, some of which have resulted in minor inconsistencies within the 1993 text. I have pointed these out in the endnotes so that the reader will be aware of them.

On a few occasions, I have omitted or added words or phrases in order to make the text easier to understand. The most significant instances are described in the endnotes. I have also noted expressions that may be unfamiliar to the reader and those for which I have been unable to find a provenance.

Unless otherwise noted, all translations from the Yiddish in the text and the notes are mine.

Shira Gorshman's Acknowledgments

My most heartfelt blessings and thanks to the friends and dear people whose hands and efforts have enabled this book of mine to see the light of day:

The gentle, noble Hebrew poet **Daniel Ben Nahum** z″l, from Beit Zera;
The tireless Yiddish poet **Meir Harats;**
The well-known writer, Chairman of the Yiddish Writers Union in Israel,
  Mr. **Mordechai Tsarin;**
The poet-essayist, the meticulous guardian of the Yiddish word, **Yakov**
  Tsvi Shargel;
His helpmate, the devoted proofreader Mrs. **Fireh Shargel;**
The hardworking, sincere publisher **Efraim Ben-David;**

The dear **Miriam Royzn,** who "banged out" almost 800 pages on her
    typewriter;
The **Sarah Idelson** group of Beit Zera;
My friend **Michal Vigodski** from Beit Avot in Ashkelon;
My friend **Yerachmiel Kaspi.**

יבואו כולם, כולם על הברכה!
[Everyone come, everyone is welcome!]
S. G.

I

Day in and day out, Hanah was trapped within her own ceaseless thoughts. Not a day went by when she didn't compare everything around her with what she'd been torn away from, thanks to Mendel Elkind. By now it was all too clear he was not the visionary she had believed him to be. Not only was he unable to see the future, but he was filled with insatiable ambition. It could be, she thought, that all of this was his elaborate way of humiliating Ben-Gurion, by showing him what a great commune he could build in Crimea from the leftist Gdudniks. Thinking about it was enough to rub salt into her very soul.

Now, day after day in the late summer of 1930, Hanah rode around on her horse and sprinkled salt on the withered grass of the clay-cracked Crimean steppe. Her goal was to entice the cattle to curl their long, bristly tongues more eagerly around the desiccated yellow fodder, which looked about as appetizing as frayed burlap. Although the salt crystals were dark, they glittered in the sun like broken glass, standing out brightly against the drab soil and dry vegetation. The horse was careful in the placement of his well-polished hooves, with their light-brown tufts at the ankles; his light-brown mane fanned out in the wind, and his round breast muscles showed clearly through his thin brown hide. Hanah did not steer; the reins lay on the horse's neck. But whenever he tried to change his gait, she would speak to him quietly and earnestly: "Now, now, Borech, I know how clever you are, but no mischief! Be a mensch!" In response, Borech would immediately resume his smooth ambling gait, and Hanah would stroke his warm neck with her small, calloused hand, grab another handful of salt out of the sack, and scatter it to make the wretched grass more appealing.

Quiet, free, aglow through and through, the vast emptiness of the steppe stretched out to the very rim of the sky. A resounding echo of Hanah's own singing returned to her ears. The melody, though wordless, was clearly a great lament about herself and all the others who'd been torn away from Palestine by Mendel Elkind. At the sound of Hanah's deep, ringing voice, Borech's ears twitched and a thin, mild whinny issued from his throat, as though he were sympathizing with the complaint of his beloved rider. Yes—beloved; for Hanah treated Borech almost as her equal. She never raised her voice to him; she carried no whip, no stick in her hand when she rode. On the morning when she had first led Borech into the stable, she'd said to Shimke:

"You see what kind of royalty I've brought home? Please make sure you don't harness him for anyone else, not even the Chairman. His name is Borech, and he's my horse."

"What do you mean, your horse? On a commune nobody owns anything, and everybody owns everything." Shimke tried to explain the matter. But Hanah interrupted him:

"Do me a favor: don't tell me what I know—listen to what I tell you! From now on, not only am I in charge of a lot of cows and sheep, I'm lucky enough to have my own horse, too. But please, keep this just between us. Yesterday, when I expressed a few words about our expulsion, Tsiperke Bril said to me: 'What don't you like about it here? Internationalism is always better than stinking nationalism!' So I'm asking you, please, try to remember that we're not in Palestine anymore. The Secret Police are our next-door neighbors."

Since that conversation, quite a bit of time had passed. Now, out on the steppe, Hanah watched Borech's narrow ears prick up and heard his thin, delicate whinny. Thinking he sensed danger, she loosened her fist in the sack of salt and momentarily forgot what to do. But everything was still the same: the steppe extended unbroken to the horizon; the reins lay loose on the horse's neck. Reassured, she began to sing again, and her bare heels, which were deeply cracked and stained with dried blood, gently rose and fell as the horse's belly heaved with his young, vigorous breathing. The age of the horse, as far as Hanah could tell from examining his teeth, was no more than four years. Hanah was twenty-three. Given the number of years a horse can live and the span of time destined for a human, she calculated that the two of them were the same age. (She also had another good reason to consider him her contemporary, but more about that later.)

By the time the Crimean sun was fully ablaze, both salt bags hung empty on Hanah's shoulders. She and Borech had already covered quite a few hectares, and the horse knew it was time to go to the verdant gully that lay near the village of Jabahi. Ever so slowly, he lowered himself down the steep slope. Hanah jumped down, landing on her tiptoes so the cracks in her heels wouldn't get any worse. As soon as she'd loosened Borech's saddle and tossed it onto the thick, soft grass that grew in the gully, the horse started running back and forth with a resounding neigh. Then he lay down on his back and began rolling from side to side, so that at one moment his legs stuck up toward the sky and the next moment they lay stretched out on the grass.

Hanah watched this performance attentively, as always. Then she climbed out of the gully and let out—not a song, but a sort of primal girl-scream; bent her knees; and rolled down the bank. She did this several times in a row. Borech stood up, and as Hanah lay in the grass, he slowly walked over and lowered his muzzle to her, his lips lifting into a little wrinkle, as though he were smiling at Hanah's playfulness. Hanah started giggling because his muzzle was tickling her shoulder.

Mischievous as Hanah was, she was already the mother of three little girls. Like all the children on the commune, they lived in the Children's Home—and like all the mothers, she went about her work free from the yoke of child-rearing. Hanah was the head of the Livestock Brigade. This was no easy task. She had enough worries about the fodder, about how the silage was to be packed into the storage towers; in addition, she had to make sure the cattle were attended to punctually, the cans of fresh milk were sent off to the health spa at Saki, the Children's Home and kitchen need not wait on any dairy products. And on top of all that, she also had to milk the cows three times a day, just like any other milkmaid. There was some justification for this: the cows that had hard udders or cracked teats, those that would not stay on their feet for even a moment, or that constantly waved their tails—all calmly allowed themselves to be milked by her.

As she milked, she would croon softly, "Hagar, stay, you little dear, you little love, a blessing on your hind legs . . ." And the dairy workers would watch in wonder as Hagar, who was known as a wild, wily thing, never once kicked over the pail that Hanah held firmly between her knees.

* * *

The sun was beaming over the wasted steppe when Hanah rode out of the gully. An uneasy feeling came over her. It seemed to her that not only was she all alone out here, but even when she arrived back at the commune, she wouldn't meet another living soul.

She had ridden out right after the first milking, at dawn. Needless to say, she hadn't eaten breakfast. Now it was eleven o'clock, and hunger tugged at her belly. She sat loose in the saddle, her legs dangling by the horse's sides, her head rocking back and forth. If someone had caught a glimpse of her at that moment, he would have been sure she was napping. But Hanah was awake and, God knows why, her mind was once again flooding with thoughts.

No one else, she thought, ever seemed to get into as much trouble as she did. "I was in too much of a hurry, didn't listen to what my parents said, and it turned out they were right. But taking back what I've done—that would be like trying to catch the wind in a handkerchief!" This brought to mind her former husband, who was fifteen years older than herself. She didn't have the slightest bit of regret that she'd left him right after giving birth to their third daughter. And, swinging along in the saddle, Hanah reflected that the men on a commune were, in one respect at least, no better than men anywhere else.

Very often she found herself turning down unsolicited attention. For example, last week after supper, Hayim from the Field Brigade had said:

"Hanakeh, let's go for a stroll, it's a shame for a treasure like you to go to waste. Being out on the steppe is such a thrill! Stars fall by the bucketful!"

Hanah didn't say what lay on the tip of her tongue, because everybody knows a mother of three shouldn't be choosy. Instead, she looked at him with a mixture of surprise and disappointment, and remarked unenthusiastically:

"Tell me, Hayimke, if I did go out on the steppe with you, would the stars stop falling? Or would the fallen stars go back up into the sky?"

Hayimke barely took in what she was saying. He shrugged his shoulders and casually tossed back:

"A no is a no."

By the time he said it, Hanah was already striding off toward the new building, where she had a room—or, more precisely, shared a room with two other women, Rivke and Yocheved. This wasn't the only such incident; there were other interested parties besides Hayim. She had even heard from Yisrolik, who was always sweaty and covered with soot from the smithy:

"Hanatchke, when someone has three children, she doesn't have anything left to protect!"

And Hanah had held her tongue.

All of this she was now remembering, and it was all very disappointing.

Borech walked slowly along, his hind feet matching up precisely with his front ones. It seemed as though he, too, were remembering something. Hanah looked at him through her lowered eyelashes and patted his neck to urge him on. Entering the commune at a trot, she noticed right away that an odd group of people were standing in the middle of the yard. It wasn't so much the people themselves who were odd as the polished wooden cases hanging from their shoulders by leather straps. Mysterious objects in cloth coverings were also in evidence, as well as large, flat rectangular packages wrapped in canvas. There were several ordinary suitcases, too.

Hanah seized the reins with her right hand so that Borech's head jerked up and he came to a halt—otherwise, she and the horse would have run right into the gathering. As she rode past the guests at close range, she turned around in the saddle and spotted a very tall young man with curly blond hair and a nose so long that she found herself thinking, "Can there actually be a mouth under such a long snoot?" She also caught a glimpse of a short, swarthy fellow with a shaggy mop of pitch-black hair and a slender woman in a low-cut *sarafan* dress. Last of all was another man—also short, but dark and handsome. He was wearing a *tubeteyke* cap on his head, and it seemed to her that a heartfelt smile arose on his longish, delicate face when he saw her spurring the horse with her bare feet.

At the stable she unsaddled Borech and said to the groom:

"Just our luck, Shimke, we have guests. As if I don't have enough to do! On top of everything else, I'm Chair of the Culture Committee. There will be the usual questions about what kind of commune this is, how it got started . . ."

Hanah would have gone on, but Shimke consoled her:

"Don't worry, Hanakeh, maybe these people have nothing to do with the Culture Committee; maybe they're surveyors."

"No, no, this place has already been measured a thousand times," Hanah declared, and went off to eat.

*　*　*

There is a saying that fate comes knocking at the door. But the door to the dining hall, where the guests were now sitting together, was already wide open when Hanah walked in. She was greeted at the entrance by a hovering cloud of flies, which filled her with disgust. To make matters worse, the dining hall had no ceiling; birds perched on the exposed rafters, and their "extraneous matter" fell thickly into the room below. The earthen floor was also rather uneven; last week it had rained, and the boots of the communards had carried in a lot of clay, which had now hardened. Not only did all of this irritate Hanah, it gave her an intense feeling of embarrassment. She walked quickly to the kitchen window, took a chipped enamel plate loaded with thick grayish barley gruel, and seated herself at the very last table—as far from the guests as possible.

Before she had managed to eat half of what was on her plate, a flock of snow-white roosters and hens let themselves in through the open door and scattered all over the room. At the same moment, Rochke walked out of the kitchen, carrying two plates in each hand for the guests. She quickly set the plates down and began driving the fowl away, but some of the spooked chickens settled on the table. The guests stood up and started waving their arms, too. The chickens flew off the table and fluttered around the room, but they were so agitated that they couldn't find the door to get out.

Hanah was too flustered to understand at first why the guests weren't re-seating themselves. She set her plate down and ran to the table where they were standing. Discovering the "calling cards" that the chickens had left behind, she dashed off to the kitchen and quickly returned with a rag and a teapot full of water. Soon, the guests had the opportunity not only to sit at a clean table but also to observe Hanah's firm, agile brown hands, her slanted blue eyes, her prominent cheekbones with a flush of pink struggling through the suntanned skin. As she worked, she pursed her full, fresh lips, which were so red they looked as though they had just been cut by a sharp knife. The guests forgot all about their gray porridge and followed Hanah's every move, spellbound.

Hanah also got a good look at each of the visitors. For a fleeting moment she glanced at the handsome one, with his long, delicate face and his gentle smile. But she made no further attempt to eat. Filled with bitter shame, she left the dining hall.

She led Borech out of the stable, hastily saddled him up, clambered onto his back, and fitted her bare feet into the stirrups. The horse set off with his floating, even gait, out onto the steppe and along the familiar trail to the herd. From a distance Hanah could see the cart with its raised shafts, the cattle, the cowherds, the milkmaids with their red or white kerchiefs. She pulled firmly on the reins, and the horse slowed his pace and came to a stop right next to the cart.

Hanah flew out of the saddle, and her powerful voice rang out over the steppe:

"Toybe, why are you wandering around like you're lost in the woods? Did you lose your cow—*again?*"

The question was full of reproach and mockery, and not without reason. Hanah was continually amazed at how the milkmaids roamed the steppe like sleepwalkers, unable to recognize the very cows they'd been milking three times a day for the past two years. How many times had she said: "Notice how the cows in the barn always press up against the same neighbors? Well, they arrange themselves the same way out on the steppe."

More than any other milkmaid, Toybe was incapable of identifying her cows. Hanah had literally led her by the hand from one animal to another and vigorously explained:

"Take a look. Gera always lies next to Viktoria, Havah lies next to Juliet, and the rest are the same way. Don't you have eyes, you damn fool? You look, but you see nothing!"

So many times Hanah had asked the milkmaids to do as she did. She explained that they should not wash one cow's udders and then start milking her right away; instead, they should wash the udders of two or three cows in a row to stimulate their milk flow, and then go back and start milking the first. That way, by the time they got to the third cow, its milk would be flowing, and the whole process would go more quickly.

Now she came up to Shifrah Grinblat and said harshly:

"Shifrah, I'm going to tell the cows they should milk *you*. Why don't you ever listen? Take your leg away from her belly!"

Hanah demonstrated, explained, scolded. Finally, she took a tin pail and went away to milk "her" cow. Soon she returned with a full pail and stepped up on the wheel of the cart as she poured the milk through the straining cloth tied to the can. Glancing at Borech, she noticed he was standing in the blazing sun, so she took off her kerchief and tied it around his head, with two corners shading his eyes. Borech stood perfectly still until she was done; then he slowly headed off to the ravine, whickering softly as though to say, "I'll come back soon."

Hanah prepared to follow him to take care of a certain personal need. Noticing this, Ruvke the Cowherd joked:

"Hantche, I'm jealous of Borech . . ."

But more than that he didn't manage to say, because Hanah gave him a withering look and, despite her urgent need, blurted out:

"Mr. Ruven, I swear on my life, there are more brains in Borech's head than in yours!"

With that, she ran off with the "honey bucket" to do what she had to do.

* * *

That was how Hanah's days went. She could barely carve out a single hour to run over to the Children's Home and see her daughters. But that hour was always the most peaceful and precious of the whole twenty-four.

For the next three or four days Hanah didn't see the guests, but she certainly heard plenty about them during her roommates' evening gossip sessions.

"The *khudozhniks* sleep on the straw stacks!" Yochve reported.

"And rightly so," Rivke approved. "Our bedbugs have never tasted such fine fare; if the *khudozhniks* used our beds, they'd get eaten alive. Yesterday they were all out in the garden, standing around with their easels. They wanted to sketch Feyge, but they couldn't convince her to stand still long enough. How can she stand still when she's supposed to be loading tomatoes into the wheelbarrow? So they got mad, grabbed their gear, and went off to the silos."

That was how Hanah learned that the newcomers were artists, and on subsequent evenings she heard more about them when her roommates discussed what these artists were painting.

"I went over and stood behind one of them," Yocheved related. "He was painting the haystacks blue, the oxen and the cart pink, and the ground—yellow. I thought I would explode with laughter! So I went off to the wagon shed. But later, after the boys had eaten and I was washing the pots, he walked right in on me."

"Which *he* was it?" asked Rivke.

"The one with the blond curly hair. 'Well,' he says to me, 'what's your name? I want to get to know you.' 'They call me Yocheved,' I say, 'but you don't have any reason to get to know me. I already have a boyfriend.' He looks at me, gives a yawn, and says, 'Oh? Good for you!' And that was that."

"You see? Just drawing pictures of us isn't enough for them . . . But why did you turn him down? If I'd been in your place, I would have gotten acquainted," Rivke remarked.

"Such brilliant women," thought Hanah, and fell asleep.

At daybreak, when she got up for the first milking, she remembered her roommate's low opinion of the artists' work. At first it annoyed her that the ignorant Yocheved thought she understood something about art; then the absurdity of this conceit made her laugh out loud as she walked through the dim, empty yard to the dairy barn. At that hour, the single tree near the Children's Home stood veiled in chilly silence; not a leaf was moving. The air was cool; the forge, the silos, the new dormitory, the sentry box, and the old house that had been built before the Revolution—all were wrapped in nighttime slumber. Then, from the barn came a clattering of milk cans and tin pails. A new day had begun.

Although Hanah was soon engrossed in her work, she was occasionally pierced by a feeling of shame at the primitive living conditions that surrounded her. "How can we teach others," she thought, "if we ourselves don't want to learn, and enlightened women like Yocheved, who have never laid eyes on an artist or a painting in their lives, make fun of them?"

Hanah grew so upset that her work suffered. She sat on a low stool with the tin pail and coaxed the cow, "Stay, Flora, my little love," but Flora wouldn't stand still for a moment. She turned her head, waved her tail, and continually lifted her hind legs, as though she could sense what was happening in Hanah's heart. Hanah was sweating by the time she finished milking Flora. After she'd helped tie up the cow, she sent the cattlemen off to the steppe with the herd; meanwhile, she and the milk-maids cleaned out the barn and sprinkled ground oats and oil cakes into the feeding troughs.

Next, Hanah went off to the stable. As she saddled Borech, she smiled at Shimke's remark:

"Hanah, no matter how much you rub him, he's still going to be a horse!"

"That's true of bipeds, too," Hanah tossed back, and led Borech out of the stable. But although she had more to say to Shimke, she took off at a gallop the moment she saw the drinking troughs: they were bone-dry. A burning fury took hold of her as she rode, knowing that the cowherds had driven the heifers and bull calves out without watering them first. She prodded Borech in the belly with her heels again and again, her breath coming in gasps as she flew over the steppe.

Just past the village of Karahurt she spotted the cowherds and the wandering young cattle. The two herders were sitting and eating with great gusto. Hanah watched as they chewed up big, chunky slices of bread and gulped from bottles of milk after every bite. She felt as though a boiling wind were filling her nostrils, as though she were being engulfed up to the neck in a sulfurous rage. She screamed:

"Get them to the well!"

The cowherds tossed their half-finished bottles of milk on the ground. They stood up calmly and said:

"They'll drink at lunchtime."

"Do it now, or there won't be a lunchtime!" Hanah was so furious that the cowherds backed away a bit. But she was no longer mistress of herself. She leapt from the saddle, lunged at the two boys, grabbed them, and started smacking one and then the other across the face and about the head as they waved their arms and tried to defend themselves. She would have tangled with them even longer if she hadn't noticed that one of them had a bloody nose. After she stopped hitting them, she used her remaining strength to yell:

"Monsters, good-for-nothings, nobodies! Go live in Vinnytsia and peddle herring! Now TAKE THE HEIFERS!"

Having shouted herself hoarse, Hanah ran back to Borech, threw herself into the saddle, and poked her heels into his belly so hard that for several moments he stood still in astonishment, then set off at a walk, before finally giving a neigh and running off at full speed.

Hanah switched the reins into her right hand so that Borech's head rose. She steered him to where she needed to be and helped drive the herd to the well. When she saw that the cowherds had pumped water into the troughs and the cattle had started drinking, she rode away, far out onto the steppe, although it wasn't long until the midday milking.

Now she didn't steer. Borech went straight to the gully, and while he was lowering himself into the bottom, she jumped out of the saddle and fell onto the soft grass. She rolled onto her belly and lay there, absorbing the peace that breathed up into her from the earth. She didn't see Borech standing with his head lowered, or the thick, frothy yellow foam that was dropping from his lips onto the ground. She didn't see anything—not only because she was lying face down, but because she had fallen asleep.

When she woke up, Borech was lying on the ground. She stroked his neck and felt that it was wet, so she let him lie there a while longer. But the sun's position was telling her it was time to milk the cows for the second time that day. So she tugged on the bridle, and Borech got up and started walking.

At the designated spot stood the cart, full of empty milk cans. The women had already started milking the cows, and Hanah took a tin pail and went to do the same. As she was walking back to the cart to empty her pail into a can, she noticed the handsome artist she'd picked out of the crowd the other day. His dark, delicate, longish face and black eyes were smiling, entreating, and expressing doubt, all at once. For a moment he looked Hanah in the eye; then he snatched the *tubeteyke* awkwardly off his head and said quietly:

"Comrade Brigadier, perhaps it would be possible to detain the herd for an hour and a half? If so, it would be very helpful."

Hanah fixed her eyes on the cap in his right hand.

"But no more than an hour and a half," she said severely, not raising her eyes. "Cows aren't people, you know. They need to graze, and they have to be milked." Then she turned her back on him and walked away, while he unfolded his easel, set up a plywood board with a sheet of paper pasted to it, and got to work.

Although Hanah had spoken so harshly to the artist, after the milking she did, in fact, tell the workers that the herd should be delayed. The cart drove away with the full cans and the milkmaids on board, and the artist stayed behind with the cows.

Hanah rode away too. First she went to the bakery, where the baker gave her a piece of fresh bread. Then she went off with Borech to the garden. There, she was lucky—the head of the Garden Brigade, Hayaleh Grinshteyn, handed her a long knobby cucumber and a tomato, asking:

"Hantche, if I came into the cow barn, would you give me a glass of milk?"

"That would be a first!" Hanah remarked, biting the little yellow tail off the end of the cucumber, spitting it out, and sinking her teeth deep into the cucumber's flesh. She smiled and looked at Hayaleh peacefully. "Hayaleh, I'm so tired. What time do you think it is? Respectable people must have eaten lunch hours ago. The communards, too."

"Eat, eat, Hantche, you must be starving," Hayaleh said. A moment later she added: "What do you think, Hanaleh—will Future Humanity look down on me for being weak? But what can I do? People are always breaking the rules, and I'm no better than anyone else. You're not the only one who comes here looking for a little something to tide you over. This garden is like honey for the bees." She reddened with shame.

Of all the women on the commune, Hayaleh was one of those closest to Hanah's heart. Hanah finished off the cucumber and the tomato with great pleasure, but she half-promised herself that she wouldn't come here anymore, that from now on she would follow the rules and eat only what all the other communards ate. When she was back in the saddle, she said:

"Hayaleh, don't worry. Future Humanity will remember you—and even if it knows you secretly shared vegetables with the communards, I'm sure you won't be judged harshly!"

* * *

Meanwhile, the artist was still busy sketching the herd. Before long, he began to hear the stamping of hooves. Soon after that, he beheld Hanah herself, hanging from the saddle with one foot in the stirrup and the other on the ground. He lowered his pencil and watched as she hopped around beside the horse. Only when she was finally standing on both feet did he turn back to his drawing.

Hanah came and stood behind his back, watching as he worked, and found herself so entranced that she actually held her breath. She was intrigued to discover that this small sheet of paper could contain such a high, clear sky and such a spacious landscape, with room left over for the herd and the milkmaids, too. Although the figures were barely sketched in, Hanah exclaimed:

"Why, of course: that's Toybel, and this is Rochke, and this is Shifraleh."

The artist paused, turned to Hanah, and calmly asked: "You recognize them? Really? Excellent!" Then he smiled so warmly that Hanah didn't have the courage to tell him that she needed him to stop working. Instead, she walked over to the cowherds and talked to them for a few moments. The artist saw the herders shake their heads. Then Hanah came back.

"Have you finished your picture?" she asked. "If so, the herd should go to the gullies, because there's nothing for them to eat here. A person can be empty, but udders should be full."

At least, that was what the artist thought she said, just before she jumped into the saddle and rode away. He didn't always catch everything that Hanah said, because in Moscow he spoke more Russian than *mamaloshen*. But he did understand that she was treating him rather like one of the cattle. Oddly enough, this didn't offend him—on the contrary, it pleasantly surprised him.

"What an extraordinary, original girl she is—and a brigade leader, too!" he thought. As he gathered up his gear, he recalled all the "clever" questions, opinions, and jokes he had heard from the workers while he was out painting in the fields, near the silos, and among the flocks. He smiled at how different—how much better—this young woman was than anyone else he had met here so far.

* * *

The long day of drudgery, not to mention the incident with the two errant cowherds, had not made Hanah's mood any lighter. Nevertheless, she walked cheerfully through the long dining hall and took a seat. The tables were nearly empty, since most of the communards had finished supper by now, but the four artists were sitting together at the very last table.

She hadn't yet finished eating when the sound of someone banging on an iron hoop began to ring out, which had to mean a General Assembly was being called (since the hoop wasn't rung for meetings of the Commune Council or the brigades).

It wasn't in the cards for Hanah to enjoy her meal that evening. She knew very well what kind of incident warranted a General Assembly. As the room filled, she watched the Chairman and the Secretary of the Party Cell ascend the stage, which Hanah privately thought of as "the gangplank." The Chairman banged on the table several times. A strange mood now took over the dining hall: people were smiling but also curious and uneasy. Here and there, little bursts of laughter erupted. Then the Field Brigade member who had recently proposed that Hanah go out on the steppe with him to "watch the stars fall" demanded loudly:

"Hantche, why did you attack the cowherds like that? Are you their Lady of the Manor? Are they your dogs?"

Hanah turned and, raising her voice to match his, she shouted out over the whole hall:

"Your opinion means less than nothing to me. But I *would* like to have a look at your teeth!"

"Silence, there will be silence!" The Chairman struck the table again and then called out:

"Communard Hanah Faynberg, approach the stage. Communard victims Dovid Shapiro and Yankel Tsukerman—you too."

Hanah stood on the right side of the stage, the victims on the left. One of them, Dovid, had tied a red kerchief around his face, and at the sight of this, the dining hall erupted in deafening, dreadful laughter. Finally, the room became quiet.

"Comrade Tsukerman," the Chairman called upon the first victim, "tell us exactly what happened."

Tsukerman told the story at length: how he and Dovid had driven the herd of heifers out; how they had felt faint with hunger . . . Here Hanah interrupted him:

"Who felt faint? You, or the calves?"

Another round of laughter reverberated through the room. After it died down again, the second victim, Dovid, related that communard Hanah Faynberg had "fallen upon him like a she-bandit" and injured him.

Having heard the allegations from the victims, the Secretary of the Party Cell called upon Hanah to speak. Hanah painted the scene like this:

"Members of the commune, I need not explain to you how much hard work goes into the raising of a cow. If you had seen how the heifers and bull calves were wandering around the steppe, weak with thirst! And meanwhile, these two hardworking Moyshe Rabeynus were sitting there enjoying a feast! I don't know if any of you would have done any differently than I did. I have no regrets. That's all I have to say!"

After this, some communards stood up and tried to downplay the significance of the matter; others came forward to speak out harshly and sharply against Hanah. When all the members had been heard, the Secretary of the Party Cell put in his own two cents. He began with a reference to an earlier case:

"In the winter, we condemned the behavior of a female communard who refused to breastfeed a small communard, a toddler, in spite of the fact that she had enough milk to do so. You remember, comrades, how we banished her from our commune for one full quarter. I said at the time that this was an excessive punishment. But now we have a truly unacceptable incident before us. If this were someone else in Hanah's place, I would be the first to say that such a person, such a man, should not be allowed to draw breath among us. I say 'a man' because we all know that Hanah Faynberg does the work of two or three men. But raising one's hand to a comrade! I propose to exclude her from the Commune Council for one quarter. I have finished."

A vote was taken. The majority was in favor of the motion that the Party Secretary had put forward. The dining hall filled with noise and commotion. Suddenly, Dovid Shapiro, the one with his head wrapped in a red scarf, raised his right hand and announced:

"I forgot to say that while she was beating us, Comrade Faynberg yelled several dirty words, and she also said we should go peddle herring in Vinnytsia. I allege that this is kulak propaganda!"

In response to this grave declaration, the room exploded in such uproarious laughter that several communards actually got the hiccups.

"The meeting is adjourned," the Chairman announced.

Efroyim the Shepherd jumped up on the stage and took his harmonica out of his pocket. He started playing something from *Carmen*, tapping his feet, and yelling:

"Friends, Hanaleh, come up on the stage, let's dance!"

Several people began whirling around in a polka, but, although Hanah was usually one of the liveliest dancers on the commune, there was no dancing in her tonight. She looked at the stage as though the people spinning around up there were crazy and walked out of the dining hall.

After taking a few steps, she heard someone walking behind her, and stopped. When she recognized the artist, she felt a pang of remorse at the harsh tone she had taken with him earlier in the day. But he had apparently forgotten all about that, because he turned to her ever so quietly and politely and said:

"Comrade Hanah, if you're not too tired and have no objections, would it be possible for me to walk with you a little bit?"

She accepted, and did not pull her arm away when his soft, warm fingers touched her above the elbow. But as they walked side by side, he withdrew his hand and, after a long silence, quietly remarked:

"This is the first time in my life I've gone for a walk with a girl who attacked two men."

"I appreciate your courage. You were at the Assembly?"

"You didn't notice we were there?"

"I saw you earlier, but I assumed you'd left."

"It doesn't matter. But please don't overestimate my courage, because I don't know quite what to make of a girl like you."

"I'll certainly take that into consideration," Hanah said. "You're wrong, however, about my being a 'girl.' Tonight you are walking with a mother of three."

She heard him gasp. They passed the smithy, the silos, then turned right, onto the steppe. Neither of them spoke; Hanah kept waiting for him to dismiss her with a "Good night, Comrade Faynberg." But instead, he stopped and asked in astonishment:

"You, three children? How old are you?"

His tone told her that he was hoping she would say, "I was only joking." Now she was the one who wanted to wish *him* a good night. But, feeling his hand on hers, she quietly confirmed:

"Yes, I have three little girls; I'll be twenty-four next spring."

As she said it, Hanah felt ashamed of her situation for the first time since she had left her husband.

It was peaceful out on the steppe, just as it always was when Hanah came out for a walk by herself. The sky was also, as always, very dark and thickly sprinkled with stars. But to Hanah it seemed as though this was the first time she had ever experienced such a high-vaulted sky, such bright stars, such indifferent silence. Overwhelmed by her own sudden shyness, by the stillness, and by his silence, she did not immediately hear his soft question:

"Where is the father of your children?"

Hanah looked at him, paused for a moment, and then said, without a trace of irony:

"What father? I had my children all by myself."

He took Hanah's hand and pulled her lightly onward. They walked like this until he asked:

"You remember how you rode into the yard that morning when we first came to the commune?"

"Of course I remember. My heart was in my throat. Why, I almost rode right over that black-haired man who was standing near the woman in your group."

"I wasn't worried about that; I almost burst out laughing when that fellow—he's called Lyova—grabbed onto his suitcase for dear life. He's a very good artist, by the way. I barely glimpsed you that morning, you turned and disappeared so quickly on your horse. Incidentally, when I was painting the cattle, I loved how your horse was standing with a white scarf tied to his head. Was it you who dressed him up like that?"

"Why should you wonder about that? It was so hot."

"I understand, but I do wonder how you handle him so well."

"If you're not in a hurry, I'll tell you where he's from and how he came to me. Although that's not the only reason I treat him so well. Anyone who beats or torments a living creature is no mensch."

"I'm not in any hurry. I don't know what you're going to tell me, but I must say, from the little I've heard so far, I know it won't be boring."

As Hanah began her story, her voice grew calm and restrained, and her well-chosen words floated out into the night.

"Seven months ago," she related, "I was out walking on the steppe by myself. I do that all the time; I know my way around. After a while, about four *versts* from the commune, in a place where there had never been any fences before, I saw stakes driven into the ground, strung top to bottom with barbed wire. It was a bright moonlit night. I went closer to find out what was going on.

"Behind this wall of barbed wire, countless horses were crammed together. If it hadn't been for the barbs, the crowding wouldn't have been so frightful, but as it was, they were so wretchedly tangled together, and their cries were so terrifying and pitiful, that it made my blood run cold.

"Then a few horses started rearing up on their hind legs. But they didn't have anyplace to put their front feet down again, except on the backs of other horses, who were already stuck to them like glue. So they just kept waving their feet in the air. I was so horrified, I ran all the way back to the commune.

"The next day I didn't have a single free minute to go and see the horses, so I told the Party Secretary about it. But he said to me:

"'What are you so upset about? They're just kulak horses!' So I say, 'They haven't even been given any food or water!' He says, 'Today or tomorrow someone will sort them out.' To make a long story short, for two days I didn't have the time to run out there, but on the third day I went out, and I was surprised and delighted by what I found.

"All the stakes had been pulled up. The barbed wire lay on the ground, and not a single horse was left. But I heard a strange noise, like someone dragging a brush over the earth. I leapt over the barbed wire and discovered one horse, lying on his side and rubbing the ground with his neck. As soon as I saw him, I took off running toward the village, which was closer than the commune. I wept as I ran; it's a good thing no one was around to see me. In the village I got ahold of some oats, borrowed a pail from a peasant woman, filled it with water, and ran straight back to the horse. He didn't touch the oats, but he drank up the water on the spot. I knew it would be good to give him a piece of sugar every day. But where could I get sugar?

"After that, I went back to see the horse every day and gave him water and a little something to eat. If I didn't have time during the day, I went at night. Until one day, I don't remember how many days later, I fed him some barley bran, and he got to his feet and followed me. He was still very weak, so he laid his muzzle on my shoulder, and we walked like that all the way back to the stable. I led him inside and told Shimke the Groom that the horse was called 'Borech' and that he shouldn't harness him for anyone but me, not even for the Chairman. So now you've heard the whole story!"

"I see, I see . . . and what happened to the rest of those poor horses?" he asked.

"They were taken away for distribution—what else? I myself have seen horses running across the steppe several times. People say horses used to run wild around here, until the collective farms caught them all."

If her companion hadn't said "those poor horses," it's possible Hanah would have asked him to walk back alone, because, as previously mentioned, she felt no connection at all with people who consider humans to be the crown of nature. In those days she often thought, "As long as man continues to abuse living things, true compassion will be a long time coming." But when she heard him say "those poor horses," she felt that this man, at least, understood her feelings and took them to heart.

"Time to go," she said. "It's dawn." They headed back to the commune, and near the cattle barn he said to her:

"I'm not going to call you Comrade Hanah anymore—and, unless you say no, I want us to meet again tomorrow."

"It's not tomorrow anymore, it's today. And today I'm going to see my children, so we'll meet a little later, like yesterday."

"You don't have any regrets?" he asked quietly.

"No, not in the least. Don't worry—for quite some time now, I've made a point of doing what I want to do, whenever possible," Hanah said, and disappeared into the cattle barn.

* * *

It was a day like any other day. Hanah rode on the steppe, scattered salt, milked, and after the midday milking, she and the cowhands and shepherds gathered up the young bulls that were to be driven to Yevpatoria for slaughter. Not only was this activity distressing for Hanah, it was also a huge bother. She stayed out on the steppe to supervise until the bulls were separated from the heifers and calves, reminding the workers over and over:

"Don't hurry them or they won't feed enough. In Saki you should water them, not only out of compassion for living things, but because they'll lose weight if you don't give them water."

After instructing the workers and escorting them for three of four kilometers, Hanah turned her horse back toward the commune. But one of the cowherds, Shmulke from Zhmerynka, caught up with her and said in a pitiful voice:

"How can I walk such a long way in my bare feet?"

"You'll walk just the same as I would."

"But you ride your horse more often than you walk. And a horse has shoes!"

"You're right. But in some cases, a horse also has more intelligence than a person. So you can envy him that, too."

"Is that so! I should envy a horse! Well, this isn't your precious Palestine, this is the Soviet Union! Here, the worker isn't the lowest person."

"Right again. This isn't Palestine. And you can't even imagine how hard we had to work there. But never mind that. I'll ask the Commune Council about getting you and the other herders some boots," Hanah promised.

Filled with annoyance that Shmulke and the others would have to spend a long day walking barefoot on the prickly stubble, she took her feelings out on Borech. He couldn't have known how Hanah came to have a whip in her hand; indeed, she herself didn't remember that when they had separated the bulls, she'd grabbed this whip from someone and waved it in the air to gather the workers. Now Borech felt it on his back and sides.

As soon as she was back in the commune yard, Hanah came to herself and lowered the whip. Shimke watched as she took the saddle off Borech's sweaty back, then he calmly reported:

"In the *stolovaya* today there's a pea soup that's really delicious."

"What's that? Soup? That would really hit the spot! Borech is sweated, so while he's cooling down, I'll go get some."

After eating, Hanah was out on the steppe again until evening. As always, she did what had to be done. Nonetheless, at the evening milking, Shifraleh, who was one of the most efficient milkmaids, noticed that Hanah's pace was somewhat slower than usual, and started teasing her:

"Hanah, why are you dragging your feet today? By the time you get the milk to the can, it will be sour."

"The milk can go sour, as long as you stay sweet, like honey," Hanah tossed back.

"Yes, me with my honey, and you with your poison," Shifraleh said.

Hanah wasn't offended, so she didn't bother to answer. She still hadn't forgotten how Shmulke had said to her, "You ride your horse more often than you walk." Also, she hadn't slept well the previous night. Although the artist spoke so little, and she didn't even know his name, a strange uneasiness had seized her and wouldn't let go. Of course, she didn't know anything for sure yet, but she had a feeling his interest in her was more than casual. With all these things on her mind, she went into the Children's Home that evening in a mood that was far from lighthearted.

Children are a comfort. Hanah played with them as her equals, and the children sensed it; not only her own little girls, but the whole pack of children took turns riding on her back as she sang to them, "A little rain, a little rain, is falling pitter-patter." Then she sat them down on the floor and told them a story:

"Once there was a granny who had a little sheep, and she loved it very much. She took care of it and cuddled it, and all her grandchildren loved the little sheep, too. But one day the little sheep got lost. Either because the shepherd fell asleep, or because the sheep was very silly and forgot the way home. A sheep has a short memory, you know.

"One day passed, and the little sheep didn't come home; two days passed, and the little sheep didn't come home. The granny became very sad. The neighbors noticed that no smoke was coming out of her chimney, and they realized she wasn't cooking any porridge for herself or any potato peels for the little sheep. So a neighbor went over to the granny's house and asked, 'What's the matter?' And the granny explained that her only sheep had gone missing.

"They searched everywhere, for one day, for two days, but the little sheep was nowhere to be found. On the third day, the granny sat on a low chair and cried. She couldn't bear her sorrow.

"Then, all of a sudden, the granny heard a long, soft 'b-a-a-a.' She hurried to the door, and then she ran outside. And what did she see? She saw her little sheep with two tiny little sheep! 'My silly, my baby!' the granny cried out. Why did she cry out like that, children? Why?"

"Because she was so happy to see her sheep and the two tiny little sheep!" the children yelled, and they danced for joy. Hanah danced with them in a circle. But after she left the Children's Home, Henke, who worked there, caught up with her and gently chided:

"Hanke, you got them so worked up that now they won't fall asleep for hours. Don't you understand that it would be better for you to come for an hour every day, instead of coming twice a week for two hours and telling them such exciting stories?"

Hanah had an answer ready, because she was sure that sometimes it's better to hear a story that gets you all worked up than to hear nothing at all and go to sleep quietly. But she didn't answer Henke; she just headed for the dining hall.

Before she had a chance to eat a single spoonful of pea soup, the cowhand on night duty appeared in the open doorway and called her into the cow barn. Not quite in the nick of time, as it turned out: in the middle of the barn lay Hagar, giving birth.

Hanah rolled up her sleeves and rubbed the cow's sides. By the time she saw a little muzzle, a pointy little tongue, and then the whole little head with a yellow hoof on either side, she had broken out in a sweat. Suddenly the cow stood up on the straw that the cowhand had laid out as a bed, and onto this straw, with a slapping wet smack, fell the calf.

By the time Hanah had wiped the calf off with a sack and carried it into the calf barn, it was getting late. Nevertheless, she headed back to the dining hall—but she didn't manage to get inside, because just then she heard a quiet, very soft "Good evening, Hanah."

"You aren't angry at me for being late?"

"To tell you the truth, it did annoy me, but now everything is fine," the artist said. Again Hanah noticed his gentle smile, which shone on his long face and in his deep black eyes. "Where will you take me tonight?" he asked, and laid his hand on her shoulder.

"I'll lead you to a lovely spot, if you want to see it, and can handle a long walk."

They walked slowly through the silence of the steppe. Not a single breath of wind blew across their faces; even the stars weren't shining. The crescent moon had pinned a single greenish star to its sharp-edged throat; a pale greenish glow spread over the whole vast space, and all the details of the earth were shrouded in a greenish veil. The line where the sky joined the earth was so near that it seemed as though you could walk straight on until you breached that shining belt and discovered how the world ended.

"Do you like this?" Hanah asked.

"I like you."

They resumed their silence.

"Where is the lovely place you promised to show me?"

"It's too bad I can't show you the place I come from. As for what it was like there, I'll tell you that when the time is right. But the spot I'm taking you to isn't far now," Hanah said, and she was gripped by a nervousness, even a sort of confusion, such as she had rarely experienced before.

She led him down into the other ravine, which she had visited more than once on horseback. They sat on the soft cool grass, and Hanah covered her bare feet with the skirt of her shiny black *sarafan*. As he moved toward her, she could hear his rapid breathing. Assailed by fear and weakness, she shifted away from him. He embraced her forcefully with both arms and bombarded her with kisses from his warm lips . . . She felt as though her heart were being extinguished and then brightly rekindled, as though she herself, on that fated night, no longer existed . . .

* * *

Her heart was pounding so hard it muffled his question:

"Do you trust me? Do you believe in me?"

"What? Yes, with all my heart."

"You should. I will never leave you," he said. "Do you want to keep sitting here, or do you want to walk around a little?"

"All I know is, I don't want to walk away from you," Hanah said.

Day had broken when they returned to the commune yard.

"I'll wait for you this evening, Hanaleh, and you should know the wait won't be easy for me," he said.

"The same for me," she confessed, and disappeared into the building where she lived with her roommates.

"Hanke, where have you been all night?" Yocheved asked sleepily.

"For some people the night is endlessly long, and for others it's short—nothing could be shorter!" Hanah thought, and, still fully dressed, threw herself onto her little bed—but she didn't get a wink of sleep right up until milking time.

* * *

After the milking, Hanah rode off to Saki. It had been a long time since she had visited the mud therapy spa, where she'd been supplying the milk for over two years now.

Borech really couldn't understand what was happening with his rider today. She hadn't stroked him once, her heels hadn't touched his belly, and she hadn't said a word to him. So he tried rearing up on his hind legs and then turning in circles to catch her attention. As a last resort, he suddenly broke into a gallop. Hanah bent down over his neck, and he felt her give him a firm slap there. Then she scolded him:

"Borech, don't start acting like a silly human!"

Riding into the yard of the spa, Hanah threw the reins over a fencepost, jumped out of the saddle, and headed for the office. The manager, who was called Fyodor Petrovich, brought her a chair. She sat down, and they got to chatting. After making the usual small talk, Fyodor Petrovich said:

"Hanah Davidovna, I've told you before how happy the patients are, how they sing the praises of the milk from the commune. How many times have I asked you to stay for lunch? But you always say you're in too much of a hurry."

"I'm afraid I don't have time right now, either, Fyodor Petrovich . . . that is, not for lunch. But I would like to ask you for a big favor. If it weren't for that, I might not have come today."

"I'll do whatever I can for you, Hanah Davidovna."

"I don't need anything for myself, of course. But the shepherds and cowhands of the Livestock Brigade have no shoes. The summer is almost over; soon the rains will begin. In short, I need ten pairs of boots, shoes, or at least *lapti*."

"This is no easy matter, but you know the saying: 'There are no fortresses that Bolsheviks can't conquer.' Since we already award bonuses to you and the rest of the Livestock Brigade every year, I'll make sure that the bonus this year will be what you request. Now, won't you stay for lunch?"

"No, thank you very much, but the cows are missing me," Hanah joked, and got up from her chair.

When she was outside standing next to Borech and raising a foot toward the stirrup, she saw Fyodor Petrovich hurrying toward her with a small white bag in his hand. He came over, held out the bag to Hanah, and entreated her: "Hanah Davidovna, this is a bit of sugar for your Children's Home. Take it, take it—it's not for you personally. Why are you turning so red?" He produced a safety pin from somewhere, handed it to Hanah along with the little bag, and walked away.

Although Hanah very much wanted to give a lump of sugar to Borech, she didn't. After hoisting herself into the saddle, she used the safety pin to pin the little sack between the collar buttons of her blouse. Then she rode quickly out of Saki, her brown legs extended so that she was almost standing in the stirrups. Her mind was focused on yesterday evening . . . "I don't even know what kind of person he is," she thought, "but I'm melting, like snow in the sun."

Hearing the squeak of a wheel, she turned her head and saw the Chairman riding along beside her. He stopped his two-wheeled gig and stared at Hanah, and, although she and her horse were very close to the carriage, he shouted:

"Where have you been?"

"In Saki spa, Mr. Chairman."

"How are things there?"

"Not too bad. Fyodor Petrovich promised boots or bast slippers for the livestock workers for the cold weather."

"If it's bast slippers, that's not much of a favor!" the Chairman said absently, and at the same time he stared very hard at Hanah's legs in their short, shiny black trousers. He looked and looked; then, to Hanah's surprise, he declared:

"It would be a sin if those trousers were longer."

"What?"

"I said, it would be a sin if those little trousers of yours were any longer."

"Oh-h-h!" Hanah finally caught his meaning. "What does that have to do with anything?" She tried to return to the subject at hand. "We have, of course, talked about incentives for the livestock workers before." Then she couldn't help blurting out, "If I'm not mistaken, it's no business of mine how much you like my drawers!"

With that, she slapped the reins, and Borech carried her off like the wind.

* * *

Toil and more toil. After the evening milking Hanah went to the Children's Home, and once again she sang, danced, and told stories with the little ones. The children almost cried when she left to eat supper. The dining hall was serving the usual barley-and-rye concoction; she slurped it down quickly and was off to the appointed spot.

She could feel her heart hammering in her temples as she spotted him pacing back and forth near the well. As she drew closer, he turned toward her, and she fell straight into his outstretched arms. The shadow of the well house prevented her from seeing his eyes, but she could hear his deep voice clearly:

"Do you still trust me, as you said last time? I was afraid you were angry at me."

"How did that come into your head? Have you forgotten what I said yesterday? I told you, I trust you. If I were angry at anyone, it would be at myself. What—do you think what happened yesterday happens to me every day?! Do I need to tell you that I love you? There, you see—I didn't wait for you to say the words I've been wanting so much to hear."

He pressed her against himself so tightly that she lost her breath. Then he released her, and off they went to the steppe. They walked slowly, not speaking a word. For a moment Hanah had a feeling that, other than the two of them, there was no one else in the world. Abruptly, she asked:

"What's your name?"

"My name is Nehemyah."

"Nehemyah. That means *comfort*," she translated from the Hebrew. "And where are you from?"

"I'm from White Russia. Now you know more about me than I know about you."

"We both know more than a little about each other, but I still have endless questions for you."

"I'd rather hear about you," he said. "You painted the story of the horses so beautifully the other night. I heard and saw everything as though with my own eyes."

"I'm from Lithuania," Hanah said. "I had a mother, but no father. One day, when my grandmother saw my stepfather beating me, she snatched me out of his hands, and from then on I lived with my grandparents."

"You haven't described your grandparents yet, but I can already tell you like them very much."

"Like them? Why, I cherish them more than anything in the world!"

"What is this word, *cherish?*"

"*Cherish* is stronger than *like*. On the commune, you'll learn to speak Yiddish properly."

"I'm already getting better at it. When I hear you talk, I remember how people used to talk back home, and words that I haven't heard in years start coming back into my head. But tell me more about yourself, about your childrenhood."

"Not *childrenhood*; 'childhood' is the correct word. But that's a long story. Instead, I'll tell you what kind of letters my grandmother, may she rest in peace, used to write to me. She herself didn't know how to write, you understand; she dictated her letters—but they sounded exactly like her. In all of them, she wanted to find out how much I was earning, and whether I had a little wooden cabin of my own, or perhaps even a brick house.

"In one letter, she asked: 'Tell me, apple of my eye, who are your business partners? You write that you are personally responsible for three hundred cows and two thousand sheep, no Evil Eye! I ask you, please, pay close attention to the accounting. You know, of course, that your grandfather is a great scholar. You remember how he taught you the Torah, Prophets, and Writings—and why not! He was constantly saying that if you were not lacking one little thing, you would certainly be a boy, because such a receptive mind as yours only comes along in one boy out of a hundred! Now he is insisting I write to you so that you will pay attention to the accounting and not, God forbid, abandon your business partners.'

"When I read about the 'business partners,' I burst out laughing. But in another letter I realized she was really talking about herself, because in that one, it said: 'When you ran away from us, we walked around in a daze. Your grandfather completely fell apart! Then, at last, we started receiving letters from you, saying that you were living with new friends in Crimea, and that you were in charge of so many cows and sheep, no Evil Eye. Hearing this, your grandfather immediately sent you a letter advising you not to rely on your memory, but to write everything down, to the very last detail. I ask you, please, write to us about where you and your partners are selling your dairy products and the wool and meat from your sheep. Furthermore, have pity and write more often, because until we finally receive a letter from you, our eyes will be crawling out of our heads with worry. We cherish you very greatly. Be healthy, greet your partners for us, with best wishes from your Grandmother and Grandfather.'"

"*Prelest!*" Nehemyah exclaimed, and burst out laughing.

"What do you mean, *prelest?* It's better to say 'what a delight' or 'how wonderful.' But let's walk a little more quickly, I'm cold," Hanah said.

"In that case, we'll go back. You need to stay warm, and get some sleep, too; it's well after midnight," he said.

Hanah's heart was so touched by his concern that she pulled her hand away from his and fell blindly upon his forehead and cheeks with her lips. If he hadn't clasped her head in his hands and guided her mouth to his own, her lips would have blundered around even longer.

They lingered there a little while, reluctant to leave, and then set off toward the commune. Near the building where Hanah lived with her roommates, she leaned toward him and said: "I'm not so much nervous about all of this as surprised. But I'm glad; I couldn't be happier. Good night." And she disappeared.

It had been such a short time since they had met, Nehemyah reflected as he watched her walk away. And they had talked so little. And yet, it was enough. Enough for him to understand and appreciate what he had found so unexpectedly. Then he remembered that they hadn't agreed where to meet the next day, and he thought vaguely, "Maybe she won't want to see me tomorrow?"

With a heavy heart he went into the old house where he was staying with the other artists. He would certainly have been able to fall asleep more quickly, and to feel better about himself, if he knew what she thought, but . . . how could he know?

Meanwhile, Hanah was lying fully dressed on her bed, unable to fall asleep for joy. Day had barely dawned when she sprang out of bed and went off to the cattle barn.

The yard was empty. The various buildings, the smithy, the silos, the lone tree by the Children's Home, the sky and the earth were all wrapped in a light mist; everything still lay in a sweet early morning slumber. Hanah walked into the barn and noticed that Yisroel from Tulchyn was standing at the far end. He was leaning against the wall that separated the bulls from the cows, and Hanah realized he was asleep. Instead of waking him, Hanah crept in behind the carts, where there was a pile of dry oat straw. She snuggled down into the straw and felt a pleasant weariness flowing through her limbs. As she fell asleep, a thought came to her:

"Such sympathy, such admiration—how unexpected this is. How did such good fortune find me?"

* * *

Hanah slept for barely an hour; then she heard the clinking of milk cans and tin pails and got up. She was so amazed at her own renewed energy that she began to sing. The cows stopped chewing their cud for a moment, so heartily did her voice ring out:

"Atop the attic sleeps the roo-oo-oof . . ."

"When a person doesn't sleep alone, it's only the roof that gets any sleep," teased Taybeleh from Babruysk as she seated herself on a low stool and started washing Yachsente's udders.

"My neighbors are already spreading rumors about me." Hanah smiled to herself, and then she set about her milking so rapidly that the other milkmaids soon fell three cows behind. They watched with envy as Hanah ran continuously back and forth, bringing pails of foaming, frothy milk to the cans.

"Hanatchke, if you're still hungry for something this morning, maybe you should go and eat breakfast," Taybeleh teased.

"Don't shout, you're frightening the cows," Hanah said. "But if *you're* feeling hungry, take a drink of milk. Today, it's allowed!"

Hanah's suggestion was so uncharacteristic that Shifraleh exclaimed, "Too bad it's so far to the nearest forest, or I'd run and see how many bears just dropped dead!" Then she needled Hanah some more:

"Taybeleh, recite a blessing, 'That from our Brigadier, sleep has departed.' But don't sample the milk; you know that would get you in trouble."

"Why should it?" joked Reyzel from Uman. "If there's a new Milk Manifesto, she can drown herself in milk if she wants to!"

"Drink up, comrades!" Taybeleh chimed in.

When Hanah walked out of the barn, her knees buckled in joyful astonishment: Nehemyah was standing near the gate.

"Good morning, my *prelest*. Yes, yes, I know, the correct thing to say is 'my beauty,'" Nehemyah called out, leaning toward her and giving her a kiss. Hanah turned a deep red.

"Nehemyah, Nehemyah!" she repeated his name softly, as though warning him of danger.

"Are you scared because you don't want your workers to see?" For the first time, he addressed her by the familiar *du* instead of the formal *ir*. "But that's silly; everyone knows already! My friends know I went for a walk with you, and I didn't deny it."

"I swear, I'm not scared and I'm not ashamed! But I can do without a lot of extra eyes looking at me when I'm kissing someone, or when someone is kissing me."

"Good; where should I meet you this evening?"

"You know where the sentry box is?" She was still addressing him as *ir*.

"Yes, I was sketching there when the shepherds were milking the sheep."

"I'll wait for you there after supper."

"Hanaleh, say *du* to me, just once, and I'll go away. Otherwise, I'll give you several more kisses. Look, they're driving the cattle this way; your cowherds will see us!"

"I'll say *du* when it comes out by itself. I have to run; I need to send the milk off," Hanah said, and she went to oversee the workers who were loading the full cans onto the wagon.

"A little more straw, Srolke. If not, by the time you get to Saki you'll have butter instead of milk!" Hanah warned, and then she was off to the bakery. She had barely set foot across the threshold when the baker, Itsik from Uman, approached her and asked in an earnest voice, but with a slight smile on his face:

"May I give you a little bread? A fresh piece for you, and a day-old piece for your handsome mount?"

"My mount? Why are you calling Borech a dirty word?"

"Who says 'mount' is a dirty word?"

"I don't have time for this, give it already," Hanah demanded. She snatched the bread from Itsik's hands and went off to the stable, shoving the bread into her mouth with her left hand while she removed the saddle from Borech's back with her right.

"Leave it, I'll unsaddle your 'prince' for you," Shimke offered. As he worked, he made the following astute observation:

"Hantche, all of a sudden you're acting completely different from usual. I don't understand what's happening to you! Just like that, you've forgotten you were removed from the Commune Council!"

"I'll give you a friendly piece of advice: Keep your mind on your work," Hanah said, and jumped into the saddle. Borech tried to do a little dance, but she pulled firmly on the reins, and he set off with a calm and efficient gait.

The cows were feeding eagerly, although the salt had all but disappeared except in a few places at the roots of the parched grass. Like peasants mowing a field with dull sickles, the beasts stretched their long curved tongues toward these spots; then they used the bristles on their tongues to snatch up the fodder before grating and grinding it with their teeth.

There was still a good hour until the midday milking, but Hanah remembered that today the maize was supposed to be loaded into the silos, so she rode there to oversee the process. When she arrived, several wagons filled with green-cut maize already stood beside the cylindrical towers; from within came the sounds of voices and a faint stamping, as though someone were dancing on feather beds. A fresh, sour aroma spread through the air, as if a huge batch of leavened rye dough were rising in a giant baking trough.

Hanah jumped down from the saddle, tied her horse to the rail of a wagon, and set off toward the second silo. She was just starting up the stairs when she heard his quiet voice: "You can't get away from me that easily. Come here, let me look at your little forehead." He was speaking so softly that she practically had to read his lips.

She came over and stood behind him. He was sitting on a low chair, and in front of him on a small easel stood a sheet of paper pasted to a plywood board. On the paper she saw the silos—but not as she was accustomed to seeing them. The ones in the picture were yellow, and they had been raised up into the air, into the sky. The wagons were dark green, the horses were pinkish, the earth was brown; as for the people, some were reddish, others pale gray. Altogether, everything in the picture looked heightened and festive.

"Come closer, you won't disturb me. I'm already finished," he said, and as Hanah stepped forward, he asked discreetly, "You like it?"

Hanah stayed quiet and looked. But to him, apparently, she was staying quiet for too long. "You don't like it?" he asked impatiently.

"What gives you that idea? I like it very much! Look for yourself: the towers are so light, so airy, they seem as if you could pick them up. And I never would have thought they could glow, like Hanukah candles." As she expressed her opinion, a rosy blush broke out on her face, right up to her forehead.

"Hanukah candles?! That's something I haven't thought about for a long, long time. I loved Hanukah so much! You're always reminding me of everything. Thanks to you, I'm remembering so many things from the past that were so beloved, so important to me . . . Did you used to play with dreidels? Probably not; girls don't play with dreidels."

"Why on earth not? My grandfather used to cast a tin dreidel for me every year. And when I was five, he taught me the Hebrew letters on it, the *nun, gimel, hey,* and *shin,* and he told me what they stand for."

"I remember now: *nes gadol hayah sham,* 'A great miracle happened there,' isn't that right?"

"Yes."

"From now on I'll start calling you 'Hanukel.' But how will I ever survive until I see you tonight?"

He watched, enchanted, how dexterously she put her little bare feet into the stirrups, how nimbly she raised herself up and settled into the saddle. Riding off onto the steppe, she and the horse soon resembled a tiny Hebrew vowel sign on a vast, blank piece of paper, and Nehemyah was left to stand and watch until this little *nikudah* dot disappeared. Afterwards he gathered up his art materials and poured the water out of the jam jar he used for rinsing the watercolors off his brushes. Then he went back to the house where he was staying with the rest of the artists.

* * *

Walking in, Nehemyah sensed right away that something wasn't as it should be. The short artist with the shaggy black hair was pacing back and forth; the tall blond one was sitting on the room's only chair with his head down, as though he had encountered an unexpected problem. Nehemyah looked wonderingly from one to the other.

"You do as you want, and as you think necessary. I'm leaving tomorrow! I don't want to eat out of the same bowl as a chicken; I never agreed that bloodthirsty bedbugs could have their way with me!" the short one almost shouted.

Nehemyah tried to calm things down. "First of all," he said, "stop shouting. Second, of course it's uncomfortable here. But we're still a team, aren't we? Yesterday, Ida left; now you're threatening to leave over a few bedbugs?"

"I'm going, too," announced the blond man. "And you?" He looked at Nehemyah.

"I'm staying. I knew from the beginning we wouldn't be living in a hotel."

"Yes, and in addition to your very accurate prediction, there's another important reason for you to stay, something you didn't predict . . . There are no secrets here, Nehemyah," the blond man remarked.

"Of course there aren't. I want . . . that is, I want . . . I won't say. But if you're my friend, you'll wish that my 'important reason' becomes permanent—even eternal," Nehemyah said.

"Don't take offense. I hope everything turns out the way you want. Now, show us what you've made."

"I don't show my sketches to quitters. Whenever I leave the room, you always look in my portfolio anyway, so why ask permission all of a sudden? Take it and look."

The blond man pulled out a sketch, took a look, and immediately started making suggestions, as was his way:

"You should have made the horses and the wagons as light and feathery as the sky; it would be more unified that way."

"You're right. The horses, the wagons, and the ground are all very heavy and crude. You see, I'm trying to move away from painting landscapes in the conventional way. But I understand why you like that sky. It's because it looks like your own skies."

"Really? Why didn't you ever say so back in Moscow?"

"You're a strange fellow! In Moscow I watched you paint from your imagination; here, I've seen how you work from nature. And it seems to me that even before you look at a sky or a landscape, you've already decided what colors you're going to take from the palette . . . Do you understand what I'm saying?"

"Of course I understand. Every person has his own approach. But right now, I want to talk to you about this sudden involvement of yours. You and I are too close for me to stay silent. Consider what you're doing very carefully. Her children will become your children. 'May you never have the bother to discover you're a father . . . ' That's the first thing. Second, she's from a totally different background than you. That's more important than it may appear. Third, well—"

"I don't know what's third," Nehemyah interrupted, "but tell me this instead: Are you so sure you aren't a father yourself?"

"What are you saying, Nehemyah?"

"I see that I've alarmed you, so I'll talk about myself instead. I am, indeed, acutely aware that I could have been a father. I'm sure you remember that I was involved with a woman from the Sculpture Department. We were, you understand, like man and wife. One evening she told me she was pregnant. I was dumbfounded. I got some money, and she got rid of it. Now, as to Hanah's background. As I understand it, you're saying she's not from a creative background."

"Yes, yes, that's exactly what I mean."

"Don't interrupt me. Tell me this: Do you think all your artistic acquaintances are truly creative people?"

"Nothing of the kind."

"I wish all the artists I know were as direct, original, and sincere as Hanah. I already dare to say: as *my* Hanah," Nehemyah blurted out.

"I see you've made up your mind," the blond man said. "But I warn you again to think this through before you decide."

"Oh, I didn't realize it was entirely up to me! Where does this assumption come from, that we men get to make all the decisions? Hasn't it occurred to you that *they* decide just as much? The so-called softer, gentler, prettier sex is no less important than we are. Think *that* through. I appreciate your warnings, but for the time being, I'm not going anywhere," Nehemyah said, and he snatched up his painting gear and left.

He wandered around on the steppe until nightfall, but he didn't encounter anything worth painting. He returned to the house with a heavy heart. That evening, he didn't meet with Hanah.

* * *

The next day, the other two artists left for Yevpatoria. In the evening, Nehemyah waited for Hanah by the cattle barn, and as soon as she came out, he announced:

"I have the house to myself. The sky is cloudy. Come to my place."

"That's good news, but even a cloudy sky is better than a well-lit ceiling. Come, let's go out on the steppe."

For several hours they wandered around, scarcely exchanging a word. Hanah could sense that Nehemyah's heart was heavy, but she asked him no questions. Suddenly he stopped, took her hands, and pulled her toward himself so abruptly that she almost fell down. "Oy!" She gave a sort of moan as she felt his lips running over her cheeks, over her eyes, along her temples, across her hair. Then she lifted her lips to him, whispering:

"Have mercy."

"Mercy? You would do better to inform me of your background, of your pedigree, O Lady of the Milk."

"Pedigree? Background? What are you talking about?" This time, Hanah addressed him as *du*.

Nehemyah began laughing so hard he could barely speak:

"Ha-ha! . . . *Background!* . . . *Creative!* . . . What nonsense!"

"What are you saying? I can't understand a word," she said.

As soon as they entered the commune yard, he raised his voice almost to a shout:

"I couldn't care less about your background! When a person is in love—or, as you would say, *cherishes* someone—nothing else matters!"

She stared at him hard and earnestly. Because the sky was overcast and there were no stars, his face was not clearly visible, but she could see his black eyes glowing like two tiny hearth fires. Then dawn came and brushed the clouds from the sky, and Hanah was able to see his face. She gazed at it with great devotion and admiration.

"Until tomorrow, my dear child," Nehemyah said.

"Until this evening, my one delight, my life," Hanah breathed straight into his ear, and ran off to the cow barn.

***

In the days that followed, Nehemyah was surprisingly content to have so little work to do. He made only a couple of sketches a day, and often both sketches pleased him. As they began their walk one evening, he said to Hanah:

"I hope my work keeps going this well."

"It will; if course it will," Hanah said wholeheartedly.

"How do you know about such things, you milkmaid, you?"

"I know from my own experience that work always goes down easier when it's smeared with butter."

"Aha, but why don't you know that you have to give me a kiss?"

"That's news to me! But you'll get one soon enough!" The next moment, she was clasped in his arms like a barrel in an iron hoop. Her heart leapt up and fluttered with painful sweetness somewhere in the dimple beneath her throat.

And then? Then they walked slowly along; she didn't take her eyes off him, because she couldn't comprehend the source of his fascinating, terrible power, which both fettered her and liberated her from herself. It made her so weak that she disappeared, she became as though submerged within him.

"Don't look at me like that, I can't bear it," he begged her, kissing each of her ten fingers in turn. But she kept right on gazing at him, marveling at how his eyes were able to penetrate her very soul.

She asked—not him, but the diffuse greenish starshine:

"Where, where does this power come from?"

"What power?"

"Your power. You aren't very tall, your shoulders aren't broad; look at how small your hands are, how thin your fingers are," she observed dreamily.

"Don't say that." He thrust his hands into his pockets. "My hands are very strong, and I'll have you know that an artist needs more strength than a farmer, or a smith, or anyone in the world! Come here, give me a kiss, a last kiss, and then run and catch some sleep, dear child of mine."

But Hanah was not destined to run and catch any sleep that morning, nor in the nights or mornings to come. More than once in those days she said to him:

"How easily my hands finish their work, how quickly everything gets done. There's no need for sleep when you hold happiness in your hands . . ."

* * *

The blond artist had been right when he said, "There are no secrets here." But it was especially true that Hanah and Nehemyah weren't a secret. The communards had seen them together in the cattle barn, on the steppe, by the silos, and at the Children's Home.

The days rolled by, and Nehemyah's departure drew ever nearer. Hanah seldom walked out on the steppe with him now. On top of all her regular duties, she now had yet another responsibility: the nearby collective farm, the Jewish Farmer, had acquired fifteen cows, and her expertise was constantly needed there. This collective farm was located five kilometers from the commune, so it wasn't easy for Hanah to get there, but nevertheless, she spent several hours there every day.

Nehemyah teased:

"You're lucky you don't have to milk the cows in Jankoy and Freidorf, too! There's certainly no lack of Jewish farming in Crimea."

"The local Jewish peasants don't need my advice. They're more experienced than I am," Hanah explained.

But it wasn't only because Hanah had more duties now that she seldom went out for walks on the steppe with Nehemyah. She felt as though she already had more than enough reminders of how soon he would be leaving. Of course, a practical person like Hanah hadn't been actively seeking a romance; now that fate had brought her one, she was amazed, and sometimes even a little frightened, at Nehemyah's constant outpourings of affection. She had never known that such bliss was possible.

Recently, when he had invited her to go out on the steppe with him, she had said:

"No, Nehemyah. Don't be angry, because I have no idea what's happening to me, what kind of magic there is hidden inside you. I was as hard as a stone; you've made me softer than a raspberry . . . But instead of going for a walk, my dearest, come and see the children with me. My children are deprived enough, God knows. They should at least get a visit once in a while."

Nehemyah, of course, wanted to be alone with Hanah, but he was diplomatic enough not to object. So off to the Children's Home he went, bringing with him some little squares of padded cloth on which he had painted colts, lambs, roosters, and hens. The children were so enchanted by the animal pictures that they didn't even notice he had also drawn captivating little groups of children on each square of fabric.

* * *

One morning during the dawn milking, Chairman Elkind came into the cattle barn. He studied the cows and the bulls, stood for a moment watching Hanah, and then said:

"After the milking, please come to my office. We need to talk about an important matter."

"Is it about the hay that's waiting at the Yevpatoria Ozet?" Hanah asked.

"Come to my office and you'll find out. A busy man like me doesn't have time to stand around explaining things to a lazy girl like you."

"You're right; I'll come."

When Hanah walked into the office, it struck her as very odd that no one was there except herself and the Chairman. He pushed a chair toward Hanah and said:

"Sit down, relax."

"I don't have time; I'll stand."

"'Never stand up when you can sit down,'" he said, quoting the well-known saying, and then began speaking in earnest. "Hanah, I've heard that you're spending all your free time with the artist, and it apparently doesn't bother him that the cattle have become lonely and sad. Furthermore—"

Hanah glared at him and interrupted:

"Furthermore nothing. There's not a thing you can say against him."

"Shut your mouth and listen; I have a great deal more experience than you. It's true that I can't say anything about this man, one way or the other; it may be that he's a perfectly respectable person. But you have to realize he's cut from an entirely different cloth than you—"

"I don't know what kind of cloth he's cut from, but I do know he's very dear to my heart."

"Stop interrupting and let me finish. Imagine how you'll feel, even in the best case, if he genuinely means what he says and takes you and the children away to Moscow with him."

"I don't know what he means or what he thinks; I only know that I'd go with him to the ends of the earth. I don't understand why that concerns you!"

"But it does concern me, Hanah. Can't you tell that I like you—that I'm attracted to you? Of course, who isn't impressed by an artist? But don't be too hasty: that kind of life isn't all wine and roses. On the other hand, it may very well be that if you stay here, the commune will send you to Simferopol to continue your education. It's somewhat difficult to predict at this point . . . Do you remember how I ran into you when you were riding back from Saki? I made some silly remark, that I liked your legs or something, and you rode off and left me sitting there, speechless?"

"Yes, I remember."

He took a long stride toward her and laid his hands on her shoulders, and she felt as though those hands were slowly sliding toward her throat. She wrenched herself away, moved toward the door, and spoke with as much calm and restraint as she could muster:

"It seems to me that you want to walk on ten different paths with only one pair of feet. You've already had children with three different women. I will not be a fifth wheel on your wagon, do you hear?!"

"Stop, Hantche, you can't walk away from me like this!"

"Enough!" Hanah shouted. "This will never happen, never in the whole world!" And she ran out of the office.

Although she still had plenty of work to do in the barn, she flew right by it and kept going, past the smithy, to the edge of the commune and across the Sabantoy Road. There she sat down on the ground, but immediately jumped up again and began pacing back and forth in great agitation, completely unable to make sense of what had just happened.

When she returned to the commune, there was the Chairman, coming right at her. She tried to get away, but his long legs carried him closer and closer. Snatching at her hand, he spoke rapid-fire:

"Hanakeh, no one walks out on me like that! When I say I want something, that's all there is to it!"

"Let go of me! You're not my lord and master; I'm not your dog. Anyway, why are you so interested in me all of a sudden? You've been Chairman for over two years. Have you been busy with riper fruit, waiting for me to mature? Oh yes, I know all about you—always looking for something new to satisfy that insatiable appetite of yours. My mother used to warn me about men like you; your motto is 'A wild bird's no trouble, but two in a cage cost double.' Leave me alone!" Hanah finished, and ran off to the cattle barn.

Nehemyah was waiting for her there. He took one look at her and asked:

"What is it, dearest, was there a problem with your work?"

"Yes, a small one."

"Well, what happened? Tell me!"

"What happened? Don't you know? You've infected me with a very strange illness: Wherever I go and whatever I do, you're right there in front of my eyes. I can't be without you for a single minute. I ask you, what will I do when you go away?"

"Excellent! That's how it should be! I will go away, but I'll return, and I'll take you back with me. I've got the same grave illness as you. Whenever I leave the Livestock Brigade, I feel like I have to see you again right this minute, right now, just to make sure you really exist . . . My poor Hanah, come give me a kiss."

"The cowhands are turning this way."

"Well, let them kiss, too! Come." Nehemyah didn't so much speak the last word as groan it. Then he wreathed her entire face with kisses: her cheeks, her eyes, her forehead, even the crown of her head. Finally he tore himself away, looked at her, and softly begged:

"My life and my breath, walk away from me a little, I want to see your movements in the light of the sun . . ."

"Whatever you order me to do, I'll always obey. And if, God forbid, you ever stop caring about me, you should tell me so right away. Wait, I want to stroke your face," Hanah said in a trembling voice, and ran into the barn.

***

As Hanah was leaving the Children's Home that evening, she found Nehemyah waiting for her.

"Hanakeh, why are you so quiet?"

"Let's both be quiet. Listen. Do you hear what's happening on the steppe? A song is playing there, about how Nehemyah and Hanah are walking there together, so secretly, so silently. And the stars are looking at them and winking; they wonder, where did such a pair come from? . . ."

"My joy, my friend," said Nehemyah, but he couldn't utter another word, because their lips were sealed together. They were as united as the sky is with the stars.

At dawn, when they came back to the commune, Nehemyah said:

"I have never, never been without you. How is this possible—how did we not know about each other? . . . Why are you crying? Don't you dare cry! I know—it's about the children. But you should know that you have no reason to cry about our children. They'll be more mine than any children are by their own fathers! Come to me, my poor child. Let me kiss your beautiful eyes, your forehead that's so small but holds so much intelligence and love. Come closer, come closer to me; all my strength is leaving me," he whispered to her.

But even this rarest of all rare loves that existed between Nehemyah and Hanah—a love that was free of ambition, of greed, of any self-interest whatsoever, and that was permeated by a single, overwhelming passion to be together—even such a love could not hold back time. More than once Hanah thought: "How did I live without him until now, and how can I stay here without him? What a terrifying thought!"

Now Hanah clearly understood that she hadn't had the slightest idea what love was before she met Nehemyah. It seemed as though fate must surely have sent him to her. She had already asked him several times:

"Tell me, my dear one, how did you know you should come here?"

"I didn't know any such thing, silly. But I first noticed you, you remember, when you cleaned up the table after the chickens got into the dining hall. That was when I knew I absolutely had to meet you. And now, even though I'm going away, my soul and my heart are staying here with you. So you mustn't worry about anything, because we'll still be together. It's as simple as that."

Hanah believed him with all her heart, but her belief could not slow the passage of time. In the evening she said to Nehemyah:

"Why were we so blind? A whole week vanished away before we got to know each other."

"Yes, a whole week! And in three days I'll be leaving," Nehemyah said in such a heartbroken voice that Hanah turned away and started crying again.

For the last three days, they went only to the Children's Home in the evenings. And it wasn't just the two of them that were downhearted: The children became sad, too, as if they could sense what was happening.

On the appointed day, Hanah led Borech from the stable. She pushed him slowly backwards between the shafts of the two-wheeled cart and hitched him up. Nehemyah brought all his gear and laid it in the wagon bed, and then both of them, Hanah and Nehemyah, seated themselves in the wagon. Hanah tugged on the reins and said a few words of encouragement to Borech—but the horse didn't budge from the spot. So Hanah jumped out and tugged on the bridle. Borech pretended not to understand. She cajoled him with words, held the reins in her hand, even gave him a light lashing with the short whip—all to no avail.

Finally, Hanah hit upon a better idea: She ran off to the stable, returned with a sack of salt, and climbed up on Borech's back. Thinking they were going out on the steppe as usual, the horse set off at once with his gentle ambling gait.

The few people who happened to be walking along the road to Saki that day smiled to see such a bizarre team: a woman riding a cart horse, while a man sat forlornly in the wagon behind her, surrounded by luggage, with a long, folded umbrella in a tight cover slung over his shoulder like a rifle. Unfortunately, Nehemyah did not share their amusement. From time to time, he merely remarked in a sad voice: "Maybe Borech is used to it by now. Try sitting near me." Hanah would obligingly jump down from the saddle—but Borech always stopped in his tracks and refused to move until she was on his back again.

At the Saki Railway Station, all activity came to a standstill as the two-wheeled cart pulled up with Hanah in the saddle. The passengers waiting for the train to Moscow watched with great curiosity as Nehemyah showered Hanah's face, her hands, and even the scarf on her head with kisses.

After the train had left, the woman standing closest to Hanah said:

"Sister, you're a lucky girl: that man is dying of love, he's pining away for you. Grab that luck by the coattails. Grab it, you hear what I'm telling you? And hold on tight, with both hands!"

Riding back to the commune that day, Hanah was restless in the saddle. The cart clattered behind her, but she saw and heard nothing. For the first time, she was late for the evening milking. For the very first time . . .

II

If it had been possible for Nehemyah to be in Moscow and on the commune at the same time, he would have been shocked to see how much Hanah had changed. Her face, her movements, and her voice seemed drained of all vitality. She herself didn't know what was happening to her. Sometimes the livestock workers would ask her a question and she wouldn't answer; she didn't even hear them. There were days when her work was the only thing that got Hanah out of bed in the morning. The steppe and the sky just didn't arouse the same joy in her as before. During the midday milking, she didn't even bother to look up at the clear blue sky or the dazzling sun overhead. But then, in her mind, she would hear Nehemyah timidly asking, "Comrade Brigadier, perhaps you could detain the herd here?" and instantly the steppe would brighten, the cows would come back into focus, and everything would return to normal.

No matter where she was—near the silos, in the yard, by the well— Hanah was always waiting. Any minute, she thought, he would come back. It seemed to her that an eternity had passed since he had gone away.

In reality, it had been scarcely two weeks since she had driven him to Saki. The memory of that day was still clear in her mind; she could still hear the stranger telling her, "Little sister, you're a lucky girl; grab that man by the coattails, don't let him out of your hands!"

"Grab him?" Hanah thought. "But where is he? Surely he's painting, and is so busy that it hasn't occurred to him to write a few words . . ."

It was a good thing Nehemyah couldn't overhear Hanah from such a distance; if he had, he would soon have heard bitter words falling from her lips. A couple of days before, when Hanah had left the dining hall after lunch, the Chairman, Mendel Elkind, had stopped her.

"Haven't you gotten any letters yet? You must understand, he's an intelligent and busy man. He doesn't have time for such trifles . . ."

"Don't worry, I will get letters, thank you very much," Hanah had answered, all the while thinking, yet again, that she really must do away with Elkind. She had even talked about this with Shimke from the stable, but he had told her:

"Hanah, let it go. It can't be done with some old hatchet, you know. You'd need a pistol."

But the Secret Police beat Hanah to it. One night in the fall of 1930, Elkind was taken away. He vanished into thin air, along with the other leftist Gdudniks who fell into the clutches of the "night patrol" gang.

That was how Hanah was prevented from becoming a murderer.

* * *

The day started out just like any other: Hanah saddled Borech, rode out onto the steppe, milked the cows, and ordered the herders to drive the cattle to the gullies. Then she rode off by herself. If the horse had been able to talk, he would certainly have spoken kind words to Hanah to soothe her troubled spirits. Instead, he whinnied several times, fanned his tail, dug at the earth with his front hoof, and broke into a gallop, as though he were trying to distract her from her sorrows. But Hanah's mood didn't improve. She rode around on the steppe until dusk, then went to see how the cows were feeding. Later in the evening, when it became cooler, she headed back toward the commune.

"Halt!" She heard a quiet command. She didn't see who had called for her to stop, but whoever it was, she wasn't inclined to obey. She flicked the reins and poked Borech's sides with her feet so he would pick up his pace. But the man who had shouted "Halt!" overtook Hanah and appeared near Borech's muzzle, as though he had sprung straight up out of the earth. He grabbed the bridle with both hands and quietly said, "Get down!"

Hanah bent forward and tore the stranger's hands away from the bridle, and Borech took off again like the wind. But she could hear the man running after them and shouting:

"That's my horse! It always was! Some rat had me sent away as a kulak, but I'm back!"

As Hanah rode into the stable, Shimke asked:

"Hantche, what's wrong? You look like you've seen a ghost!"

"It's nothing. Borech just got a bit wild," Hanah said, and walked off to the cattle barn.

The milkmaids also noticed that Hanah was upset.

"Are you ill?" Toybke asked.

"What gives you that idea? I'm just exhausted."

"We were wondering why you didn't get here on time. We've already milked our third cows."

"It's nothing serious, I'll catch up," Hanah said, almost calmly.

After dinner, Hanah went for a walk with Hayaleh and told her what had happened.

"It could very well be," Hayaleh mused. "There's no shortage of malicious people around. Maybe someone informed on him out of spite, and the horse really was his. But it's yours now. Forget about it," she added.

But Hanah couldn't forget about it. She didn't get a wink of sleep the whole night. She kept seeing the man in his tattered jacket with his bare, hairy chest showing through the holes, and she kept hearing his quiet command: "Get down!"

After the morning milking, she went to the stable and immediately discovered that Borech was not in his usual place. Shimke happened to be heading toward her.

"Did you give Borech to someone?" Hanah asked him.

"I don't know where he is. I thought you took him, but then I noticed that the saddle is still here."

"Stop pulling my leg; you gave him to someone, didn't you?"

"Who's pulling your leg? I was starving, so I went to get some breakfast. I come back—Borech is gone!"

"Are you sure he was here before you went to breakfast?"

"What kind of question is that?"

"Sometimes people nap on the job."

"Sometimes, maybe, but not this time. You should report it to the police. But he must be around here somewhere. You could probably catch him if you put salt on his tail."

"We'll see," Hanah remarked, but she knew very well who had taken Borech away.

The horse had indeed vanished into thin air. Hanah had no choice but to ride to the midday milking in the wagon, with the rest of the milkmaids. Everyone was talking about the theft, but Hanah stayed silent. Then, unexpectedly, her roommate Yocheved came running over with an envelope in her hand. She ran straight up to Hanah and cried out, "A letter for you!"

Leaving the milkmaids to their own devices, Hanah took the letter and headed off to the nearest silo. Her heart was pounding so hard she could barely tear open the envelope. When she did get it open, she sat down on the bottom step, closed her eyes, and didn't move for several moments. Finally, she pulled out the letter.

My wonder, my life, my Hanukaleh! Today is the twelfth day I've been alone. I did not even imagine I would long for you this much. I can't get any work done. And of course one must work. Yesterday I almost went to the Kursk Railway Station to buy a ticket, but I didn't, I just went back to work as usual. I'm hoping that at the beginning of November I'll finish my assignment, and in April I will be able to come and get you and the children. Now it's the end of September—count with me: October, November, December, January, February, March! April doesn't count, because the first week of April I will come to you.

Now listen carefully! Before my departure, I left a little booklet under your mattress; it is called an *akkreditiv*. When you go to Saki, you should bring this booklet with you. Take it to the bank, and somebody there will give you a form and tell you how to fill it out. Then you'll give them the certificate, and they will give you some money. The certificate is for three hundred rubles. You can do whatever you want with it, but I advise you to buy a padded jacket, some shoes, and a warm scarf. I didn't give you the certificate in person because I knew you wouldn't accept it, but I am sure you love me and will do as I ask. In Crimea it must be getting chilly by now, and you are running around barefoot and naked. Also, as you see, I have enclosed an envelope with my address. Write to me immediately.

Here in Moscow I have friends who are well-known Yiddish writers, and I've been speaking Yiddish with them. I even wrote a few words in Yiddish and showed Dobrushin. You should remember him, because he and another writer came to the commune once. He told me he knows you. He also told me that I write very fine Yiddish, but that I shouldn't mix in so many Russian words.

I entreat you, write immediately. I kiss you many more times than I did when I was with you. I cannot live without you, my child, my delight, my *prelest*. In my next letter I will write about what I plan to do so that you and the children can be with me as soon as possible.

Your lonely Nehemyah

It goes without saying that Hanah read the letter over several times. When she finally understood what the word *akkreditiv* meant and realized that Nehemyah was attempting to send her money, she was genuinely frightened. And she quickly came up with a plan.

It so happened that she had to be in Saki the next day. When she arrived at the health spa, she and Fyodor Petrovich settled the bill for the milk; he assured her that the spa would transfer the money into the commune's account by the end of the week. As always, he also invited Hanah to stay for lunch. As usual, she declined. Fyodor Petrovich apparently sensed that Hanah was upset, so in his discreet way, without asking her any direct questions, he remarked:

"It seems as though you're a bit uneasy about something."

"You're not mistaken; today I came here on foot."

"The management took away your horse?"

"The horse was stolen."

"Did you report it to the police?"

"Yes. So far they haven't found any trace of it."

"Do you suspect someone?"

"No."

"A curious crime. The thief didn't take anything else?"

"Not even the bridle or the saddle, although they were lying right outside the stall, one step away from the horse," Hanah said.

"It's hard to imagine why someone would do something like this, but the times are very unsettled right now. A lot of fugitives are lurking around. There have even been cases of people being sent away who were not really kulaks. It may be that such a person took your horse."

"How do you know, Fyodor Petrovich, that such people are lurking around here? And how do you know that such mistakes have been made?"

"I tell you, I know. You aren't a child anymore, Hanah Davidovna; you should understand that in every village there is someone who envies his neighbor's house or his neighbor's team. So he writes down whatever comes into his head, sends it to the authorities, and the next thing you know, his neighbor has disappeared from the village. The times are very, very hard right now. And until the new collective farms get up and running, the situation will continue."

Fyodor Petrovich's face was grave. Hanah was not so disturbed by his words, however, as to forget about the booklet. She took it out from under her headscarf and passed it to him as though it were something disgusting. He examined the booklet for a moment, then looked at Hanah in surprise and said:

"I don't understand; why are you giving this to me?"

"A man with whom I recently became acquainted left it for me, but I can't accept it. I don't know how to send it back, and I don't want anyone at the commune to know about it. I wanted to ask if you would be so good as to go with me to the post office to mail it back to him."

"Do you have the address?"

"Yes."

"Let's go."

Sending off the *akkreditiv* in a registered envelope, generously paid for by Fyodor Petrovich, lifted a huge weight off Hanah's heart.

"I'm so grateful to you, you can't imagine. But . . . for me it is . . ." She trailed off, too embarrassed to admit she had no way to repay him.

"Hanah Davidovna, I understand. My few kopeks? That's nothing. All I want is for you to stay just the way you are; nothing else matters to me."

"Goodbye. I have to go. Before long, it will be time for the evening milking—and now, of course, I'm a pedestrian."

* * *

Hanah managed to get back to the commune on time. After the evening milking was done and work in the barn was finished for the night, she went to the Children's Home. She spent upwards of an hour there, then headed off to see the Secretary of the Village Council to borrow a pen and ink, two sheets of blank paper, and an old newspaper. With these, she returned to the barn.

"You can go lie down in the calf barn for a little while," Hanah told the cowhand on duty. "There's some fresh straw in there."

When the man had left to catch some sleep, Hanah found a small board and sat down on a wagon wheel beneath the light of a lantern. She spread the newspaper on the board, wiped her hands on the pinafore of her *sarafan,* laid the stationery on top of the newspaper, and began to write.

Nehemyaleh, Nehemyaleh! Your letter delighted me greatly, my dear. But I would have been even happier if I had received it earlier. Sometimes, you know, a person even sends a telegram when he senses the other person is worried. Eleven days have I waited as though it were one long hour. You should never, never do this to me again! I am addressing you as *ir,* not *du,* because only a complete stranger would treat me like this!

Now I have to tell you that I have sent back the booklet, or as you call it, the *akkreditiv.* When you receive it, you should write to me at once. I marvel that such an idea occurred to you. How did it even enter your head? Don't you know that I am already rich, don't you see that I don't want to be any richer? . . . Why didn't you write to me about what kind of assignment you're working on? Do you think I won't understand? If so, you are mistaken. Write me precisely what you are making and for whom, and I will understand right away.

Now I want to tell you what has been happening with me—not with me alone, but with me and the sheep. Last week I was out on the steppe. The sheep were grazing not far from the cows. Suddenly, black clouds covered the whole sky, and there arose such a storm that the cows started to bellow, and the sheep wouldn't stop bleating. In a flash there came floods of rain, it poured down by the bucketful, and the sheep broke into a terrified run. All of us together—the shepherds, the cowherds, and I—couldn't stop them until the rain let up. We all came back to the commune soaked to the skin. A few dozen sheep got away, but I didn't notice that until the next day, when I went out on the steppe for the midday milking. Never have I seen such a thing before. And I finally understand why people say "foolish as a sheep."

I am also very angry about something strange that you wrote to me: "Don't count April." That's easy for you to say, but for me, each day is like the seven years that Jacob tormented himself because of Laban. But of course you don't know what that means. Ask Dobrushin, he'll tell you. I do indeed know him and remember him. Send him my warmest greetings.

I walk around like an invalid. I yearn for you so, I can't even describe it. On top of that, I have another great heartache: Borech was stolen. When we see each other again, I'll tell you why and how. I wait with impatience for your next letter. There can be fewer "dears" and *prelests* in it, as long as there are more signs that you know what's happening with me,

your lonely, lucky Hanah

As soon as Hanah had dropped the letter into the mailbox by the office, she began waiting for a reply. During this period, her work kept her in such a constant rush that she had time for only four or five hours of sleep a night—which was a blessing in disguise, since it kept her mind off Nehemyah's absence.

Meanwhile, here is what was happening on the commune: As previously mentioned, the old Chairman, Mendel Elkind, had been removed, and another man was sent in his place. The communards speculated that Elkind had been sent away because he had cared nothing about their living conditions. As for the new Chairman, red-hot rumors about him quickly began to circulate. The workers from the Field Brigade claimed the new Chairman didn't know the difference between oats and wheat. In the dining hall, Shifraleh the Milkmaid reported that the new Chairman had come into the barn, looked at the cows, and then gone over to the bulls and asked why they had such small udders. The communards laughed until they wept. They wondered why such a man, of all people, had been sent to oversee them; they'd heard that in Simferopol he had been the director of a garment factory.

Later, it turned out he wasn't such a hopeless case after all. He began to get a feel for running the commune, and as a result of his innovations, conditions were completely transformed. Hanah would no longer have to be ashamed of the place in front of guests.

* * *

This time, she didn't have to wait long for a letter. Nehemyah wrote:

My dearest, my only Hanukeh, I received the *akkreditiv* and your letter. I might have expected many things, but this? . . . All I wanted was for you to be more warmly dressed and not go barefoot. What in the world am I going to do with you? Luckily, I can't be angry, but it was wrong of you to offend me like that. I thought you were my wife and I was your husband. It turns out I made a mistake. That's why, when I come to the commune, I'll give you a good thrashing!

Well, enough about that. You ask what kind of assignment I'm doing. I'm making illustrations for a Russian textbook. Soon I'll be ready to turn them in. Up until now, I haven't written in detail about my work because I thought it wouldn't interest you. From now on, I shall always write to you about everything. And you, my *prelest,* should also write me more about yourself and about the children. (You may write about the cows and the sheep, too.)

Why should I need to ask Dobrushin about that? I studied the Torah, you know! When you wrote about Jacob, I remembered the whole story. Laban was a scoundrel. Not only did he exploit Jacob, he also tricked him into marrying his daughter Leah with the bad eyes. But no one will fool me like that. And the one I've chosen for myself will be mine forever. Is it not so, my life?

Now I must tell you that I've taken another job, because when I bring you and the children here, there will be no money to spare. (By the way, it's unfair of you to think that just because I tried to send you some money, I don't know how rich you are in the things that really matter. Indeed, I am well aware that in this respect you will be giving me some of your wealth. If I hadn't understood this, I would never have chosen you as my wife.) In any case, I took this second job because it's possible that I won't receive any more official assignments for some time. This way, I won't sit idle. I can find work for myself here as I did on the commune, remember? There are plenty of opportunities to paint from life in the city, too. True, there are no cows and no steppe, but there are people, houses, streets—and those are also a part of nature.

I think you understand how important my work is for me. But just to be sure, I feel I must make it very clear to you, once again, that there is nothing in the world more important and more serious for me than my work.

Here it is, almost the end of October; soon it will be time for the November holidays. For me, too, the days drag by; they're very long and boring. How am I going to survive the minutes until I get off the train at the Saki station and hug you?

I am sending you a little money so you can buy the children whatever you want. For yourself, you should buy nothing; go barefoot! Dobrushin asked me to send you a greeting, my only, my most beloved Madame Rothschild!

Your Nehemyah

Hanah did accept the small sum of money from Nehemyah, and, since the November holidays were indeed approaching, she bought some sweets and divided them between the Children's Home of her commune and that of the Jewish Farmer, where she was still very busy.

To this day, people talk about that holiday on the commune. The new Chairman found some milled boards somewhere, and real floors were laid down in the dining hall. He also found oilcloths for the tables. The night before the celebration, the workers slaughtered six sheep that would not, in any case, have troubled this sinful world for very long. On the holiday itself, the baker created such enormous loaves of braided challah that they had to be brought into the dining hall on special carrying boards. Fresh fish were also purchased in Yevpatoria, and the cooks made real gefilte fish. And Hayaleh the Gardener contributed the last pale, crooked cucumbers of the season.

Guests also came to the celebration from the Red Guard commune. They brought a pile of homemade pork sausages and two large casks of wine. And Fyodor Petrovich came, too. He brought a big wreath of pretzels, several paper bags full of candy, and a box of apples for the Children's Home. After the opening speeches, Fyodor Petrovich announced that he had also brought boots for the Livestock Brigade, just as he had promised Hanah. He added that since he knew Hanah Davidovna better than he did the other communards, he was giving a special thanks to her for the milk, which was always so rich and had never once gone sour in the entire two years that the Saki spa had been receiving it.

Once the formalities ended, the feast got underway. The communards had never seen such well-laden tables. The braided challahs, the gefilte fish, and the greasy pork sausages drew them like a magnet. The dinner continued until the light of dawn.

After the celebration, when Hanah was seeing Fyodor Petrovich off, he leaned down from his wagon and asked:

"Have you read the newspaper article 'Dizzy with Success'?"

"Yes."

"I expect that quite a few people will be leaving their positions now," he remarked seriously. At the time, Hanah did not understand his meaning, but later she comprehended it very well . . .

* * *

After the morning milking, Hanah sat down to write a letter.

First of all, I want to take the weight off your mind, my dear, my only Nehemyah. You can rest assured that when I come to live with you, I am not going to sit around and wait for you to earn all the money. You have, of course, seen with your own eyes that I am no lazy woman. There may not be any cows or steppes in Moscow, but there are mills, factories, and other facilities where workers are needed. You write that when we are together, we won't have any money to spare. Although it's been three years since I've laid eyes upon a single kopek, I realize you are right about this.

I'm glad you wrote that your work is more important for you than anything in the world. I know that being an artist is not the easiest way to make a living, but believe me, it would never enter my head that an artist and his family should live better or more comfortably than any other hardworking people. Furthermore, it seems to me that you wanted to scare me a little bit with the prospect of poverty. You should know by now that I don't scare easily.

But if you feel that my children and I will put your career at risk, I'm telling you right now that, as unhappy and lonely as I would be without you, you are free! You are not obligated to give up your beloved art for our sake; remember this!

Lastly, I want to tell you that with each passing day I love you all the more, and that without you, my life is no life at all.

Your faithful, well-wishing Hanah

Having finished the letter, Hanah put it in an envelope, dropped it into the mailbox near the office, and went off to milk. And the next day, and the day after that—each day was exactly like the one before: work, and more work, and in between, the joy of Nehemyah's letters. And his letters came more and more often, and Hanah had nothing but pleasure from them.

Here is what Nehemyah wrote next:

My one and only, my dearest, I read over your last letter several times. What can I tell you? You threw a stone straight at my head with your three words "you are free." If you knew how that hurt me, you would never allow such words out of your mouth.

I didn't want to offend you or frighten you, I wanted you to know that an artist walks a thorny path. I must tell you again that art is more precious to me than anything in the world. And that my work is my priority. I'm telling you this now because I will never speak of it again.

Why don't you answer my letters right away? What do you do in the evenings? After all, now you have back all the free time I used to take away

from you! The days are short now, but the nights are so long and lonely.
I send you enough kisses to fill all the days and nights since we parted.

Yours, and yours alone, from You Know Who

Then came a period when Hanah did not receive a letter for almost
three weeks; she was convinced she would never get another. But there is a
saying, "God sends the remedy before the plague," and that year, the cows
started to calve early, in the middle of December. Hanah began staying
in the barn all night, since she couldn't abandon the man on night duty,
Shloyme from Zhmerynka, who had never even owned a goat, much less
birthed a cow.

It is late at night. Venera is calving. She stands still, stands still . . .
Then, all at once, she lies down on the floor, stretches out her neck, turns
her head to one side, and rubs the ground with her cheek. Her belly towers above her; something is continually rolling around inside it. Suddenly
she stands up again, emits a deafening and pitiful bellow, and looks with
detached astonishment at her own belly, as if she wants to discover what's
in there, breaking her backbone into pieces.

Hanah is already doing everything that can be done, and it seems to
her that there will never be an end to it . . . She strokes and rubs the cow's
belly from the shoulder blade all the way to the pelvis as sweat falls from
her face onto Venera's hot, damp hide. Hanah is exhausted; her strength
is nearly gone. Then the cow falls to the ground again; all four legs stretch
out at once. Hanah jumps up. There is a loud, wet smack, and with the
last of her strength, Hanah catches a damp, shiny black bull calf. She
wipes the calf off with a clean sack.

"Mazel tov!" says Shloyme. He lifts up the calf, gives a groan, exclaims,
"Damn, it's as heavy as lead!" and carries it away to the calf barn.

Hanah walks along the gangway between the stalls until she comes
to the corner where the two fathers of all the calves are standing. Amur,
a light-gray Swedish bull, is lying down. Mishka, a dark-red German, is
standing and growling. Hanah assumes he's growling from hunger, so she
takes a shovelful of oat bran and carries it around behind Mishka's feeding trough. But as she is pouring out the bran, the bull wheels around and
points his horns directly at Hanah's chest. It's a miracle she doesn't drop
the shovel. But she doesn't back down: she hits Mishka right on the mouth
with the rim of the shovel. He jerks backward. Deathly afraid, Hanah

slides out between the trough and the wall. A dreadful scream escapes her throat of its own accord and continues until she hears Shloyme's stammering voice.

"What? What is it?" Then, seeing Hanah, he exclaims, "That scream was enough to wake the dead!"

"Go back to sleep, it was only a dream," Hanah says, almost indifferently. But not long after this, she convinces the Chairman that Mishka should be sent to the slaughterhouse.

* * *

No type of task, duty, or obligation can grip someone by the throat the way a personal problem can. Although Hanah was not one of those people who think only about themselves, she was now so unbearably bitter about Nehemyah's long silence that she didn't know what to do. Even visiting the children didn't make her feel any better.

The Crimean winter began with mild weather. After a brief spell of snow and rain, the sun shone again and warmed the short days. At this time of year, there was less work to do: the cows were milked only twice a day, and Hanah traveled to Saki only once every two weeks. The spa was now being run by someone new; every time Hanah went there to settle the accounts, she compared the new manager with Fyodor Petrovich, and this did nothing to alleviate her unhappiness.

No letter, no letter from Nehemyah . . . and then, she received a telegram:

MEET THE 25 DECEMBER, COACH 5, I KISS YOU, YOUR NEHEMYAH.

Hanah made arrangements for the milkmaids to milk "her" cows on the designated day. After midnight, she hitched a pair of oxen to a wagon and drove off—or, more accurately, rattled off—to meet Nehemyah. The oxen walked slowly; the wheels squeaked; the wagon, seemingly disconcerted by the unexpected journey, groaned in its every plank. Hanah sat as though on a hot skillet. The night was a starry one, but she saw nothing. The steppe was monotonous enough even in the daytime; now all its details were hidden in darkness. Other than the measured strides of the oxen, the squeaking and groaning of the wagon, she heard nothing; other than the bony necks and backs of the oxen, she saw nothing. From time to time throughout the cold night, she would get down and walk alongside the cart rails. She didn't bother lifting her eyes to the sky, and it seemed to her as though she would keep walking and walking and walking at this maddeningly slow pace forever, and miss Nehemyah's arrival. In her impatience, she occasionally broke into a run, passed the oxen, and then ran back.

For all her worrying, she arrived at the Saki station two hours before the train was scheduled to arrive. Recalling that a shipment of oil cakes for the cows was waiting to be picked up, she left the oxen and cart at the railway station and walked over to the Zagatzerno Grain Elevator. In the yard stood wagons from the Red Guard commune, the Jewish Farmer collective farm, and the Youngwood commune. Two men from Red Guard were sitting in a wagon, wolfing down their food in a manner that made Hanah feel ill. One of the communards recognized her and shouted, "Come on over, there's enough for you too!" and he held out a big chunk of pork and a slice of wheat bread.

As soon as Hanah swallowed the first bite, she felt so warm that she unbuttoned her jacket.

"There, that'll warm you up, eh? No need to thank us. Come sit up here in the wagon. No one gets out of Zagatzerno in a hurry; you'll be eating lunch with us, too. We're not as delicate and fussy about our food as other people. That's how we manage to eat three meals a day," joked the communard, and he winked at Hanah.

"At lunchtime I'll be part of a twosome," Hanah informed him.

"What good is a twosome? Don't go away; we'll be a threesome," the man teased again. But Hanah didn't hear him; she was hurrying back to the railway station. She suddenly had a feeling that Nehemyah was already waiting for her. But when she arrived, there was still no sign of the train.

The last minutes dragged by as though through tar. Hanah waited and watched so eagerly that when the train finally did pull in, she ran right past the fifth coach. Breathlessly, she turned back and fell straight into Nehemyah's outstretched arms. He spun her around as though she were a child. Then he set her down, looked at her, sprang forward, snuggled against her coat, tore himself away, looked at her again, and asked in alarm:

"Hanukeh, are you well? I don't even recognize you. You look pale, and you're so thin!"

Hanah wanted to reassure him, but she began to cry so hard that she couldn't utter a word.

"Crying? What's the matter? We'll never be apart again." He spoke quietly and kissed her eyes and her wet cheeks.

Now, on the way back to the commune, the oxen stride carefully and slowly; the wheels squeak; the wagon creaks; the sun grows warm; the withered grasses tremble in the breeze; and in the bed of the wagon they sit as a couple, the two of them together. "My soul, my dear child, my joy," murmurs Nehemyah. "My little sun, my dream, my breath—and my life," babbles Hanah straight into his ear. Then they look wordlessly at each other for a long time, as if they can see straight into each other's souls.

The two mute oxen, the sky, the steppe, the bright sky belt softly clasping the dark seam of the earth—everything is inevitable, just like Nehemyah's and Hanah's first meeting. As the oxen move along, their wasted jaws grind slowly over the sparse regurgitated straw. They walk evenly, with no notion of what is happening behind them in the wagon . . .

* * *

Back at the commune, Hanah persuaded the new Chairman to transfer her roommates, Cheved and Rivke, to the women's dormitory. And the next day, she and Nehemyah became the proprietors of a "private" room.

In those days, just as today, it was impossible for a person to be completely cut off from everyday life. Hanah went to milk the cows that evening, as always—but on this particular evening, she arrived in an exceedingly festive mood. The milkmaids and the cowhands, it seemed to her, were unusually well behaved and friendly, and the work went as smoothly as butter.

After completing the milking and the rest of her chores, Hanah ran straight back to Nehemyah. He took a blue dress out of his suitcase, held it up to her shoulders, and declared:

"You should see yourself—you look beautiful!"

Then he tossed a thin cream-colored fringed scarf over her shoulders and beamed. He had also brought little dresses and shoes for the three girls. But here Hanah objected:

"Are my children supposed to go around the commune dressed to the nines?"

"What do you mean, 'your' children? They're ours! Anyway, I've brought gifts for the other children, too. That's the first thing. Second, we'll be leaving the commune soon enough. Why do you look so surprised? Of course we're going to leave. Come, sit near me on the bed."

So they sat on the bed and didn't do any talking for quite a while. Then Hanah suddenly remembered that they hadn't eaten supper, and asked:

"Nehemyah, aren't you hungry?"

"Are you?"

"I feel so good, I don't even want to eat."

"Whether you want to or not, we should go," he said.

The dining hall was now completely transformed. The tables were set with the colorful oilcloths the new Chairman had brought in for the November holidays; the wooden floor was spotless, and no rafters protruded overhead—they were hidden under a ceiling of milled boards. The window frames and doors were painted bright colors. The food also wasn't anything like the swill they'd eaten over the summer: on the tables stood pickled tomatoes, farmer cheese made from sheep's milk, and fresh bread, and near each aluminum cup of tea lay a cube of sugar.

The majority of the communards had already eaten. But those who were still sitting at their tables when Hanah and Nehemyah came in cried out:

"A toast to Hanah! Comrade *khudozhnik,* just look at her, you've breathed new life into her!"

"What do you mean by 'her'? Are you referring to my Hanah?" Nehemyah asked calmly. His words made the proper impression—the room grew quiet at once.

After eating, Hanah and Nehemyah went to the Children's Home and delivered the clothes, toys, and candy he had brought from Moscow. The scene that followed is hard to describe. That evening, the children went to sleep two hours later than usual.

When Hanah and Nehemyah left the Children's Home and arrived back at their door, they caught the sound of happy voices inside. Opening the door, Hanah let out a joyful cry. Not because Hayaleh, Shimke, and Efroyim the Shepherd were inside; not because a table and several chairs had been brought in—no, Hanah cried out because the room was unrecognizable. The window was adorned with a curtain of yellow netting, the table spread with red chintz. In a jam jar stood a bouquet of everlasting flowers, which can keep their color for years without water. There was even an electric lamp illuminating the scene. Taking in all this magnificence, Hanah scolded Hayaleh:

"Is this your work? Did you take malaria pills before giving us your mosquito netting?"

"But isn't it pretty?" Hayaleh asked, and burst out laughing.

The door opened, and in came Leybke-Charlie the Tractor Driver, Shachne the Smith, and Ruvke the Salesman.

"Ruvke, we're all hoping you'll come through for us tonight," Hayaleh said to him.

Ruvke gave her a look and disappeared back out the door.

They sang a lot of songs, and more than one person said "Mazel tov!" to Nehemyah. Then Hayaleh brought in a pitcher of soda water, and at the same moment, Ruvke reappeared carrying a clay pot full of anchovies, a loaf of bread, and, in a paper bag, a half-melted clump of pale pink candies. The feasting began right away, and the atmosphere grew homey, just like at a real wedding. But the most joyful one of all was Hanah. She started singing so lustily that Nehemyah, who had been sitting beside her on the bed, got up and stood before her, never once taking his eyes off her.

"When will you make it official and go under the chuppah?" Hayaleh wanted to know.

"First of all, nobody goes under the chuppah anymore. Second, we'll go to the chuppah when my Hanaleh wants to." Nehemyah waved off everyone's curiosity.

It was long past midnight by the time they all left. Hanah was finally able to ask:

"Nehemyaleh, why didn't you write to me for so long, and why did you come back so much earlier than you said you would?"

"You wrote me in no uncertain terms that I should shower all my affection on my drawings! So I did, and I was able to finish the assignment much sooner than expected. Now you know why I came back so early . . . so come here and give me a kiss."

"All right, you did the right thing. I can't even describe how wonderful you are! But don't be in such a hurry—I'll give you a kiss already."

* * *

The time passed; the toil did not diminish. Hanah would come back from work so tired that she was practically falling off her feet. Then one evening when she walked into the room, she found a second cot there.

"Where did you get this from?" she asked Nehemyah.

"I went to the place where they're putting up the new building," he said. "I talked to the carpenters, and they gave me a few boards—see, I raised them up on bricks. I got a straw mattress from the dormitory, and the bedsheets I brought with me from Moscow."

Nehemyah had hoped that having a cot of her own would enable Hanah to get some real rest—a few hours at a time at least. But often, instead of sleeping on her cot, Hanah would sit down with Nehemyah on his, and the stories would come pouring out of her mouth as though of their own accord—stories about her childhood, about the shtetl. Hanah had such an excellent memory and such a facility with words that story-telling came naturally to her. Now she told him more about her family:

"I didn't have a father, and I don't even want to think about my step-father. I'm fond of my mother, from a distance, but as a child I couldn't stand the sight of her. She knew very well that my stepfather beat me, and she never defended me. Finally, as I told you, my grandmother found out I was being abused and took me away, and from then on I lived with her and my grandfather. My grandfather was utterly without malice, and he was very well respected, too—he had *smiches.*"

"What is *smiches?*"

"It means he was authorized to be a rabbi. I remember once, all the most important men in town came and asked him to be rabbi of the shtetl. But my grandfather said to them, 'Go in good health, thank you for the honor, but I would rather make a living from my trade, from masonry; I'm not worthy to be a rabbi because of all my *aveyres.*'"

"What does *aveyres* mean, Hanaleh?"

"Nehemyah, you're not letting me tell the story. Try to remember the words you don't understand and ask me about them afterwards. Now listen. In the summertime, my grandfather's job used to take him away from home for the whole week. He built fireplaces and ceramic tile stoves for the gentry. My grandmother taught herself how to dye cloth to make some extra money, but my grandfather was always scolding her about it. 'You don't have enough to do during the week, so, God forbid, you work on Shabbes, too? Why do you need to move heaven and earth for a few extra kopeks?' But that didn't help; my grandmother did what she had to do. And she never let me sit idle for one minute, either. I had to weed the garden, clean the house, help carry water—because for dyeing you need a lot of water. Naturally, I would rather have been running around outside with all the other girls, but I had no time for that. So I used to quarrel with my grandmother, and then I used to run off to my Uncle Hirshe the Miller, and then . . . well, it would take too long to tell you what happened then. At the age of fourteen I ran away from home, and at eighteen I traveled to the commune in Palestine."

"Now I understand why you wrote me such quarrelsome letters. I wasn't anything like you. I was a quiet, obedient son; I studied hard in school and drew pictures of everything I saw—and on every possible surface, too. As a result, I got my share of spankings, because I drew on the walls with coal, and on the table with chalk, until my mother couldn't stand it anymore. My father had died of consumption, and she had a houseful of children to raise. My older sister studied pharmacology and went off to Kostroma to work in a chemist's; one day she sent me some money, and I went to stay with her. A lot of intellectuals from Petrograd and other cities came to Kostroma in the twenties; there was a painter there, Nikolai Nikolaevich Kuprianov, who had just opened an art school. To make a long story short, my sister took my pictures to him, and he accepted me at his school. In nineteen twenty-two he went to Moscow and became a professor in Vkhutemas, and he encouraged me to apply there. So my sister gave me two herrings and half a loaf of bread, and off I went to Moscow. I passed the entrance exam with flying colors and, as you can see, I've become an artist. But it's very late; we should go to sleep now."

More easily said than done. Hanah had barely slipped out of his arms and into her new bed before it was time to run across the yard to the cattle barn. A few pale, cold stars were still visible in the sky. Hanah ran with her jacket unbuttoned; today she didn't feel like the silence was closing in on her.

In the barn she didn't hear what the milkmaids were saying, didn't even hear how the tin pails and milk cans clattered. As though surrounded by pealing bells, she was deaf to everything but the newly awakened yet long-awaited feelings that completely consumed her.

* * *

Hanah's days now flowed by in constant joy. As soon as she finished her work in the cattle barn, she would run back to "her" room, where new and wonderful things materialized daily. Nehemyah could not, of course, paint outdoors in such cold weather, so he stayed inside and made watercolor and pencil portraits of the communards. When Hanah came into the room, he would lay out what he had made that day on the beds, and Hanah would be beside herself with delight. She often exclaimed:

"Nehemyaleh, don't put them away yet. This one is obviously Leybke-Charlie, it looks exactly like him!"

Nehemyah would always smile, but once he quietly remarked:

"Hanukaleh, you still don't understand the work; that's why you keep praising it."

"You're right—but what else should I do, since I like it so much?"

"You like it? Then just look at it. You don't have to say anything."

And that was how Hanah learned to look at art without saying a word.

* * *

In the evenings she and Nehemyah often went to see the children. He would cut up squares of paper and draw pictures of horses and foals to bring to them. Not infrequently, these evenings ended with tears because the children didn't want Nehemyah and Hanah to leave.

With each passing day, Hanah felt all the more strongly that she couldn't live without Nehemyah. And she could tell it was the same for him. If she happened to be delayed at work for some reason, he would show up at the barn. After this had happened several times, Hanah found a work jacket for Nehemyah, and he started helping to muck out the stalls and crumble oil cakes into the feeding troughs. Other times, he would stand there with a sketchpad and pencil and draw the milkmaids and the cows.

One day, Shloyme, the cowhand on night duty, said to Nehemyah:

"Commune life certainly seems to suit you. Instead of taking Hanah and the children back to Moscow, maybe you should stay here with them. After all, you know the saying: 'A wild bird is no trouble, but two in a cage cost double!'"

"Commune life is very good," Nehemyah conceded. But he had already made up his mind to take Hanah and the girls back with him.

In those days, whenever Hanah traveled to Saki, Nehemyah would come along. But one day when it was very cold and snowy, she persuaded him to stay home. He worked indoors the whole day, and in the evening he set out on foot to meet Hanah at the edge of the commune—but a heavy snow was falling, and he had to turn back.

When Hanah finally returned from Saki, she found Nehemyah standing outside their building. He opened the front of his overcoat, wrapped her inside it, and breathlessly asked:

"Where have you been all this time?"

"Have you eaten yet, Nehemyah?"

"Who cares about eating? I thought I would lose my mind with worry!"

"Well, I did eat, as it happens. Come inside, I have good news!" Hanah said, so cheerfully that Nehemyah felt a little hurt. But once he heard what Hanah had to tell him, he was no less delighted than she was.

"I don't know whether you heard what happened with Fyodor Petrovich, the previous manager of the spa. He's such a good person; he's the one who helped me send back the *akkreditiv*. But he disappeared a while ago, and I didn't know what had happened to him.

"Well, to make a long story short, today I go to Saki, go into the spa office, and—Fyodor Petrovich is back! He told me they'd removed him from the spa and put him in charge of purchasing chickens and ducks for the collective farms. But before long, they realized it was a mistake and sent him back to his old job. So today I not only ate lunch at the spa, I drank a little glass of whiskey there, too."

"That's certainly a good reason to have a drink! . . . Now take a look at what I made today." Nehemyah laid out his latest drawings for her.

"I like these, and these, too—but of course, you said I should look without talking," Hanah remembered. Nehemyah smiled at her. He loved how she unerringly pointed to the pictures that he himself considered the most successful.

Now that Nehemyah was spending so much more time with Hanah than before he went away, he had a more complete picture of her as a person. But he also noticed some things that worried him. He saw that Hanah was not quite the same person she had been before. He no longer heard any peppery words from her about her work; she didn't reprimand the milkmaids or get angry at the cowhands. And as she had promised, with him—with Nehemyah—she was now so accommodating, so obedient, that it actually disturbed him. Nehemyah didn't want her to act like this; her old rebelliousness was dearer to his heart, and he didn't understand why she had changed so much. More than once he thought back to the trial in the dining hall after she had beaten the cowherds for neglecting the cattle. Nowadays, he was sure, she would never raise her hand to anyone, even for such a grievous offense.

One day he came right out and asked her:

"Hanukaleh, why have you become so agreeable and so quiet?"

"How can I explain it to you? Obviously I see what a quiet person you are yourself. You do your work and you hold your peace. True, not everything a person says in a quiet voice is clever, and not everything a person shouts is stupid. But I've discovered that when I speak softly, the brigade obeys me just as much as before. So if I don't yell at them, why should I yell at you? Is that so hard to understand? It's not that I've become more agreeable; not really. I just want to be as good and as quiet as you. Whenever I hear a yell coming out of my mouth now, it hurts me, and I promise myself that I'll never, never yell again."

"Oy, my darling, what a *prelest* you are!" This time Nehemyah was the one yelling.

Hanah had said that even when she didn't shout, the brigade still obeyed her. But it wasn't only because she was quieter. There was a more important reason for their newfound respect, and this reason had a name: fate. The milkmaids, the shepherds, the cowhands—all of them saw and felt that Hanah had been touched by the Divine Presence. They could tell she was surrounded by something that elevated her above other people, and not one of them wanted to cause her grief.

Meanwhile, time was rushing by. On New Year's Eve, several friends came to their room to celebrate with Hanah and Nehemyah. Leybke-Charlie strode back and forth across the room, chanting:

"On every other night of the year, our throats are dry. Where can we get something to drink on this ni-i-ight? . . ."

"The thirsty shall be refreshed; the hungry shall be satisfied," Froyim the Shepherd called out.

"Oy, I'm dying of hunger," Hayaleh suddenly realized.

"Go take a lick of snow from your garden—unless it's against the rules," joked Shachne the Smith.

At these words, the door opened, and Shimke the Groom appeared. The right side of his jacket was bulging out, and he took from under it a round loaf of bread and a thick square packet of butter wrapped in a rag.

"Where did you get that?" everyone cried at once.

"Go ahead and dig in, my good people!" Shimke said. Then he explained: "I had to wait at the Saki station for hours to pick up the Chairman. Finally, who do I see walking toward me but Shapiro, the teacher from the Chebotarka Agricultural Institute, carrying his briefcase. 'Why are you standing here?' he says. 'Come with me.' And he leads me to the wagon that's waiting for him. To make a long story short, the wagon driver from Chebotarka gave me this food."

"You dummy, you could have eaten it all yourself," Hayaleh pointed out.

"Advice that comes too late is a stone on the heart," Shimke joked. "Anybody got a knife?"

Although they ate little that night, and drank nothing stronger than water, they stayed together until the light of dawn. Then they made a toast: that the year 1931 would be a lucky and successful one, that there would be a good harvest, and that a lot of little communards would be born. At this point, for some reason, Hayah suddenly burst out laughing; she laughed so hard she got the hiccups.

"Don't laugh, Hayetchke, give me a fresh cucumber instead," Shimke said glumly.

But no one heard this because Hanah was singing "I Go Out on My Balcony" and "Little Star, Little Star, Herald of Blue." She sang until it was time for the morning milking; then everybody left.

When Hanah came back after the milking, she saw that Nehemyah had fallen asleep in his clothes. She covered him with his overcoat and the borrowed work jacket. Then she stole away again and returned with a bowl of split pea porridge from the kitchen. Nehemyah was awake by then. Hanah sat on the narrow bed next to him, and they both ate—a spoonful of porridge for her, a spoonful for him.

* * *

As previously mentioned, the new Chairman was not nearly such a schlimazel as the communards had thought at first. On top of all his other administrative duties, he managed to find time to call in a disinfection brigade from Yevpatoria, and after that, not a single bedbug was to be found on the commune for love or money. Under his leadership, two sheep or a young ox were slaughtered every rest day to feed the workers, and all the children had shoes and coats. But just as life was becoming so much easier and more comfortable, a rumor started spreading that the commune was to be converted into a collective farm. People started giving notice that they were leaving.

Although Hanah knew she would soon be departing with Nehemyah, she did not issue any such announcement. She kept on working, the same as always. For Nehemyah, the days were also not unproductive: already he had accumulated dozens of watercolor portraits and drawings. One day Hanah said to him:

"Nehemyaleh, do you want to exhibit your work? We're about to transfer the calves into the sheep shed, and then we'll be cleaning out the calf barn and whitewashing it. After that, you can hang your pictures there."

"What are you thinking? First of all, there's no glass to cover the pictures; second, I don't know if the communards really need an art show."

"First of all," Hanah mimicked him, "I'm not asking if the communards need an art show; I'm asking if *you* do. Second, it's not summer anymore; there are no flies. Even without glass, what harm can come to your pictures if they hang on the walls for two or three days?"

"I really would like to see my work on the walls—but how would it look, in the calf barn?" Nehemyah murmured.

Hanah didn't discuss the matter further with him, but she arranged everything just as she had said. And when Nehemyah walked into the calf barn, he was amazed to see how bright and clean it was. Once he'd agreed to the plan, the Commune Council gave special approval to the two communards for their project, and a few days later, the art show opened.

The first to arrive were the teachers from the Children's Home with the older group of children. Next came the laborers. They started off by circling quietly and politely around the room, as though they had been to any number of art shows before—but then the cries began to ring out: "Hey, that has to be Shimke!" "I'll be damned, is this Froyim?" "And there's Hayaleh!"

"Quiet down!" shouted the Chairman. Then he turned to Nehemyah and asked him, loudly enough for everyone to hear, whether he had ever exhibited his work in Moscow, and whether these pictures had ever hung in a museum. Nehemyah answered the Chairman's questions and then talked to the visitors at some length about his work.

For almost a week the pictures remained on display, and it wasn't just the communards who came to see them. The students from the Chebotarka Agricultural Institute came, and so did workers from the nearby collective farms. Visitors even arrived from the Saki spa. After a while, the Chairman said to Nehemyah:

"If you want, another exhibition of your work can be held in Simferopol. The public there is quite cultured. Simferopol is my home city, and I can arrange it easily."

"Thank you very much, but transporting an art show to Simferopol while getting married would be rather difficult," Nehemyah said, smiling.

It didn't help that Hanah also started nagging him:

"You don't paint pictures just for yourself, you know. Simferopol is a big city, and it's winter—the perfect time for an art show! I can take a few days' leave and help you out."

But Nehemyah stood his ground. For the rest of her life, Hanah would always wonder why she had not been able to change his mind. His decision was final.

* * *

Hanah didn't consider most of her co-workers to be particularly special people. But it did occasionally sadden her that she would soon leave the commune and have to live among an entirely different set of people, in a new place that she didn't know or understand. Although not all the communards were friendly with one another, Hanah had some very close, dear friends here—including Hayaleh Grinshteyn, Shimke the Groom, Leybke-Charlie, and Froyim the Shepherd.

There were also some people on the commune that Hanah couldn't stand. One of these was Feyge Dimenshteyn. Hanah had given her the nickname "Feyge the Rabbi's Wife," and the name suited her so well that whenever Feyge wanted to speak at a meeting, everybody would start shouting, "Quiet, the Rabbi's Wife wants to shoot her mouth off!" Feyge was a tall woman with gray eyes and thin, mousy hair. She had a little girl—but who the girl's father was, nobody knew. People often speculated about this, but one day after supper, Shimke put the matter to rest:

"What's the big mystery? Obviously, the Rabbi's Wife must have made her little girl without a man's participation . . ."

People laughed—Hanah loudest of all. Unfortunately, someone told Feyge about this, and she resented it for a long time.

Now that Hanah and Nehemyah were living together, Feyge's long-simmering grudge had ignited into a burning rage. She bad-mouthed Hanah continually, and people all over the commune reported to Hanah what Feyge was saying—often in even stronger language than Feyge had actually used.

One day, while Nehemyah was painting Feyge's portrait, she took the opportunity to say:

"Comrade Nehemyah, I assume that in Moscow a man has to search high and low to find an unmarried girl? Otherwise, you certainly wouldn't have had to come here to look for a bride."

Nehemyah studied her and said quietly, "Go to Moscow, comrade; you'll see for yourself." Then he abruptly stopped painting. "I'm finished," he told her.

"I have a day off tomorrow—should I come back?" Feyge asked.

"Thank you, but that won't be necessary."

* * *

Hanah had no time to think about anything besides work. So when Nehemyah said he wanted them to leave in February, it didn't even occur to her to ask where they were going to live. If Nehemyah said they were moving to Moscow, she assumed he must know what he was doing.

One day, Hanah was astonished to hear Nehemyah say:

"I've submitted a marriage application to the Village Council; we'll register there and then leave right away."

"Why go to the Village Council? You know who you're in love with, don't you?"

"I know and you know—but I submitted an application, and that's how I want it to be."

And that's how it was. On the fifteenth of January, 1931, Nehemyah had Hanah put on the dress he had brought her from Moscow. Then he draped her in the cream-colored scarf, its fringes falling magnificently over her padded work jacket. Shimke and Leybke-Charlie served as the witnesses. There was also no lack of "relatives" on the bride's side: Hayaleh, the Chairman, and the whole Livestock Brigade turned out in full force. Nehemyah shaved and put on a necktie for the occasion; Hanah's friends ordered her to take off her jacket, and they all declared that the blue dress suited her very well.

In those days there were no government wedding palaces, so the Village Council office had to accommodate the entire wedding party. The guests were squeezed together like sardines in a can.

"Quiet!" commanded the Secretary of the Village Council, and he stamped the marriage license so slowly and earnestly that all the young people burst out laughing.

"A fine time to laugh!" the Chairman scolded.

From the Village Council building, the attendees led the newlyweds to the dining hall, and the celebration began. Froyim shook heaven and earth with his harmonica; Hanah had to dance with everybody; someone even spun Nehemyah around the floor in a polka. Not until late at night did Hanah and Nehemyah leave the dining hall.

* * *

At the end of January, the commune's only motor truck stood outside the Children's Home. Onto it Shimke loaded Hanah's "fortune," which fit into one yellow wooden suitcase. Then Hanah's daughters were led out of the Children's Home, followed by Hayaleh with a white bundle in her arms containing three little pillows. Everyone on the commune came to see the family off. They did not depart without tears, without words of farewell, without cries of "Travel safely" and "Come back to visit . . ."

When they arrived at the railway station in Saki, Fyodor Petrovich was there waiting for them. He had brought two loaves of bread and several jars of jam, all wrapped up in a blanket. He also helped carry their bags, and then sat in the coach with them until it was time for the train to depart.

Nehemyah settled the children in their seats and secured the luggage. Then he stole a look at Hanah and asked uneasily:

"Why are you so sad, Hanaleh?"

"I don't know why."

"Have you forgotten that we're together?"

"I know, but my heart still aches."

"Perhaps you have regrets?"

"God forbid."

Nehemyah didn't ask any more questions. For him, too, it was a rather sad day. Nevertheless, he drew all kinds of entertaining little pictures for the children as they rode along. The eldest girl, Pereleh, was not shy around him, but the younger two sat very close to their mother.

And their mother—their mother was like a stranger. It seemed to Nehemyah as though she had grown thinner just since the start of the journey. Whenever the train stopped at a station, he would run out of the coach to buy something to eat, but all the station buffets were completely out of food. So, as it turned out, the bread and jam that Fyodor Petrovich had brought proved very useful. Finally, in Kharkov, Nehemyah got lucky: he was able to buy some *pirezhkes* filled with plum jam, and two smoked herrings. But Hanah ate almost nothing, and, looking at her, Nehemyah lost his appetite, too.

The journey to Moscow lasted nearly four days. Hanah spoke very little. Occasionally she would murmur a word or two, more to herself than to Nehemyah:

"It's getting dark; they've finished milking the cows by now."

At night Nehemyah used to climb down from the upper berth to check on her, and every time, he would find Hanah awake.

"Hanaleh, my *prelest,* give me a smile, I can't stand to see how sad you are. Talk to me—say a word, at least."

"I cherish you so, and you don't even get a word! Don't worry, it will pass. Everything will settle down. Nothing can change in an instant."

The only ones who were enjoying themselves were the children. Already they seemed to have shed their commune life like an old skin. They were constantly throwing themselves at Hanah, shouting "Mamaleh!" and squealing with joy and laughter.

* * *

On the evening of the fourth day, they finally arrived in Moscow. The railway station was buried in snow. Nehemyah went off to find a sleigh driver, which took quite a while. When he returned, Hanah and the children climbed into the sleigh and rode through a maze of long, long snowy streets. Just when it seemed to Hanah as though they would keep riding and riding forever without getting anywhere, the sleigh turned in to a courtyard, and Nehemyah said:

"Hanaleh, help the children down. We're here."

Nehemyah spent what seemed to Hanah like a long time turning the key in the door, then opened another door that wasn't locked and led her and the children into a small room. It took another long while for him to carry all their things inside. Finally, he lit a Primus stove and made some tea.

After the children had finished their tea, Nehemyah spread some newspapers on the floor. Then he threw some old overcoats on top of the newspapers and lay down to sleep.

III

Hanah was not asleep, but that didn't make getting up any easier. The darkness of the small, narrow room pressed in on her from all sides; the frost-covered windows didn't admit a single drop of wintery morning light. Even pushing off the blanket was an ordeal from within the depths of the rump-sprung sofa. Slowly she lowered her feet over the edge and sat up; then she just stayed there for a while, peering around, but seeing nothing. When she finally slid her arms into her shiny black peasant blouse, her hands didn't make it all the way through the sleeves. She stood up like this, hands trapped, head lowered, sighing heavily from time to time. Somehow she just didn't fit in here, in the same way that a tree, for example, wouldn't be able to grow here if someone were suddenly to plant one.

Finally, Hanah pulled her hands through the sleeves of her blouse and started putting on her long overcoat, which was made from the fabric known as "devil's skin." Now all that remained was to put on her fur boots, a single one of which was more than large enough for both her feet. And there she was, in her full commune outfit, standing between the children, who were sleeping on the floor, and Nehemyah, who lay breathing so evenly and appealingly on the dreadful old sofa (which, in her opinion, should be thrown away as soon as possible).

Hanah didn't know what hour it was by the clock, but she was sure she had gotten up right on time for the dawn milking—with the difference that on all those past mornings, she had known exactly what to do, whereas now she had absolutely no idea how to begin her day. She looked around again, but her sharp eyes drilled vainly into the thick darkness. It seemed to her that the walls must be very close. She reached out one hand but found, to her surprise, that it was able to move freely, without touching the wall.

She took a couple of steps in one direction, a couple of steps in another, and finally located the doorknob by touch. She turned it, stepped across the threshold, and found herself in the kitchen. At the sight of the weakly glowing electric bulb that hung just below the ceiling in its wire cage, a sense of pity arose within her. Pity for this light that could barely breathe through the dark metal mesh. And a thought came to her: "Even a lantern is better than a light like that."

Some sort of voice, speaking words that Hanah couldn't quite understand, broke through her thoughts, and the figure of an older woman emerged. The figure repeated the words:

"You need the toilet? It's over here."

Hanah eyed the woman, hastily backed toward the door, and retreated into the little room.

The children were still sleeping. Nehemyah was still breathing lightly, evenly. Hanah understood at last that she had gotten up too early. She shook the enormous boots off her small feet and lay down, fully dressed, on the floor beside the children. She lay with open eyes, as though she could still see the pathetic glow of the light bulb through its dark grid. The milkmaids, she knew, were milking their third cows by now. And she heard, then saw, and then heard again the soft hissing of the milk falling into the pail, so vividly that she was lulled into a doze. And this light doze carried her back to her childhood . . .

All at once she notices her grandfather sitting by the door, his yarmulke trembling slightly. Reverently, he grasps a page from the open Gemara with two fingers and bends forward over the tiny print. Lower and yet lower sinks his head, until his yarmulke is practically falling over his eyes.

He grabs at the yarmulke, straightens it, rocks back and forth, mutters softly, absorbed, detached from everything and everyone. And now her grandfather disappears, and it's a summer's day. The apple trees in the orchard are decked out in pinkish-white blossoms, the green leaves flutter like butterflies. Her grandfather is tearing out every blade of grass from around the trunks of the trees, and he says with deep piety, as though reciting a prayer:

"Help me, little daughter. There is a horseradish plant growing near your foot."

She tries to obey, but the plant won't budge from its place. Her grandfather presses his right foot down on the edge of the shovel, gives a grunt. The shovel cuts into the earth, and a moment later a pale, longish root with hairy whiskers emerges. Her grandfather lifts it out, shakes off the dirt, and quietly instructs her:

"Little daughter, my little love, go and take this to your grandmother so she can make horseradish for the calves' foot jelly. The day after tomorrow is Shabbes, you know."

Now, before her eyes stands the cherry orchard: the shiny green cherries hang from the branches, and the currant bushes are covered with buds. The bees are extremely busy. Her grandfather stands leaning on the handle of the shovel, looking benignly at everything around him, and whispers to her:

"You see how He works. He doesn't know what to do first."

"Who?" Hanah asks, looking around.

"Who? The turkey and the bear! Look at those bees. Thanks be to Him in heaven. I am honored to see His creation."

Hanah woke up, but everything she had seen stayed before her eyes. She wondered why her heart ached so. This wasn't the first time she'd had this same experience: almost every time she was confronted with some sort of trial, her childhood would float back to her, and along with it, her favorite, her dearest, her most beloved person in the whole world—this grandfather of hers. And every time it happened, her mood became lighter.

Every time, but not now . . .

"Mama, where are you?" The eldest girl, Pereleh, was awake.

"I'm right beside you, my child."

"Mamaleh, stay here so I can touch your face. It's so dark I can't see you. Why isn't there a lamp here, like at the Children's Home?"

"You've forgotten, we're in Moscow now."

"I know. I don't have a bed to sleep in anymore."

"Don't worry, my darling, don't worry—you'll have a bed. But be quiet now. You'll wake everybody up."

"I want them to wake up; I'm hungry!"

"Hanukel, give Pereleh a lump of sugar." Nehemyah's voice sounded through the darkness.

* * *

That was how Hanah began her first day in Moscow.

Of course, it's easy to say "Hanah began her day." But she had absolutely no idea what to do first. It was lucky that Nehemyah was there to help her. Taking the reins into his own hands, he calmly instructed:

"Hanukel, take your time, leave the bedding for later. Get the children dressed, and I'll run out and buy some milk."

By the time Nehemyah came back with the milk, the bedding was in order, and Hanah had washed and dressed the children, too. The three girls sat in a row, each holding a lump of sugar, and the room was soon filled with their boisterous little voices.

After having a bite to eat themselves, Nehemyah and Hanah left the children in the room and walked over to the market on Arbat Street, where a tram happened to be passing. Startled by the loud noise, Hanah tore her hand away from Nehemyah's and took off running. He chased after her, grabbed her hand again, and spoke to her quietly and sternly:

"Why are you running away? You have to understand, you're a pedestrian; you can go in any direction you want. But the tram has to stay on the rails. So don't be afraid—it can't run you over."

When they came to the market, they stopped near a potato stall, and Nehemyah gave Hanah a little purse with three rubles in it. Noticing the bewildered look in her pure blue eyes, he reassured her:

"Don't be scared, my child. I'll be right back. Keep your eye on the purse, and stay right here. Don't go wandering off, or you'll get lost. Just behave yourself and have a good time."

"Should I spend all this money on the potatoes?"

"Are you serious, Hanukel? We wouldn't be able to carry that many potatoes! We would need a wheelbarrow! Just remember what I told you: Stay right here."

Hanah followed him with her eyes until he disappeared. Then, looking around, she was delighted to notice a young couple nearby, standing at a little table not far from the potato stall. On the table were stacks of tiny, sharp-edged tin molds. And the pair were cheerfully and boldly singing: "Nye prokhaditye mimo! Nye prokhaditye mimo! Formochki dlya pechenya, palchiki oblizhetye!" This means "Buy some little molds for making delicious pastries!"

Hanah was enchanted with the little molds; she wanted to buy three of them for the children. And the couple pleased her every bit as much as their wares. They were so cheerful, so young, so strangely dressed that Hanah couldn't take her eyes off them, and she couldn't decide—were they engaged, or already married? As she stood there gazing and gaping at the pair, an old woman suddenly came up to her, gave her a hard slap on the shoulder, leaned forward, picked something up off the ground, and disappeared. Hanah wanted to go after the woman and say a few choice words to her, but she remembered that Nehemyah had ordered her not to move from the spot. And just then, she saw Nehemyah himself coming back with the groceries he had purchased. He asked:

"Haven't you bought the potatoes yet?"

Hanah didn't answer; her tongue was paralyzed. She had just discovered that her right hand was empty. All of a sudden she understood why the woman had given her such a hard smack and then immediately bent down. She looked at Nehemyah and found him gazing back with sympathy and curiosity. Beginning to sob, Hanah said:

"Darling, it wasn't my fault at all. I stood right here the whole time, just as you told me to. But then someone gave me such a shove! I dropped the little purse, and she picked it up."

"It's gone, my child. But don't cry," Nehemyah consoled her. "You'll learn soon enough that in Moscow, you can't be caught napping; you have to keep a clear head. Because around here, it's all too easy to fall, even if someone doesn't push you!" Nehemyah gave Hanah a kiss, and then he bought some potatoes. Before long, they were back at their room.

When they arrived, the children started shrieking and whining as though Hanah and Nehemyah had been gone for a year. Hanah calmed them down and busied herself making everyone something to eat. It took her a while to decide what to cook, but the potato soup that she eventually served pleased Nehemyah and the children very much.

After lunch, when Nehemyah had gone out again, Hanah began inspecting her surroundings. Opening a second door that had been closed since they'd arrived, she discovered another small room. "This will make things easier," she thought. She carried everything out of the room, opened the ventilation pane, and swept the dust off the walls and the ceiling with a broom. When this second room was all tidied up, she led the children inside and closed the door. Then she got to work on the first room. By evening, both rooms were gleaming.

When Nehemyah came back from the city, he stepped onto the newspapers that Hanah had laid outside the door and stopped short.

"Come on in, don't be afraid," Hanah teased.

"My comfort, how did you manage this?" Nehemyah marveled. But when he noticed that the second room was also clean, he remarked rather sadly:

"Why did you have to clean the other room, too? It's not ours, you know."

"Whose is it, then?"

"I must have told you I live with my friend. You remember, the blond-haired artist who was at the commune with me?"

"Of course I remember. But where is he now?"

"He went to Kiev to make set decorations for a show."

"Is he coming back?" Hanah asked in a tone that suggested she very much hoped not.

"I can see you don't want him to, but yes, he is coming back. Actually, he wrote to me that he's bringing his new wife with him, because he just got married down there."

"So I did all that work for nothing? How infuriating! If your friends could only see what a garbage dump they had under their bed!" Hanah fumed.

"Well, at least they won't be able to prosecute you for theft, since they didn't see you throwing their garbage away," Nehemyah joked.

* * *

With each passing day, Nehemyah saw all the more clearly that Hanah was indeed no lazy woman. Of course, he had known this all along, but he continued to marvel at her industriousness.

"Come, sit down for a minute."

"With you? For as long as you like," she'd say agreeably. But a moment later she would be off again. Nehemyah often stopped drawing to observe how she washed carrots, peeled potatoes, chopped cabbage, scoured the teapot with sand. No matter what she was doing, her hands were always in motion; they flew like birds from one task to another. As a child, Nehemyah had often seen his mother and his older sister working in the kitchen. But when it came to shaving such long, thin, curly peelings from a potato as Hanah did, or making such short work of a carrot—he had never seen anything like that.

"Go and do your work—why are you staring at my hands?" Hanah would say at such times.

"Give me the knife for a minute. I want to peel a carrot for you."

But watching him, Hanah would say:

"What are you doing? You keep cutting it in the same place. Give it here. See, one scrape and it's done."

He saw that she was right, but he wondered:

"How did you learn to do that?"

"What's to learn? It's just common sense. Don't torment what's in your hand; don't waste what someone worked so hard to produce."

Such a thing might have seemed trivial, but it taught Nehemyah how fortunate he really was. The housework always got done, as though of its own accord; everything was completed on time, because Hanah never sat with idle hands. Whenever she did have a free hour, she would take the children to the Zoological Garden, or simply out in the yard, to give Nehemyah some quiet time to work.

The children were, of course, like all children: they got into everything. Nehemyah repeatedly told them not to touch the table where he worked, but to no avail. No sooner would he leave the table for a moment than the children would be there. They would grab his paper and pencils and make such a mess that Nehemyah had to come up with a solution right away. So he gave the children their own paper, paints, and a pair of dull scissors. He arranged these materials on the sofa, and they kept the children occupied for hours at a time.

As previously mentioned, the eldest girl, Pereleh, was very attached to Nehemyah. But the other two, Beylkeleh and Reyzeleh, still rarely approached him. One day, Hanah heard Beylke say to Pereleh:

"Why do you call him Papa? The auntie from the kitchen told me he's nothing but a stranger to us."

Hanah said to the children: "The auntie from the kitchen doesn't know anything. If he weren't your papa, he wouldn't have come to the commune. And you, Beylke-Bulkeleh, shouldn't talk to that auntie anymore. You should love your papa, because he loves you." But in her heart, Hanah didn't feel entirely at ease.

That evening she was washing a load of clothes for the children, and the neighbor woman was standing nearby at the Primus stove, singeing the hair off some pigs' feet. Hanah decided this was the right moment to say a few words to her.

"If you don't mind, I'd rather you not talk to my children."

The woman stopped cleaning the blackened trotters and, waving her knife in the air, she proclaimed:

"If I've met one stuck-up aristocrat like you, I've met a hundred! I don't tell *you* when to talk and when to shut up!"

Hanah now had a complete picture of what a magnificent neighbor she had, and she never spoke a word to her again. She also stopped letting the children leave the room by themselves; instead, whenever she had the time, she went out with them.

In addition to all the other activities that kept them busy during this period, Nehemyah started teaching Hanah Russian. Soon she could read the language quite fluently, and write it fairly well. This was also a good form of entertainment for the children. They used to sit as though under a spell whenever Nehemyah read aloud in Russian.

Artists and poets frequently came to visit, and some of them looked at Hanah as though they were staring into an empty void. And then they would ask, "Nobody is in?"

"Nobody," she used to answer, feeling as hot and flustered as though she had a fever.

One day, Nehemyah came back from somewhere and immediately saw that Hanah was upset. He asked:

"Has something happened?"

"What can I tell you? Kornblum was here, or Kornveyts. I don't remember what his name was. He looks at me the way a person looks at a flea, and he says: 'No one is home. I'll come back later . . . ' So I say to him, 'Who are you talking to, then, if no one is home?'"

"Good for you!" Nehemyah said. "You should always do that. Let them get used to it."

"Whether they get used to it or not, what kind of pigs are these people?"

"Hanukel, I'm sorry to say that having an intellectual profession is not the same thing as being a sensitive person. But you'll adjust after a while, too—you're not a child anymore. Don't take things so much to heart."

Soon after this, Hanah learned that there was a special treat in store for her: Nehemyah had purchased tickets to *Turandot*. The evening of the opera, she put on the blue dress that he had brought to the commune for her—the "wedding dress," as she called it. But she still didn't have any dress shoes, so she wore her enormous fur boots. When they arrived at the opera house, she didn't even notice how strangely people were staring at her feet. As soon as the overture started, Hanah completely forgot herself. She saw before her eyes such pageantry, such brilliance, such rich colors, that from time to time she would give a loud cry, as though she were out on the steppe. Nehemyah had to keep tugging on her sleeve to remind her to be quiet.

After the show, when they were walking down the street, Hanah threw herself at Nehemyah. She kissed his cheeks, his temples, his forehead, and in a voice breathless with gratitude, she gushed:

"Oh, what a wonderful thing you've shown me! All the streets and houses look so ordinary now! Take me to the theater all the time!"

"Dear comfort of mine, try to be a little quieter. We're on the street, you know; people are looking at us. Certainly we'll go to the theater again. Oh, my dear soul, you appreciate everything, you feel everything! Do you still love me as much as you did on the commune?"

"Do you even need to ask? No one in the world ever loved anyone so much!" Hanah cried.

And it was true. The two of them were truly united: there was only one body and one soul between them.

* * *

More and more, Hanah was adjusting to her new life. Fortunately, not all the artists and poets who came to visit looked at her as though they were staring into an empty void. One artist, who came more often than most, even had a strange custom: he would kiss her hand. When she remarked upon this to Nehemyah, he explained it to her this way:

"Remember how I told you that in Kostroma there was a teacher named Nikolai Nikolaevich Kuprianov who taught me to paint, and later he summoned me to Moscow to continue my studies? Well, he comes from the aristocracy. And that's not the only reason he's such a noble and refined person. Pay attention to him; you'll see."

Frida Blyumberg, an artist who sometimes came to visit, soon became very friendly with Hanah. She often brought little toys for the children, too. One day she said:

"Hanah, perhaps you'll be offended with me, but I want to suggest something to you. My mother is the director of a kindergarten. A job may be opening up there soon. Perhaps you could go and work there. It would be better for your children, too."

"Why should I be offended? On the contrary, I'm very grateful to you. That would be wonderful!" Hanah said.

Meanwhile, one day followed another, and there was no lack of work to do. Nehemyah had no official assignment, but nevertheless, he sat painting and drawing at the table all day long. Hanah would see him sitting there hour after hour, and the thought would often cross her mind: "I must have been fated to have such a conscientious husband; he's so dedicated, he's exactly like my grandfather."

This was true, with the difference that her grandfather had spent his days rocking back and forth over the pages of the Gemara, whereas Nehemyah, with pencil or paintbrush in hand, would strive and struggle until the desired image appeared on the paper. And when it did, it was always as fresh and lively as if it had been made in the wink of an eye.

Hanah said nothing to Nehemyah about her conversation with Frida. But apparently Frida told him about it herself. And soon afterwards, Hanah went off to work in the kindergarten.

※ ※ ※

The sky grew higher and brighter, the days longer, but for Hanah they were as short as ever. The tramway ride to the kindergarten, which was located on Rogozheska, took more than an hour. At first Hanah worked as a helper in the kitchen, but by the end of the month, she was often the one at the stove. The cook, Ksenia Timofeyevna, was constantly leaving her post. She used to say:

"Hanah Davidovna, I have to run out someplace. Cook a rice pudding for the children."

"Sure, why not? Give me rice, sugar, milk, and butter."

"Everything except the butter is on the table."

Why "except the butter" Hanah didn't need to ask. She already knew that the rice pudding "did well enough without" that ingredient fairly often. Where all the butter was going was evident from the appearance of the cook; looking at the woman's round, well-fed body, Hanah would think, "My dearest friends should be so lucky . . ."

Nevertheless, everything would have been fine if there hadn't also been a third person working in the kitchen. Her name was Yevdokia, and she did all the unskilled labor. Whenever the cook went out, Yevdokia would voice her resentment:

"Ugh, what a bloated carcass! She gobbles and guzzles 'til her hide nearly bursts. She could at least say to me once in a while, 'Here you go, Duska, have a bit of butter, take a lick of cream.'"

Hanah listened and held her tongue. But then the cook began to make such offers to Hanah herself:

"Hanah Davidovna, take a bottle of milk home with you. If you don't want any milk, have a couple of herrings. Or a jar of plum jam."

Not only did Hanah not take anything, she pretended not to hear.

There were times when Hanah had to accompany Ksenia Timofeyevna to the base to get supplies, pulling a small wagon along behind her. At such times, the cook would pour her heart out:

"Hanah Davidovna, you think I don't know? That Duska makes my eyes crawl out of my head! It's not like the others would turn down a marrow bone if they had the chance. And no one sees how I have to drag heavy objects, and lift whole sackfuls of sugar, and stand over a hot stove all day!"

Hanah listened in silence. She had never seen Ksenia Timofeyevna drag anything. One day she asked the cook:

"Why don't your children attend the kindergarten? You keep saying you have two children."

"My children are fine right where they are. My husband stays home with them; he doesn't drink, and he doesn't waste money. My children do perfectly well without kindergarten."

As time went on, it became more and more evident to Hanah how self-serving the cook was. Ksenia Timofeyevna sensed her disapproval and began to avoid taking Hanah with her to the base. But to take Yevdokia along—that would be even worse! The cook became so disgruntled that she spent most of one staff meeting yelling, "I'm not a horse, I will not drag everything back here all by myself!"

Finally, the Director, Yelizaveta Abramovna, agreed to hire a new "factotum"—that is, a person who would bring supplies from the base, chop wood, carry in coal, heat the stove, and pick up around the building. The Director's only stipulation was that "the person should be a man, because the roof is already flying off from all the screaming in the kitchen."

* * *

By this time, Hanah had learned quite a bit of Russian, and she always brought a Russian book along on her rides to and from work. During the week, her daughters boarded at the kindergarten, but on Saturday evenings Hanah brought them home, and they spent two nights with her and Nehemyah. On Sundays they would all go for a walk in the Zoological Garden, or to the Pushkin Museum of Fine Arts on Volkhonka Street. During one visit to the museum, Hanah suggested to Nehemyah:

"You go wherever you like with the children, and I'll walk around by myself. Then I'll show you which paintings I liked best."

Later, when she led Nehemyah to paintings by Cézanne, Pissarro, and Degas, he approved with a smile:

"That's excellent, Hanukel. Looking at great paintings really suits you; you're glowing!"

"You're right. Next Sunday, maybe you can take the children somewhere else, and I'll come here by myself."

So that's just what they did. And when she left the museum after her visit, Hanah had the same feeling of disappointment in her heart that she used to have at the end of Shabbes, or after a holiday, when her grandmother removed the tablecloth and they all went back to their everyday lives.

* * *

With the passage of time, the love between Hanah and Nehemyah only increased. Nehemyah never failed to meet Hanah at the tram when she came home from work in the evening. But there is a reason for the saying "The more one has, the more one wants . . ."

One day, Hanah complained:

"I suppose it must be easier for you to meet me at the tram in the evening than to walk me there in the morning?"

"Hanukel, have a little mercy. You know how late I go to bed."

"It seems to me that a person doesn't need to stay up until after midnight talking about art. The important thing is to *make* the art. But if you went to bed earlier, and you still didn't escort me to the tram in the morning, I know what I'd have to do."

"What would you do?"

"Try getting up earlier, and you'll see!"

Although Hanah was able to joke like this, she wasn't the same person she had been on the commune. If Nehemyah hadn't been so wrapped up in his own worries, he would have noticed and tried to soothe her. It wasn't the amount of work that was weighing on Hanah, it was the city itself—the enormous buildings, the noisy tramway, the throngs of people. More than once she thought, "How miserable it is for so many people to be crammed together in one place!" And the situation in the kitchen did nothing to improve her mood. Yevdokia was always rubbing salt in the wound with her complaints about the cook: "Such a parasite! Everything for her and only for her! Just once, I wish she'd offer me a piece of meat or something." Then, still burning with rage, she would turn on Hanah:

"Why are you keeping quiet? You have eyes, you see what goes on! Why don't you talk to the Director about it? Never mind, I'll do it for you. We have to strike while the iron is hot!"

Hanah couldn't bear it. Of course, she knew there were thieves, liars, flatterers, and two-faced characters everywhere. But she had never experienced them at such close range before. She kept remembering all the times when Henke from the Children's Home had come to the barn to fetch the milk. Sometimes Hanah would say to her, "Here's a pint for you; drink up!" But Henke would always take the pint, pour it into the pan with the rest, and say, 'That's one more pint for the children."

* * *

By this time, the Moscow artists and writers had adjusted to the fact that Hanah was mistress of the apartment. And two poets used to visit from Minsk, too: the blond artist's brother, and a famous man with a head of terribly curly hair. Hanah was delighted with his poems; when he read aloud, she would hang on his every word. But having him as a houseguest was intolerable. Wherever she looked, wherever she turned, she found strands of his stiff, curly hair—even in his empty tea glass!

"Goodness, how will I survive until he goes back to Minsk?"

"Hanukel, it's true that when he leaves, you won't find any more of his hair—but you also won't hear any more of his poems."

"You're right—the hair is the sacrifice I have to make for the poems."

Often, Hanah couldn't clean up the apartment when she came home from work because people would already be there, sitting on the sofa, the chairs, and even on the windowsills. A lively debate would be in progress about the impressionists, or the Renaissance, or the 1920s and modern art. There were some Sundays when the visitors stayed so long that Hanah couldn't even bathe the children. And then, on Monday morning, exhausted and sleep-deprived, off she'd go with Nehemyah and the girls to catch the tram.

* * *

At least things had now become a little calmer at work. Ksenia Timofeyevna had indeed acquired a new unskilled worker: a man, just as the Director had wanted. His name was Makar, and he was tall, broadshouldered, and energetic. If it weren't for the beard and mustache, he would have looked a lot younger. Hanah estimated he was about thirty. The work around the kindergarten was child's play for him. The yard around the building was always clean. Wood and coal were brought in on time. The supplies that Hanah had previously fetched in three trips, he brought back all at once. Although the weather was now quite mild, Makar still wore his sheepskin, and the flaps of his rabbit-fur cap dangled over his ears.

Whenever the cook called him for lunch—"Makar, *kushat!*"—he would leave his sheepskin in the corridor, seat himself on an overturned bucket, and eat slowly. The crumbs that fell onto the painted floor, he would gather up and put in the pocket of his quilted vest. After eating, he would go to the faucet and drink deeply, with gusto. The cook always offered him a glass, but he wouldn't take it—he just wiped his mustache and stepped outside with a single stride of his long legs. There, he would shake out his pockets, and the sparrows would feast on the crumbs.

"What an excellent young man. So spirited. Whoever takes him for a husband will be lucky," remarked Ksenia Timofeyevna.

"What would be the point, when he has no passport?" Yevdokia scoffed.

"And if you came from the country, would you have a passport? All of a sudden you're so clever! Remember how you cried and begged me to hire you? Remember how you sobbed that you would work for nothing but a piece of bread?"

That was how the cook and the kitchen helper used to talk to each other.

Hanah often looked at Makar and had a strange feeling: it seemed to her that if she were to see him out in a field somewhere, she would certainly remember where she knew him from . . . but this feeling lasted only a moment. And she didn't ask him any questions; she knew he would only act as if he didn't hear, or didn't understand.

One Saturday after lunch, Makar went off to the public sauna with a bath whisk, came back flushed, took a good long drink from the faucet, polished off an entire bowl of millet porridge, and then said calmly to Hanah:

"Hanah Davidovna, you fit in here about as well as I do. You think I don't notice? Duska really has it in for you."

"That's a little harsh," Hanah said quickly, because Yevdokia was standing nearby on a ladder, washing the windows. Just then, the ladder wobbled a bit, and Makar called out:

"Get down! Get down, I tell you!"

Hanah stopped turning over the cutlets in the skillet; she couldn't have been more surprised if all the pots on the stove had suddenly floated up into the air. Those words, that voice had instantly transported her far, far away. There was no doubt in her mind that it was this man, and no other, who had chased after her on the steppe when she was riding her horse; this man, and no other, who had shouted, "Get down!"

Just before leaving work that evening, Hanah calmly, and with seeming indifference, asked:

"Makar, where did you come here from?"

"The place I came from is a place I've never been."

"If you don't want to tell me, you don't have to."

Makar gestured toward Yevdokia, as if he didn't want any extra ears listening. And for once, she took the hint. After Yevdokia had stepped out of the kitchen, Makar gave a little cough. Then he inhaled, as though forcing the words into his mouth, and said quietly:

"Where am I from? I told Ksenia Timofeyevna that I was from Kerch, but I'm really from a village not far from Saki. I won't be a kitchen drudge for long. You want to know exactly where I'm from? I'm from Jabahi. There were some Jewish communes near our village. One day, an enemy of my father's informed on him; he claimed my father and grandfather were kulaks, and had us all sent away. That lie was eventually exposed, but my parents didn't survive, and neither did my wife. But I came back to Jabahi. One day, I saw a Jewish commune woman riding my horse. But I couldn't catch up. Oh, if only I'd gotten my hands on her!"

"What would have happened?"

"Don't ask! At the time, I was dying for a sledgehammer! Well, I did take my horse back, though. I sold it, and then I had enough money to come here. Someone at the base told me they're getting ready to build a ball bearing factory here. I'll go and work there."

"But you're a farmer. How will you get by without any land?"

"I'll get by well enough. We're through with land. Even if I knew that every ear of grain was made of gold, I wouldn't be a farmer anymore. Well, enough of this. I'm going out to rake the yard."

That night, Hanah told Nehemyah the whole story.

"Incredible!" Nehemyah remarked. "If anyone else had told me this, I would have laughed."

* * *

What Yevdokia had said to Hanah about informing on the cook—"I'll do it for you!"—made Hanah burn with rage. She herself frequently considered talking to the Director, because both the cook and Yevdokia were now stealing food almost daily. But there is a saying: "If you carry the water jug long enough, the handle will break off by itself." One evening, two women and a man entered the kitchen. They took Ksenia Timofeyevna away, and three days later she still hadn't returned.

When Hanah finally did see the cook again, it wasn't in the kitchen but in a courtroom. The most remarkable thing about the trial was that Ksenia Timofeyevna's husband showed up unannounced. He asked for the court's permission to testify as a witness, and when the judge agreed, he spoke as follows:

"I wouldn't have come, Your Honor, but I can't remain silent. Ask her, Comrade Judge, how many times I told her not to carry so much food home. We couldn't even eat it all! But in any case, I beg Your Honor not to sentence her too harshly, because she is a mother of two children. That's all I have to say."

The sentence was not a harsh one, but it wasn't light, either. Ksenia received a two-year suspension. In the meantime, the person in charge of all the cooking and supplies for the kindergarten would be . . . Hanah.

Obviously, hard work was no novelty to Hanah. But now she was busy late into the night. And the late nights were only half the problem: it was impossible to endure Yevdokia's selfish demands. When everyone else on staff was eating leftovers from the children's lunch—she wanted a piece of herring. When everyone else was eating soup—she wanted a piece of raw meat to take home so she could cook whatever she pleased for supper. Finally, Hanah couldn't stand it anymore.

"Dusya, you know very well that I'm not a butcher. If you don't want to eat what the rest of us are eating, go talk to the Director about it."

"Yes, now I can do whatever I please, even though things turned out so well for Ksenia on account of . . ." Yevdokia's voice trailed off.

"I won't try to guess what you're implying. But I do know that, as *you* see it, anybody who steals supplies and gives you a share is doing the right thing. I won't talk to you about this anymore. Eat—don't eat—it's not my problem!"

Three or four days later, Makar was sitting on an overturned bucket, as was his habit, and smoking a cigarette. Hanah was in the supply closet. Suddenly Makar gave a shout:

"Hanah Davidovna, come quick, look what that witch is doing with your purse!"

Hanah came running in time to see Makar prying her purse out of Yevdokia's hands. Then she saw him reach into the purse and pull out a big chunk of butter and a bag of sugar. Hanah raised her arm, and she would have given Yevdokia the same treatment as the two cowboys who hadn't watered the calves—but Makar grabbed her hand just in time. With his other hand he restrained Yevdokia, ordering Hanah to run for the Director.

And that was the end of Yevdokia's plot to incriminate Hanah.

* * *

It became harder and harder for Hanah to work. Because she always finished up so late, Nehemyah started coming to the kindergarten in the evenings to escort her home. If she was still busy when he arrived, he would wander around the yard, and the time would drag for him like a lead weight. On the tram ride home, he would sit very close to her, taking great pleasure and pride in her company. He would gaze and gaze at her, and murmur in wonder: "Hanukel, where did I get you from? Look at me,

I'm talking to you; why are you looking at that young fellow over there? What do you need him for? . . ."

On Sundays, their door never closed. Very early in the morning, poets and artists would begin arriving, as well as people who were simply attracted to art. There was, for example, a tall, heavyset young man who didn't write or paint, but who never stopped lecturing others about how they should conduct themselves, how they should always be honest and not allow an impure word to cross their lips. The previous Sunday he had shown up at seven thirty in the morning and spent two and a half hours preaching a sermon about honesty. Nehemyah had listened and listened, and finally remarked:

"Nosen, I know all of this is very important, but shouldn't you be talking to people who are actually in the habit of cheating, or picking pockets?"

Although Hanah was in the kitchen, she overheard this, and burst out laughing. Nehemyah ran in, shrugged his shoulders as if to say, "He's really not a bad speaker," and then ran out to buy some bread. When Hanah went into the room to set the table, she rolled with laughter to see Nosen, still dressed in his overcoat, lying on the worn-out sofa and snoring like a lumberjack—not at all like the philosopher who had been expounding so deeply just minutes before.

Another person who used to visit on Sundays was Nikolai Nikolaevich, Nehemyah's old teacher. A typical visit would go like this:

Nikolai Nikolaevich comes in, takes off his hat, bends forward, and gives Hanah a kiss on the hand. If she's doing something with her hands, such as washing the dishes or peeling potatoes, he gives her a kiss on the elbow instead. He never sits on the sofa, but always in a chair. From the large front pocket of his jacket he takes out a live white mouse with beady pink eyes, and calls the children over to see it; their jumping and screaming are enough to make a person deaf. After a while, Nikolai Nikolaevich strokes the children's heads, puts the mouse back in his pocket, and begins chatting with Nehemyah about a show he saw recently, or Van Gogh's letters to his brother Theo, or some other art-related subject. Hanah listens attentively, although she understands very little of what he's saying. When he goes away, Nehemyah escorts him to the door, then comes back and shares his admiration with Hanah:

"What a wonderful person! He carries himself so modestly and acts so informal around me, just like a brother."

"You're right. But why does he have to kiss my hand, or some other part of me? Three Sundays ago I happened to be doing the laundry when he came in, and he kissed me right on the forehead! I was so embarrassed!"

"You have nothing to be embarrassed about," Nehemyah reassures her. "Don't be upset with him." Then they both get busy tidying up the room.

On many Sundays the children went unbathed, and Hanah couldn't do the laundry, because the family would be hosting the two poets from Minsk—the blond artist's brother and the man with the frightfully curly hair. One day the brother, Zelik Akselrod, read one of his poems aloud:

And so begins your story,
A life that drags you with it,
You expected so much,
It comes to an end—
All but a little song.

Hanah was quite taken with it, but she asked:
"It's very short, isn't it?"

"If it's a good poem, the length doesn't matter. But several good short ones are better than one," he explained. Then, noticing that she was holding a broom in her hands, he teased: "Let go of that thing, Hanaleh. Don't be annoyed with us, relax a little. It's all right to leave some of the dirt for next week." And turning to the curly-haired poet, he recited:

Kharik, you should not crown us
We have laid out the pieces here
And positioned ourselves for checkers.

"Stop that," the curly-haired man rebuked him. "Don't break the braids off the rolls, you filthy pig!" But Zelik was already chewing away with gusto. And nearby stood another visitor, the critic, who had just slipped into the room like a shadow and, in a voice that could barely be heard, greeted Hanah with a soft, polite, friendly "good morning."

Now the curly-haired poet took hold of the critic's nose with two fingers, and the critic, whose name was Gurshteyn, protested quietly and mildly:

"What are you doing? Enough; don't pinch so, if you please. That's very unpleasant. Hey!"

The other man released his nose, the critic covered it with his hand, and the discussion went on as though nothing had happened. They argued about poems. One said that Hofshteyn's poems were better, another said Halkin's were. Then they drank tea. More poems were read. If Nikolai Nikolaevich happened to come in during such a gathering, he would not take the white mouse out of his jacket pocket; instead, he would shrug with disapproval and drop a word to Nehemyah:

"Kakoy shum, kakoy shum, poshli na Volkhanku," which meant "What a racket, what a racket, come to Volkhonka Street instead."

Very often after such gatherings, Hanah had to clean and scrub until midnight, but she still had to get up at five o'clock the next morning. She often felt as though she were falling off her feet. And all the while, time was passing, spring was starting to push its way up, and the work at the kindergarten just kept coming and coming. Hanah applied herself to making sure the food for the children was properly prepared, and everyone agreed that it was much tastier now that all the ingredients were actually going into the pot.

With regard to their apartment mates, everything had happened just as Nehemyah had predicted: the blond man and his new wife had come back from Kiev and were living in the adjoining room. Hanah now knew that the man's name was Yakev, although most people called him Yashe—or simply Yak. His wife's name was Bronislava Yosipovna. Yakev called her Bron. To her face, Nehemyah addressed her by her full name and patronymic; behind her back, he referred to her as "Madam." She was of greater than average height, and her small head was covered with straight bobbed hair that looked as stiff as wire—although apparently she hadn't been to the hairdresser's for quite a while, because this stiff, thick black hair of hers hung down to her shoulders. When she walked, her high bosom thrust forward, while her flat hips scarcely moved at all. But although her appearance was so striking, the most remarkable thing about her was how utterly dull her eyes were.

Naturally, Hanah did not neglect to mention this to Nehemyah on the evening of the woman's arrival.

"You're right, my comfort," Nehemyah agreed. "How did you notice that so quickly? Her eyes are exactly like two worn-out buttons!"

"Oh, I can't stand you! Of course you'd noticed it already—you're an artist, after all."

"Now I know we're truly man and wife. I can tell from your tone that you resent me."

"What are you talking about? Why should I resent you? On the contrary, I cherish you all the more," Hanah asserted.

These days, Hanah couldn't reproach Nehemyah for not escorting her to the tram in the mornings because he came out with her every day. A typical morning went like this:

The tram is coming. Nehemyah runs along behind her and warns:

"Hanukel, be careful! Don't run across the tracks, don't run! Do you hear me?"

"I hear you; I'll be careful. Go home, you can still catch some sleep. I won't run, I won't run! Why would I want to pick a fight with all these trams and carriages?" shouts Hanah with one foot on the platform and the other on the step of the tram.

"Get in the car already, don't just stand there yelling," he orders—and then he does, in fact, go home to catch some more sleep.

Hanah takes a seat in the back, because at such an early hour the tram is nearly empty. She takes out the book that Nikolai Nikolaevich recently brought her. As she reads, she occasionally bursts out laughing, causing the sleepy passengers to stare at her in surprise. Arriving at work, she sets a pot of millet porridge on the stove, cranks some meat through the grinder, and lays pats of butter on the children's small, shallow plates. Then, hearing the door open, she turns and sees the Director, Yelizaveta Abramovna, come in. The Director looks thoughtfully at Hanah and wants to know:

"Why are you so cheerful? I heard you laughing to yourself just now."

"Well, you see, I can't stop thinking about the prince."

"What prince?"

"The prince that tried to make a match with a true princess but, unfortunately, couldn't find one, no matter what he did. Until one night, during a rainstorm, in wandered a soaking-wet princess, right into the emperor's house."

"I have no idea what you're talking about," Yelizaveta Abramovna confessed.

"What's not to understand? The princess was standing near the door of the palace, soaked to the skin. Someone let her inside, and the clever old empress said, 'We shall soon see if she is a true princess or not.' And as she said it, she pulled all the mattresses off the bed, placed a pea on the bare bed board, and then laid twelve feather beds on top. And what do you think happened? The princess didn't shut her eyes the entire night because of that pea. And the next morning, her sides were covered with black-and-blue marks."

"Oh, this is wonderful! It's 'The Princess and the Pea!'" Yelizaveta Abramovna exclaimed, and she burst out laughing. Then she marveled:

"Hanah Davidovna, are you reading Andersen for the first time?"

"I'd never even heard of such a writer before."

"I'm jealous; you have so much pleasure in store for you! I was only nine years old when I read those stories, but I remember them to this day," the Director said, and she headed toward the door. But Hanah called after her:

"Yelizaveta Abramovna, you can eat breakfast now; I've done the calculations, and there will be more than enough food for the children today."

"No, no, I don't want any special privileges," the Director said, and left the room.

Just as she went out, Makar came in. He seated himself on an over-turned bucket as usual, and Hanah handed him a big bowl of porridge.

"You know, Hanah Davidovna, this is the last breakfast I'll be eating with you. Yesterday I was over at the site where they're building the ball bearing factory, and tomorrow I'm going to start working there."

"Maybe you will, maybe you won't. Either way, here's a glass of sour milk to go with your porridge."

"I love sour milk. Back home, my mother used to cook potatoes in their skins, and she would always put out a big bowl of sour milk. We could have as much as we wanted!" Makar reminisced.

"Eat faster! One foot here and the other at the base, because whoever gets there fastest can use the grinder first," Hanah hurried Makar. She was constantly hurrying him, and herself.

* * *

On the commune, Hanah had often visited her children at unsched-uled hours, and had always been allowed in. Now, however, she saw the girls only on Sundays, because the teachers at the kindergarten explicitly forbade her from seeing them during the week. One teacher had even gone so far as to say:

"Do you think, just because you work here, you can come in and see them whenever you feel like it?"

Being separated from her daughters wrung Hanah's heart, and she would often break down in tears. Indeed, tears now welled up in her eyes quite regularly. If someone else was in the kitchen, she would hold them back, but if she was alone, her feelings would overwhelm her and she would have a good cry, taking care that her tears didn't fall into the soup pot or onto the bread she was slicing. Then she would wipe her face and reproach herself: "Brave girl! You call yourself a mother? You need a mother yourself!"

It was also very hard for Hanah to come home from work now, even when Nehemyah accompanied her, because she had a strong sense that the neighbors considered her a fifth wheel on their wagon. Although neither Yakev nor Bronislava Yosipovna ever spoke an unkind word to her, Hanah felt at every turn that she was taking up too much space. Several things made it clear that they did not consider her their equal. For one thing, as soon as she started doing the laundry on Sundays, Bronislava would sail in with a big bundle of dirty clothes in her outstretched arms. She would toss the bundle on the floor near Hanah's feet and say, smiling:

"Would you do these along with yours? It's only a few things."

Usually, Bronislava dropped off her laundry when Nehemyah was out somewhere with the children. And Hanah never said a word to him about it. But there is a saying: "Every rope has an end." One Sunday, Nehemyah and the children happened to stay home because it was raining. Hanah was standing by the tin tub, doing a load of wash, when Bronislava walked in from her own room carrying a big bundle of dirty clothes in her outstretched arms. She threw it near Hanah's feet and, as always, continued on her way, casually tossing out the words:

"A few more for you."

Nehemyah sprang into view from his place on the sofa. With one stride, he was standing between Hanah and—as he called her—"Madam." He glared at Bronislava, hardly knowing what he was doing; as though of their own accord, his feet started kicking apart the pile of clothes she had thrown on the floor, and at the same time, he shouted in a voice quite unlike his own: "When a corpse sneezes, and you say 'bless you'—*that's* when Hanaleh will do your washing!" Then he turned to Hanah and said: "Hanukel, I can see this isn't the first time. Why didn't you tell me? What—when she moved in, you didn't know you'd be living with a pig, you didn't buy a slop pail?! *Ach,* poor child of mine." He spoke these last words in a low, soothing voice, and stroked Hanah's hair.

After this incident, Hanah literally couldn't look at Bronislava—not even at her dress or the shiny pumps on her feet. And it made her sick to her stomach whenever she overheard Bronislava in the next room saying, "Yakev—Yashenke—come help me take off my shoes." And her husband always obeyed! Hanah would often mimic the whole scene for Nehemyah, and he would laugh himself silly and then exclaim:

"Bravo, Hanukel! You've got such a great ear—you've captured them to a T!"

* * *

It turned out that "Madam" was a career woman. She started working at a monthly journal and hired an old woman to come and do the house-work for her. One day, when the men weren't at home, Bronislava turned to Hanah and inquired:

"Tell me, if you would be so good—why don't you want to go and live in the suburbs, near your children's school? Do you actually enjoy living in my apartment?"

Hanah didn't say a word in reply. She wasn't surprised at the rudeness of the question; she already knew, more or less, what to expect of this career woman—although that didn't make her any easier to deal with. But it did surprise Hanah to hear that Nehemyah was not even the official tenant of the little room they lived in.

The next day at work, she had trouble focusing on her job. The Direc-tor watched how absently Hanah was spooning sour cream into the little dishes, and when the task was done, she asked nonchalantly:

"Hanah Davidovna, are you just tired today, or has something hap-pened at home?"

"I'll tell you about it after work, if you have some time."

"Good; I'll be in my office."

It was not from idle curiosity that Yelizaveta Abramovna had asked about Hanah's personal life. And likewise, it was not because Hanah was ready to pour her heart out to just anyone that she offered to talk the matter through with Yelizaveta Abramovna. Hanah wasn't afraid to confide in her boss; she knew that the Director saw and appreciated what kind of person she was. They had sat together on many evenings, figuring out the accounts, and little by little they had opened up to each other. Gradually, Yelizaveta Abramovna had come to understand how Hanah had found herself in her current circumstances.

That evening, after the Director had heard what Hanah had to say, she sat thinking for a moment. Then, as though weighing every word, she began:

"I understand that your husband needed to do a lot of serious thinking before he brought you and the children here. But didn't you ever ask him if he'd found a place for you to live?"

"It didn't even occur to me. He's not a little boy, you know; he's almost thirty years old."

"But surely you see what demands you've placed on him? He's never been a father before, whereas you were already a mother . . . But don't be too downhearted. It will all work out somehow."

"I don't bear any ill will toward anybody. And I understand very well that this neighbor of mine needs me and my children like a hole in the head. But I can't go back to that apartment anymore; if I had anyplace else to go, I would never set foot there again!"

"But that's where your husband is, and you say that you love him."

"Very much! But should love force a person to be humiliated and insulted? The reason I've told you all this is because I was hoping you would let me sleep here, in the corridor, until I can find someplace else to stay with my children."

"Why sleep in a corridor? You can stay at my place for a while. But you can't decide anything without your husband; he has to know about all of this first. Both of you are equally responsible. Listen to me: first of all, go home tonight, just as you do every night. Second, don't tell him about the neighbor, what she asked and what she said. Talk it through with him simply and straightforwardly—bring him around to the idea that it's necessary to get an apartment of your own, and that it's easier to find one in the suburbs. Your oldest girl will be starting primary school in the fall. The way things are now, where will she be able to sit and do her homework? Enough; I don't need to tell you what to say."

Hanah realized the Director was right. When Nehemyah came to meet her that evening, he didn't notice anything unusual. But at home, after they had finished their tea, he sensed that Hanah was upset. When Yakev and Bronislava had retired to their room, he invited Hanah out for a stroll, and when they were on the street, he asked quietly:

"Did something happen at work?"

"What gives you that idea?"

"I can just tell. What happened?"

"I was wondering if you would notice."

"What is it? Do you feel sick?"

"I don't have time to feel anything—and I don't want to share an apartment with *them* anymore!"

"I don't want to, either. But for the time being, I don't see how we can move. I haven't told you about this yet, but I submitted an application to the Artists' Union."

Hanah ignored this. "We're going to have to find a place of our own sooner or later. The Director of the kindergarten—you know, Frida's mother—told me we may be able to get an apartment outside the city."

"I'm certainly willing to move. But you need to be patient; it's not so easy to find a place. Also, I should tell you that the room we're living in now is actually mine. Which means that you're not really living with them; you're living with me, in my room. I used to have a big, bright room of my own; then one day Yakev came to see me, and he kept talking and talking until he convinced me to move in with him. And when I did, he made me an official tenant here."

"Nehemyaleh, I don't understand any of that. But when I tell you I can't stay here anymore, I want you to understand what I mean: I will not live under the same roof as Yakev's wife. Whatever kind of room you can get, even if it's only five feet wide, I'll be happy. I'll whitewash it, I'll tidy it all up—we'll finally be able to breathe again."

"Don't worry. I promise I'll look for a place. Now come inside, and don't be so sad. I can't stand to see you like this. You know very well that I'd do anything to make things better for you."

Back in the apartment, Hanah didn't say another word. They put out the light and lay down to sleep. The next morning, Nehemyah had a complaint of his own:

"Hanukel, why don't you ever wear your wedding dress? It's high time you threw away those old commune clothes. And I gave you a new pair of shoes on the Eighth of March. So why are you still going around in those boots?"

"If it bothers you, I'll wear the shoes. It's all the same to me."

"Put them on now, then."

"I don't have time right now."

"Why not? You're just sitting there."

"I'm sitting here because I want to remember my dream. Shh—I remember it now. I'm going across the steppe at night. It's a gloomy night, pitch-black. I walk and walk in the darkness, until suddenly the sun appears. It rises slowly, slowly, as though some powerful giant is pushing it up out of the darkness. The light spreads, and then I hear the distant sound of galloping hooves. A faint neighing. The sound becomes clearer, and now I see a herd of horses running across the steppe. They run with heads tossing and mouths gaping so that I can see their teeth, and their hooves beat the dry earth like a drum. I start running along with them. I grab the mane of a pure-black horse, but he gives a twist of his neck, the mane slips out of my hand, and I fall to the ground. There is a stamping and a whinnying above me; I press myself against the ground with all my strength. A dreadful wave of neighing passes over me, and my back hurts so much that I wake up from the pain. Is it the bright steppe that's throbbing, or is it my heart? Yes, of course it's my heart, it's practically jumping out of my chest."

"Hanukel, my comfort, you truly are a poet!"

"You'll laugh at me," Hanah said, "but I often have the urge to set down what I know in writing—to record what I've seen, and what I see around me now. Just a few words, to remember all of this. Sometimes I want to write about my life so strongly, it feels like there's a heavy, heavy weight pressing down on me, and I can't get it off. It's much more of a burden than working with my hands."

"Hanukel, you should never do that. You *must* not do it!"

"What are you saying, Nehemyah? I shouldn't write? Why?"

"You have to trust me on this. The kind of people who write about their private lives are loathsome, they are . . . in a word—you shouldn't do it! I love you so much, I refuse to share our love with strangers . . . Listen: I'll *postareven* to find a *kvartir*—I mean, I'll try to find an apartment—and after that, I'll get more work than I do now—make more money. You'll leave the kindergarten; you'll be my homemaker and my beloved. Believe me, it will be excellent!"

"I know you love me. I know that no matter where we live, things will be excellent. I love you more than I do myself. But on the other hand, you sit at your table and you work. You tell stories with pencils and brushes about what you see—so why are you saying I shouldn't do the same thing?"

"My comfort, we already talk about everything you see. Now let's go to the tram, or you'll be late." Nehemyah brought her back to reality and walked her to the platform. And as always, when she was already standing on the step of the tram car, he warned:

"Be careful, don't run across the tracks!"

* * *

Whether or not it's true that an angel flicks an infant on the nose when it first glimpses the light of this world, it is certainly true that each person has his own share of luck; this Hanah understood. She had never given much thought to the question of whether she'd received a lucky flick from an angel at birth . . . but she often wished her life were a little easier than it was. For the moment, however, there was no prospect that her burden would be lifted.

In the stores, the shelves were stocked with packets of coffee made from acorns. Bread could be purchased only with a bread card; fabric and footwear only with an employer's order. In the kindergarten, too, Hanah could clearly see that the mothers who came in to drop off and pick up their children were troubled. Yelizaveta Abramovna often said to her, "A woman will be coming in here; give her two cups of rice and a bit of margarine." And as she watched how eagerly the woman took the food, Hanah's heart would ache.

Now she was faced with a new problem. She had not yet told Nehemyah about it, but she knew she was pregnant.

"Just what I need. How can I bring a baby to live with 'Madam'?" As Hanah's hand stirred millet porridge with the big wooden spoon, her mind was stirring up discontent with itself. "A mother in this city isn't even allowed to love her own children. On the commune, my little birds received the same care I would have given them myself; here, they're like seedlings transplanted into alien soil. They've aged ten years, and so have I!" She drove this last thought from her mind, because if the children were transplanted seedlings, then she was surely an uprooted tree.

The city, the streets, the trams, the coachmen, the houses, the crowds of people—everything here seemed utterly strange to her. "In the daytime, the sky is dark with smoke; at night people don't look up at the stars because they're tired and want to go to sleep. At dawn, nobody watches the sunrise because they're too busy running to work; in the evening, they don't notice the sunset because they're in even more of a hurry to catch the tram home. So many people, such a lot of houses, such a rush, such a hurry, so much unhappiness, so many people crammed together!" Hanah kept thinking.

How could she have felt otherwise? Her grandfather's house had been next to a field. The field was close to a forest. Everyone in the village knew one another. People greeted each other eagerly, described what they had cooked yesterday and what they were planning to cook today. When a child had a stomachache, the whole street knew about it; when there was an outbreak of measles or chicken pox, all the mothers sewed tiny linen bags, filled them with naphthalene, and hung them around the children's necks to ward off disease. In the summertime, Hanah often went into the forest with her grandparents to gather birch twigs, which they tied into bundles for bath whisks. Her grandmother knew that chamomile was good for the bowels, mint for headache, thousand-leaf for the joints. Hanah helped her gather the herbs and bind them together. Countless bunches of dried linden blossom and hare sorrel hung on nails in Grandmother's bedroom. Grandfather used to complain: "Those weeds of yours come into my dreams. You say they help with all kinds of sleep problems, but I'm telling you, the only thing they help me do is sneeze." (Here he would do a perfect imitation of sneezing: "*Ah-choo, ah-choo!*")

On the commune, there had been no forest. But there had been a steppe; a high, wide-open sky; a free, fragrant wind. No wonder, then, that Hanah's tiny room in Moscow felt like a cage, and the kitchen at work like a vise. On the other hand, when a person is blessed with an aptitude to contemplate and understand her surroundings, that person can at least take pleasure in her own thoughts. In this respect, Hanah differed from most people, who trudge mindlessly along under the yoke of day-to-day life and their own experiences.

When the Director sent a mother into the kitchen for food, Hanah would often dole out a little more rice than she was supposed to. One particular woman used to come more frequently than the rest. Hanah started treating her to a little bowl of porridge or a glass of tea. After this had happened a few times, the woman confided to Hanah that she was a single mother, that her husband had run off somewhere and forgotten all about the two children he'd left behind. Hanah listened and sympathized. She knew from the Director that this was not the only such case; there were several children in the kindergarten who had no fathers.

Hanah frequently reminisced about the Children's Home on the commune. There, it would never have crossed a worker's mind to swallow a single bite of food meant for a child, because the mothers rightly expected their children to be well nourished. And she kept remembering what one of the caregivers, Henke, had said when Hanah offered her a drink of milk:

"Don't treat me better than you treat yourself."

What a contrast, then, with the teachers here at the kindergarten, who said to Hanah: "Don't be stingy, give us another two spoonfuls, we work hard enough with the children." At staff meetings, Hanah complained of this selfishness more than once, but it was like beating her head against a wall.

Another subject that was frequently on Hanah's mind these days was Nehemyah. "It's clear that I was destined to be lucky: a husband like Nehemyah is a rarity, and I should value him. But he's never experienced any kind of loss; everything that he's ever had, he still has. And that includes me."

One day, she asked him:

"Nehemyaleh, tell me, what did you think would happen when you came to take me and the children back with you?"

"I thought I would bring you here, and the children would live with us—not at a kindergarten. Of course, I didn't know Yakev would come back from Kiev so quickly, much less with such a 'Madam.' I know you don't like it . . ."

"I like *you*, so I'm happy. That goes without saying!" After a pause, she said:

"I've been wondering whether to tell you this or not, but you'll know soon enough, in any case. Where will we find room if there's . . . another child?"

Hearing her own words, Hanah felt scared. But Nehemyah fell upon her, kissed her face and hands, and wanted to know everything:

"Hanukel, are you sure? Are you absolutely certain?"

"Stop, Nehemyah! What will we do, where will we find room? This place is always full of people yelling and smoking. Bringing a baby here would be impossible."

After this, Hanah's heart was uneasy—oh, so uneasy. And her work didn't go easily, either. Makar really had taken a job at the ball bearing plant. True, another man had been hired to help around the kitchen, and the Director had told Hanah to stop pulling cartloads of heavy supplies, because she knew Hanah was expecting. But the supplies weren't going to come into the kitchen all by themselves.

One day, Yelizaveta Abramovna came in to help Hanah sort through the grains and dried peas. It wasn't hard for her to see that Hanah's heart was troubled. So she spoke to her quietly and discreetly:

"Hanah Davidovna, if I can help you with anything, I'll do so with pleasure."

"I've thought about turning to you for help. But I'm not sure I want that . . . and anyway, it's too late."

"It's never too late to help."

"In this case, it is too late: it's already my fourth month."

"Your husband knows?"

"Yes."

"Well, as I've told you several times, you should stop going to the base for supplies. And don't be so downhearted and worried. Even a blind rooster can find a seed; your husband will find a solution to your housing problem. I'll say it again: Stop pulling the supply wagon!"

"I'm surprised you're so concerned," Hanah said. "You know this isn't my first time."

"And I'm surprised at *you*. You talk like a little child! In certain things, every time is the first time."

Although these words struck Hanah right to the heart, she was so sure of herself that she continued going to the base with the kitchen helper, and always pulled the wagon herself. She often wished she could get rid of the pregnancy—but as soon as she remembered how happy Nehemyah was, how eagerly he was awaiting the baby, she tried to dismiss these thoughts. She knew very well how devoted, how loyal, how attached to her Nehemyah was. Nevertheless, the longer the pregnancy went on, the more heavy-hearted and bitter Hanah became.

* * *

The days grew longer, brighter, and warmer. Hanah worked as before, and as before, she and the girls made the long ride home every week on the tram. And each time she returned to the room, she would marvel anew at how much grease and filth had accumulated there in a mere six days. The oilcloth, the windowsills, even the backs of the chairs were completely smeared with grease. As she washed everything down with hot water, Nehemyah consoled her:

"Hanukel, don't let it bother you. This is all from *their* butter."

"Where are *they* getting so much butter?"

"They shop at the commercial store."

Sundays would fly by, one-two-three. No sooner had she laid the children down to sleep than it would be time to wake them up and get them ready for school. Each week, this was a bitter struggle: the children cried and would not let her dress them. By the time she arrived at work, she was exhausted, and the new week had only just begun.

Hanah often started her day by going to the base for supplies; even though she made three trips with the wagon instead of one, the process wasn't easy for her. Yelizaveta Abramovna was a wise person, and what she had said was correct: "In certain things, every time is the first time." Hanah felt worse now than during her three earlier pregnancies. Back then, she had been able to eat and drink just like anyone else. Now, she could only keep down fluids . . . everything else nauseated her. She couldn't bear the smell of the dishes she cooked. Every so often she had to run out of the kitchen to catch a breath of fresh air, because if she stood over the stove for too long, her heart would start pounding as though it were about to jump out of her chest. It was really because of the kitchen odors that she was now so enthusiastic about going to the base.

Nehemyah had come and helped her out with the supplies a few times, but now he had a commission. He still met Hanah at the tram when she came home but had no time to do more than that. On Sundays, he would take over some of the housework so she could spend a few hours with the children in the fresh air. But then, as it turned out, the Artists' Union gave him a two-week residency, and off he went to a creative retreat in the suburbs.

One day, Hanah was walking slowly along the sidewalk with a rope wrapped around her hand so the heavily laden wagon would stay balanced and not get away from her when the street sloped downhill. She had been unwell all morning; her limbs felt as though they were filled with lead. Earlier, she had also felt a little lightheaded, but on the way to the base this dizziness had subsided.

Now, on the return trip, she suddenly felt a pain in her lower back. With the last of her strength, she dragged the supplies the rest of the way to the school. By the time she reached the yard, she had no strength to pull the wagon any farther. A contraction seized her, and at the same time something hot poured out of her, and she fell to the ground.

* * *

When Hanah came to herself in the hospital, she didn't ask "Where am I?" She remembered right away what had happened. The ward nurse noticed that Hanah was trying to turn onto her side, and she warned sternly:

"I know you're uncomfortable, patient, but lie still, because your operation was only yesterday."

"What kind of operation did I have?"

"Before they gave you the sedative, you must have heard the doctor say they had to remove the child. In any case, everything is in order now. Lie still so you won't have a hemorrhage."

At the nurse's words, a cold emptiness pierced Hanah's heart and spread to her limbs. She turned her face to the wall, and hot, painful tears began pouring from her eyes. The nurse came back over to her.

"Patient, get ahold of yourself right this minute; don't get hysterical. They say you're likely to make a full recovery."

Hanah stopped crying, insofar as she was able to, and told the nurse:

"You should only be allowed to take care of healthy people. No one else can handle that warm bedside manner of yours."

After this, Hanah couldn't be bothered with the nurse anymore. Instead, she lay in bed thinking about what had happened to her. But more than anything, she thought about her children: "This bad luck must have happened to me so that I would understand how devastated my children would be if they should ever lose me."

. . . And meanwhile, what was happening with the children?

The three little girls never stopped asking their teachers and Yelizaveta Abramovna:

"Where's our mama? Why didn't she come to see us yesterday, or the day before? What happened to our mama?"

"I told you, your mama is ill. When she gets well, she'll come back to you."

"We want to visit her in the hospital," all three girls said in unison.

"You know you're not allowed to go to the hospital."

The smallest girl found a solution to this:

"We'll tell the doctor that we're sick, too!"

On the sixth day after the operation, Yelizaveta Abramovna convinced the head doctor to allow her to bring Hanah's children to the hospital. The moment the door to the ward opened and the children saw their mother in bed, they tore themselves away from Yelizaveta Abramovna and ran straight to Hanah. Then they all burst into such bitter tears that the other patients in the ward, and even the nurse, who was always so harsh and humorless, began crying just as hard as Hanah and her daughters.

Overhearing all this lamentation, the doctor walked over to the children and said in mock amazement:

"This is the first time I've ever seen children who don't love their own mama!"

At this, the children started crying even louder. Eventually, somehow or other, the doctor managed to convince the girls that he had a surprise for them in his office. And he did, in fact, give them something: caramel candy. Once their mouths were full, the children stopped crying, and he was able to warn them that if they started again, he would not let them visit the hospital anymore.

As soon as the children had left with Yelizaveta Abramovna, the doctor gave Hanah a scolding for causing such a disruption. Meanwhile, she lay there wishing she hadn't agreed to let Nehemyah go away to the artists' retreat.

The next day, Yelizaveta Abramovna's daughter, Frida Blyumberg, came to visit. She told Hanah:

"I went to see Yakev, to find out Nehemyah's address. Then I sent Nehemyah a telegram and told him which hospital you're in. By the way, have Yakev and his wife been to see you?"

"Not so far. That's no surprise; they need me like a frog needs an umbrella. But don't worry; I'm not at all lonely here. Your mother comes every day, and you come. And yesterday, Yevdokia brought me a bottle of milk and some pretzels. So I can do without Yakev and his Bronislava."

* * *

Day by day, Hanah felt better. She was already starting to walk around the ward. She tried talking to the doctor about getting discharged from the hospital, but he wouldn't hear of it. Hanah didn't understand why he was so opposed to the idea, but there was actually a good explanation: Yelizaveta Abramovna had conferred with the doctor. She had told him about Hanah's situation and convinced him that he shouldn't be in any hurry with the discharge. Of course, she didn't tell Hanah about this, any more than she told her that on Sundays, she was now taking the three girls home with her to bathe them and give them the care they needed.

One afternoon, Hanah was sitting on her bed, reading Tolstoy's *Strider: The Story of a Horse*. Although she was deeply engrossed in the book, she couldn't help noticing that something unusual was going on around her. First the ward nurse ran through the room, then one of the orderlies, and then the other orderly. Soon afterward, the doctor himself ran by. After that, it was quiet again. Later, when one of the orderlies came in to serve the evening meal, Hanah asked:

"What was all that disturbance this afternoon?"

"Disturbance? Oh, that's quite a story! A young man came in to see his wife, but the orderly from the third ward told him it was bad news, that his wife had died. So he fainted dead away—they were barely able to revive him. He's still lying in the admissions office. I'm going to look in on him now. It's so pitiful, I can't begin to tell you."

"What did his wife die of?"

"I don't know what the orderly told him; I don't work in that ward. But it turns out his wife didn't die at all! The doctor really gave that orderly a piece of his mind for spreading a falsehood like that!"

Hanah immersed herself in her reading again. A little while later, she closed her book, but the entire scene she had just read stayed with her. She remembered each word of the story, practically saw everything right before her eyes. And she had a sudden realization: "If I were a horse, they would have dragged me away, too, when I fell down in the yard." Then the thought that had been plaguing her almost incessantly came into her mind again: "If only I had obeyed Yelizaveta Abramovna and not pulled the supply wagon, this terrible thing wouldn't have happened."

As Hanah lay there in bed, this thought kept going around and around in her head. She was so distracted that she didn't hear the door open, but she did take notice when the nurse called out:

"Comrade Faynberg, someone is here to see you."

But the nurse's words were unnecessary, because Nehemyah was already standing at Hanah's bedside.

"How are you feeling, how are you feeling?" he blurted out, clearly agitated.

"I don't feel too bad. But why are you so pale?"

The nurse came over and warned Nehemyah:

"You'd better behave yourself. Before this woman came in here, she was slaving away like an ox at home and at work, while her own husband turned a blind eye. And now you come in and go all to pieces, you're sick to your stomach for more than an hour, and then you raise the roof with all your carryings-on!"

Hanah suddenly guessed the identity of the distraught husband she'd heard about earlier.

"Yekaterina Pavlovna," she said to the nurse, "you can see he's behaving himself very well now." Then she turned to Nehemyah and said:

"There's a chair; sit down. What happened?"

"Oh, it was nothing, they just told me you were dead."

"Well, as you can see, I'm alive. Sit down! How did you hear where I was? Did you get Frida's telegram?"

"The telegram must have gotten lost somehow. Frida herself came to see me. But now I don't understand anything! Oh, how could I have gone away? I should have been there, I should have picked you up with my own hands . . ."

He wanted to say more, but Hanah interrupted him:

"Please, don't be so hard on yourself. What difference does it make whether I was picked up by your hands or someone else's? There's no reason to faint, nothing to cry about. Wipe away your tears. Believe me, I've already cried enough for the both of us. Come, bring your chair closer; why are you sitting so far away? You know, a lot of people were running around here earlier; there was a big commotion. And right after that, the orderly told me that some young man had fainted because he'd been told his wife was dead. But it never occurred to me that it was you!"

"You're right, there's no point in crying. Tomorrow I'll go and look for an apartment. That's the most important thing right now. You won't have to work anymore—that is, you'll still have plenty of work to do, but not in some big institution."

It seemed as though Nehemyah had barely spent any time with her, but the duty nurse was already telling him it was time to leave. Not long after he'd left, Yelizaveta Abramovna arrived. She was very surprised when Hanah requested several pieces of paper.

"If you need to write a letter, I'll bring you an envelope, too."

"Thank you, but I don't need an envelope. I just want to write something," Hanah said evasively. Although she was very attached to the Director, she kept wishing she would leave, because she had a strong feeling that there was something she needed to focus her mind on. And indeed, as soon as Yelizaveta Abramovna left, Hanah immediately had a vision from early childhood.

It is a wintery Shabbes evening. On the table stands a big bowl of potatoes in their skins. A second bowl is filled with sauerkraut. In the middle of the table lies a porcelain platter of baked herring, and around the table sit various neighbors. Etel Haykel, the glazier's wife, has already finished her meal and is standing near the warm stove. No one else is watching, but Hanah sees Etel pull up her undershirt to warm herself better. Hanah's grandmother apparently notices what she's looking at, however. She mutters at Hanah:

"You dirty thing, looking at something you shouldn't!"

All of this appeared so clearly in Hanah's mind that she broke into a big smile. But a little later, she started to wonder: "Why did Nehemyah say I mustn't write anything when I told him I wanted to? He shouldn't have said that writing is wrong. I can't understand why he objects so strongly, but I know one thing: I won't obey him!"

* * *

Nehemyah did just what he had promised. He went off to Udelnaya to look for an apartment, and he was lucky: he didn't need to search for very long. On a side street not far from the train station, he found two rooms for rent with a private entrance. The rooms were bright and fairly spacious, but Nehemyah was even more pleased with the landlady than with the rooms themselves. He liked her from the moment they met. First of all, she spoke Yiddish better than he did; second, she asked him right away:

"When are you moving in?"

"As soon as my wife is discharged from the hospital."

"Why didn't you tell me your wife was sick?"

"I didn't think it was important."

"Well, whatever you thought, I won't take any down payment from you now. Please, put your money back in your pocket. I'll make a deal with you: the fifth of May is a week from now, so let's say that in a week, you come and see me again and let me know whether you need the apartment or not. If I don't hear from you, I'll rent it to someone else, because there's no lack of people looking for a summer place—my door never closes! But since you need the apartment in the winter, too, I'll wait for you."

"Why don't you want to take the money now?"

"Don't worry about it. For some people, money is important; for me—it's just a word."

From Udelnaya, Nehemyah rode back to see Hanah, and although it was not a visiting day at the hospital, the nurse let him in, grumbling:

"Go in already, go ahead! If I don't let you in, you'll probably faint again!"

Nehemyah pretended not to hear. He strode over to Hanah's bed and announced:

"Hanukel, you are now the mistress of two rooms."

"Far from Moscow?"

"No, no, not far from Moscow, and not far from the train station, and both rooms have doors, so I can sit and work just like a count!"

"Well, if you're going to be a count, I'll be a countess. Today the doctor told me they're going to discharge me at the beginning of next week."

"In that case, I'll go back to Udelnaya tomorrow, so the landlady can prepare the rooms," Nehemyah said, and he left.

His next stop was the home of Nikolai Nikolaevich, where he told his old teacher about the whole situation with Hanah. Nikolai Nikolaevich listened closely, shaking his head from time to time and saying, "Tsk, tsk, tsk." Afterwards, when he was showing Nehemyah to the door, he murmured as though to himself: "I was just over at Yakev's. Neither he nor his wife said a word about Hanah's being sick. I can't understand such behavior." Then, abruptly, he asked, "Do you need any money?"

"No, thank you."

"Send a message to the Moscow Artists' Union that you are literally out on the street and need their support. It's the simple truth."

"Yes, I'll do that."

"Tell me, has Yakev or his wife visited Hanah Davidovna in the hospital?"

"Not once. But don't worry: Hanah isn't on her own." As Nehemyah spoke these words, he realized for the first time how much Yelizaveta Abramovna and her daughter Frida had done for him. A few days later, Nehemyah ran into Yelizaveta Abramovna in the hospital ward and told her he had rented an apartment. She answered in a low voice, so that Hanah couldn't hear: "In the beginning, you should help out around the house as much as you can. Hanah Davidovna needs to rest." And a little later, as they walked out of the ward together, she brought the matter up again:

"It's important for you not to assume that Hanah has endless reserves of strength and can deal with anything that comes up, the way she could before. We're going to have to pay a lot of attention to her, because she's one of those people who feel that no matter how much they take upon themselves, it's not enough."

"Thank you, I'll keep that in mind."

"You need to do more than keep it in mind. Whatever you can't do yourself, tell me and my Frida about it, and we'll help you. Excuse me for saying this," Yelizaveta Abramovna added, "but it seems to me you don't completely understand Hanah. A while ago she retold one of Hans Christian Andersen's fairy tales to me with so much taste and understanding that I was really astonished. This is a true gift; she communicates with such fresh, original feeling that I wouldn't be surprised if, in time, she proves to be exceptionally talented. You're very fortunate: such a thing doesn't happen often." Yelizaveta Abramovna said all of this to Nehemyah not only to show him that she understood more about Hanah than he did, but also to demonstrate how highly she valued Hanah's abilities.

Now Nehemyah busied himself with getting the new apartment in order. This turned out to be easy: the landlady gave him two beds, two tables, and several chairs, so all he needed to do was find a few cots for the children. When Hanah walked in and saw the room, which even had a jar of narcissus flowers on the table, she clapped her hands with delight. A couple of days later Nehemyah brought the children in, and, at last, they all had their very own home. There was only one thing that detracted a bit from Nehemyah's happiness: he felt that Hanah was not being entirely open with him about something.

And he was right. Hanah had used the paper Yelizaveta Abramovna had brought her in the hospital to write a little story about how her grandmother used to treat her neighbors to supper on Shabbes evenings—in winter, with baked potatoes and sauerkraut, and in summer, with cold sorrel soup. She wrote the scene exactly as it appeared in her mind's eye. And one day, when Nehemyah wasn't home and Frida happened to come for a visit, Hanah read the story aloud to her. Frida laughed and said she loved it. But Nehemyah didn't find out about Hanah's new pastime for quite a while.

Hanah wrote another little story, about how she had taken lessons with Shmuel the Rabbi as a child. A boy named Meylechke Senders used to sit near her in the schoolroom, but he could never remember a single word of Torah. So Hanah used to whisper the answers to him, and in exchange, Meylechke would give her a groschen every Friday. In this way, she eventually saved up two kopeks and was able to buy herself some halvah from Vichne the Confectioner. Arriving home with this special treat, she hid behind the woodpile and ate and ate until she felt like she was going to throw up. Then she hid the rest of the halvah among the logs and went inside.

In the house, she encountered none other than Vichne the Confectioner herself, and immediately felt a cold shiver run down her spine: Vichne must have told her grandparents how she'd spent her ill-gotten money! Sure enough, her grandfather turned to Hanah and asked: "Did you save some of your snack for us?" Her grandmother didn't say anything—she just gave Hanah a couple of good smacks. After that, Hanah always hated halvah, right up until the present day.

By this time, Hanah was addressing Yelizaveta Abramovna simply as Leah, and it turned out that not only did Leah speak Russian, she also spoke very fine Yiddish—a lot better than Nehemyah had been able to do only a short time ago. When Hanah read the story about the halvah to Leah, she roared with laughter. Then she asked:

"Have you read that to Nehemyah?"

"He says I shouldn't do this."

"Do what?"

"He says I shouldn't write."

"You aren't obeying him, of course."

"I'm not obeying him, and I never will!"

And so the years went by, until eventually, Hanah was pleased enough with her writing that she stopped tearing it up.

* * *

They were extremely lucky with regard to their new landlady. Hanah and Nehemyah addressed her as Rozaliya Salomonovna; the children called her Grandma Reyzeh. She was truly like a mother to Hanah and Nehemyah, and like a grandmother to the children. The three little girls had positively come back to life since moving in with Hanah and Nehemyah full-time; there was a new glow about them, and their laughter and playfulness made everything around them feel homey. Hanah was amazed.

"Nehemyah, I can't understand it; I don't even recognize them! Ever since the day they were born they've lived in one Children's Home or another. I had no idea they could be so happy."

Hanah was feeling better, too. The fresh air in their new neighborhood certainly helped. She and Nehemyah had been a little worried about the rent, because they'd been sure that Reyzeh would raise it during the prime summer months—but she never said a word about it. Nehemyah and Hanah had many opportunities to compare Reyzeh with Yakev's wife, because Reyzeh's behavior was the exact opposite of Bronislava's. For example, when Hanah wasn't home, Reyzeh would gather up all the clothes in Hanah's rooms that looked as though they needed washing and put them in with her own laundry. Then she would wash the whole load of pillowcases, towels, and children's clothes together. The fact that Hanah protested each time made no difference.

"Why should it bother you, sweetie? It's not as though I set up the tub just to do your laundry. I started washing my own things, and I thought of yours. So what did I do that was so terrible?"

When Reyzeh did the baking on Friday mornings, she always made several extra challahs so there would be some left over on Sunday to serve to Hanah's guests. Sundays were when Frida and her mother, Leah, came to visit, as well as Nikolai Nikolaevich with the white mouse in his pocket. Reyzeh's baked goods were always put to good use.

Meanwhile, summer was approaching, and here it was, already June. One day, Nehemyah told Hanah that the Artists' Union had given him a field assignment.

"What do you mean? You're going away?" Hanah was distressed.

"Darling, I go away every summer. If not, how would I have met you?"

Hanah acted as though she hadn't heard. She went off to the kitchen to light the Primus stove and extinguish her resentment. "'I go away every summer,' he says. But this summer is completely different from the others. Doesn't he understand that?" she thought. But although Nehemyah hadn't mentioned her illness, he understood very well that this whole situation could have been avoided. Indeed, he was eating himself up with guilt, and kept thinking: "If only I hadn't listened to Yakev; if only I hadn't agreed to move in with him. If I'd had my own apartment in the first place, none of this would have happened." And, of course, when Nehemyah had applied for the field assignment, it hadn't occurred to him that he shouldn't travel this year. But it was too late to decline the job now.

In spite of their looming separation, life went on as usual. The children were healthy and well fed; Hanah managed the household prudently and thriftily; Nehemyah was full of enthusiasm for his work. Grandma Reyzeh helped them out however she could. But a person never knows what fate has in store. One day, when Hanah was reading on the front porch, a woman and a man arrived. They hurried past her without a word, bumping her with their suitcase as they entered the house. A few hours later, Hanah overheard a conversation coming from Grandma Reyzeh's room, and she surmised that the landlady's adult children had come to live with her.

Hanah had assessed the situation correctly, but she didn't realize that she and Nehemyah would have only a couple of days to find another apartment. They left the children with Grandma Reyzeh and went out apartment hunting in the Moscow suburbs. With relatively little trouble, they found a small room in Lyublino. Naturally, Nehemyah postponed his work trip to help with the move. By the time they had gotten organized and bought a few furnishings, it was already August. Then one day, out of the blue, Yakev came to see them and handed Hanah a letter. Hanah was very surprised, but as soon as she tore open the envelope and read the first few lines, she understood what had happened: it had been sent to her old address, because the writer had no way of knowing that Hanah had moved. Here is what was written in the letter:

Hanah, Hanatchke, my warmest greetings, you wonderful friend! You, who went away and tossed us out of your mind and your heart, like so much garbage! Someone like you should really go around grunting like a pig, instead of speaking human language . . . You need not wonder how I found out where you live. When Yocheved cleaned out your room, she found an empty envelope in your bed with a Moscow address. Truth be told, I actually expected you to send me a word or two. Then I started thinking: the minute she gets married, she forgets me! Don't you even remember how eagerly you used to gobble up the cucumbers in my garden? No finer, prettier ones exist in the world!

It should be crystal clear by now that I would never write to you if I didn't have to—but, as the saying goes, need breaks iron. Who else can I turn to? Who else do I have? I keep asking myself, who? . . . The first thing you need to know is that the commune is no more. As soon as we became a collective farm, most of the communards left. Those who stayed got married as quickly as they could, because the Collective Farm Board announced it was going to distribute cows, but only to people who were married. When I heard about this, I said I wanted a cow, too—if not a milker, then at least a pregnant cow, and if not a pregnant cow, then a heifer. But the Chairman of the collective farm told me: "Hayah, if you want a cow, get yourself a husband!" I laughed very hard at that, but when I saw what kind of matches people were making, I laughed even harder. Efroyim married Zeldke; Ayzik married your old roommate Yocheved; Shimke the Groom married Mineh—you remember, the one who worked in the Children's Home. I myself, as I'm sure you can understand, did not want a husband, and I therefore remain cowless.

Because of all this, I am asking you to find out whether it's true that a ball bearing factory is being built in Moscow. For weeks now I've been hauling vegetables to Saki, and I always stop at the well in Temesh to water the oxen. Along the way, I started seeing one boarded-up house after another. So I asked a peasant woman at the well: What's going on here? She told me that someone in the neighborhood had received a letter from his nephew in Moscow, saying you can earn a good living there. The nephew, Makar, says they're up to their ears in work, and that he's helping to build a big ball bearing factory. Apparently he used to be dirt-poor until he found menial work in some kind of kitchen, but now he's living in a barracks and doing as well as anybody. So Makar's uncle dropped everything, boarded up his doors and windows, and bang!—off he goes to Moscow. When other people heard about it, they did the same thing. You wouldn't even recognize Temesh now. It's a ghost town.

So do me a favor, Hanah, and write back right away. I even ask that you find out the address where they're building this ball bearing factory. I'll go straight there, without visiting you—I don't want to bother you, seeing as how you haven't found one free hour in the past five months to write me a few words! Take care. In spite of everything, I still think about you and love you.

Hayah from the Garden Brigade

Hanah read the letter aloud to Frida and Leah, who had just walked in. They laughed, but then Frida asked sadly:

"What will become of the family farms? Who will sow and harvest the crops if all the peasants run off?"

"Some will leave, but others will stay," Nehemyah reassured her.

Soon after this, Nehemyah finally left for his field assignment. When he bade Hanah goodbye, the kiss she gave him was so weak and unenthusiastic that he knew it would have been better to stay. But when Hanah came back inside after Nehemyah's departure, she didn't actually feel that his absence would be such a bad thing. Indeed, she knew just what she would do in the coming days.

At this time of year, the nights were still not very long, and as soon as the sun came up, Hanah began to write. Then she would tear up her work, write some more, and then tear it all up again. But one day, she suddenly started writing about a black hen:

The wicked old hen was constantly running into the house, and the old granny who lived there had to chase her around and around to get her out. Whenever the granny sifted flour, the hen would jump right up on the table, and clouds of flour would fly up to the ceiling. But one day, the hen disappeared. The granny searched and searched, but she couldn't find her anywhere. A few days later, the granny needed something in the attic, and when she reached inside an old trunk, she came upon the hen. The hen scratched the granny's hands with her sharp claws and flew out of the trunk, flapping and squawking as if she had gone mad. The granny reached back inside, and her hands touched some little bottles, spools of thread, and other small things, all warm from the hen's body. She realized that the hen was seeking a place to hatch a brood of chicks. So she tossed everything out of the trunk, brought fifteen eggs into the house, and laid them in the bottom of the empty trunk. And sure enough, it all went just as she had hoped. The wicked old hen hatched out fifteen chicks . . .

This story, Hanah did not tear up.

* * *

Writing came easily for Hanah. The problem was that she loved to read even more than she loved to write. It often happened like this:

Hanah is sitting and writing. Suddenly, without realizing how it's happened, she's holding a book in her hands. And once she's started reading it, she can't put it down!

Books became such a problem for Hanah that she started hiding them from herself. Even so, she read a great deal. And, moved as she was by Yiddish writers like Sholem Aleichem and Peretz, Opatoshu and Vaysnberg, Hofshteyn and Halkin, she was just as likely to be moved to tears by writers like Chekhov and Tolstoy, Cervantes and Dickens. "The Woman Mrs. Hanah" was one of her favorite characters. When Andrei Bolkonsky died in *War and Peace,* Hanah mourned as one mourns a dear friend; when she read in Dickens's *David Copperfield* that "there is no grass anywhere as green as the grass in the churchyard where my father lies in eternal rest," it wrung her heart. Recognizing the symptoms, Nehemyah would ask:

"Hanukel, what kind of misfortune happened in classical literature this time?"

"Misfortunes happen in classical literature because they happen to us, and to everyone!" Hanah would answer earnestly. "To Father Goriot and Tevye the Dairyman alike!"

Nehemyah now understood that when Hanah was writing, he should not say, "Come to bed; nothing will come of your scribbling, in any case." When he woke up the next morning, she was often still sitting at the table, hard at work; he would pretend to be asleep. The longer this went on, the more concerned he became. He found himself reminding her more and more often to eat something. In the evenings, he used to put a glass of milk, a piece of bread, or a lump of sugar on the table for her.

After his field assignment ended, Nehemyah often traveled into the city with the pieces that the two of them had agreed were his best, Hanah having duly inspected each sketch and painting several times. But he never stayed in Moscow overnight. Many evenings he took the last train back and, arriving home, he would knock twice at the window. Then he would press his face against the glass, while Hanah stood and looked at him from within. They would smile at each other for a moment, and then Hanah would run and open the door.

From Lyublino, they moved to Tsaritsyno, from Tsaritsyno to Perlovka. Everywhere Hanah lived, she was a careful, thrifty housekeeper, and when times were hard, she managed their budget accordingly. Never again did they have such a wonderful landlady as Reyzeh, but wherever they were living, she would come to visit them, always bringing them something, and often taking the children out somewhere. She had aged a great deal, but she never complained.

"Even though I'm a boarder at my son's, I am still, with God's help, the mistress of my own room," she said. From these few words, Hanah and Nehemyah had a good idea what kind of a son Reyzeh had.

* * *

At the beginning of 1937, the Artists' Union gave Nehemyah an apartment.

At the end of the same year, Hanah gave birth to a son.

IV

Hanah dubbed the four lean years before the war "my seven years of abundance." She called them this in the hope that it would make them better. When talking to Nehemyah in those days she often quoted the saying:

"What good to me is a golden goblet if it's full of tears?"

She said this not, God forbid, because she was lacking anything. Indeed, if their own well-being had been enough to make her and Nehemyah happy, they would have had no cares in the world. But . . .

When they moved into their new apartment, they didn't throw a housewarming party. They weren't in the mood to celebrate. Too many of their friends were missing. Never again would Hanah see the curly-haired poet from Minsk, and others were gone as well. Hanah and Nehemyah were so depressed that sometimes whole days passed in nearly unbroken silence. When Frida and her mother, Leah, made one of their frequent visits, they would all sit around the table together—but there was more silence than conversation.

* * *

The sun rose, the sun set; Hanah was never free of the routines of everyday life. But her work became much less hectic after they moved into the new building. Here, they had the luxury of occupying two whole rooms—and the distance between the rooms made it all the more convenient. Hanah, Nehemyah, and their three-month-old son slept in the larger room, at the front of the building. At the other end of the corridor stood the second room, where the three little girls slept—or, more accurately, where they made a racket.

The two older girls, Pereleh and Beylke, went to the Jewish school in Maryina Roshcha. They were good students. But that did not stop them from having some fun with their little sister, Reyzeleh, after they finished their homework. Several times a day, the woman who lived on the other side of the wall from the three girls would come and knock on the door of the big room, and when Hanah opened it, the woman would wring her hands and complain:

"Go take a look at what your little trio is doing now. They're going to break their necks! Oh, this is just my luck! It was so quiet here until you came. *Hospodi!*"

"What am I supposed to do? They're children!" Hanah would answer.

"So if you have children, why didn't you make the Housing Authority give you a suite? When the artists who lived here before you had children, they were given a bigger place on Maslovka Street, and better benefits, too. So why didn't you? If your husband were as good an artist as those people . . ."

When the neighbor started talking like this, Hanah would shut the door. But eventually she and Nehemyah moved the three girls into the big room, and they themselves moved into the small room with the baby. After that, the neighbor seldom knocked on the door, and seldom compared Nehemyah with those other artists. And the girls were also less likely to come in and disturb Nehemyah's work. The big room was forty meters square, which gave them plenty of space to play; the only furnishings were three small cots, three small chairs, and a big low table. Often all the bedding wound up on the floor, because Pereleh and Beylke liked to show Reyzeleh how the acrobats in the circus stood on their heads. This kept them so busy that they didn't have time to run into the small room and see what was going on at Nehemyah's work table.

To be sure, things were much easier for Hanah here than on the commune. But she still didn't have a single moment to herself. The girls attended the early shift at their school, so Hanah had to get up an hour and a half before they did to cook millet or barley porridge or roast some potatoes for their breakfast. Right after that came the hardest part of the morning, because getting the girls out of bed was like pulling teeth. Once they were finally up, dressed, and fed, they had to be walked to the tram. After getting them onto the car, Hanah ran breathlessly back home and up to the third floor. She made breakfast for Nehemyah, gave him a quick kiss, and saw him out. He was always in a rush now, because he was working as a teacher at the Institute of Art. Hanah would stand in the doorway and watch as he made his way down the stairs, and she would warn him, just as he had warned her in the past:

"Nehemyaleh, don't rush; don't pick a fight with the tram!"

"Aye-aye, Commander—but as you know, *I'm* not the one from the country! Now go lie down and get some rest while the baby is sleeping."

But she didn't have time to lie down, because now the baby was up and wanted breakfast.

To list everything Hanah managed to accomplish, to calculate how many kilometers she walked in a day, would be no modest undertaking; indeed, the amount would be unbelievable—especially given that, as already mentioned, she also spent the whole night writing. As she wrote, she would sometimes hear Nehemyah calling:

"Hanukel, it's almost dawn!"

Hanah, however, would continue to sit and write. Then Nehemyah would say:

"My dearest, come here. Get some rest . . ."

And then, early one morning, Nehemyah suddenly walked out.

Disconcerted, Hanah followed him—but only with her eyes. Although she stopped writing, she remained seated at the table. When Nehemyah came back, it was already well into the morning. He did not eat the breakfast Hanah served. And for the first time since they had been together, they didn't speak a single word to each other for several days.

* * *

Nehemyah's discouraging predictions about Hanah's writing failed to come true. One day, during the period when he and Hanah weren't speaking to each other, Frida came to visit. Nehemyah happened to be out. As always, Frida was warm and kind, and Hanah read her a little story she'd written about going into the woods to gather mushrooms. When she finished reading, Frida asked:

"Do you have another copy of that?"

"No; why would I need one?"

"If it's not too much trouble, copy it over for me. I want to read it to my mother. Has Nehemyah read it?"

At this question, the blood rushed to Hanah's face.

"Why are you turning so red?" Frida asked in surprise, but Hanah didn't answer. Someone else might not have paid much attention, but Frida sensed something was wrong. She looked closely at Hanah and said quietly:

"This happens. I know an artist who put his wife through hell because she wanted to work—she was an artist, too. And things ended sadly for them. They had to separate."

"Over that?" Hanah asked uneasily, but she didn't say anything more. She had a feeling that her friend knew all about what was going on between her and Nehemyah. As Frida was getting ready to leave, Hanah changed the subject by asking about Yelizaveta Abramovna.

"Why doesn't your mother work at the kindergarten anymore?"

"You know as much about it as I do. My mother used to be the Director of Education in a model school, but as things turned out, she had to leave that position . . . That's when she started working at the kindergarten. Now, she's unemployed again," Frida answered with tears in her eyes, and added: "Make a copy of the story; don't forget. I'll give it to her the day after tomorrow."

Scarcely three months after Hanah gave Frida a copy of the story, the latest issue of *Zay Greyt* was delivered to her from Kiev—and there, in the journal, was her story "Hunting Mushrooms"! Of course, much has been said about the pleasure a writer feels at seeing his name in print for the first time. Suffice it to say that for Hanah, too, this experience did not disappoint. Indeed, she went around drunk with joy. A few days later, when Hanah received her honorarium from Kiev and went to put it in the drawer with the housekeeping money, Nehemyah happened to be nearby. Watching her, he burst out laughing. His reaction sobered Hanah up a little bit; she imagined what she must look like, carrying the money in her upraised hand as though it were some precious treasure—and then she, too, began to laugh hysterically. She fell upon Nehemyah and kissed his whole face; she grabbed the baby from his crib and started carrying him around the room in a wild dance, all the while singing, to the tune of her grandfather's Shabbes hymn, "My life, my treasure, my little son, my dearie, the apple of my eye!" She caught Nehemyah's hand, made him twirl around with her, and kissed him again. Then, to keep the baby safe, she laid him back in his crib before continuing to "cut a rug," as she called it.

Soon it was time for Hanah to go and meet the girls after school. As she was feeding them their lunch, the youngest suddenly started begging:

"Mama, sew a dress for my doll!"

One-two-three, the little dress was cut out and sewn together. Then the children went outside to play, the baby fell asleep, and Nehemyah went off to the Art Institute. Hanah suddenly remembered that she should write a letter to her old friend from the commune, Hayaleh Grinshteyn.

A good day and a good year to you, dear Hayaleh! Don't think I've forgotten you, or didn't want to answer your letter. What can I say? Some days, I just don't know where the time goes. The very best solution would be for you to come and stay with us. Then you would see with your own eyes that I'm not such a terrible person. I'm certainly not the monster you seem to imagine. You may think I'm just making excuses, but the truth is, I'm so busy, I roll around like a pea in a sieve from morning 'til night, and every day seems like Short Friday to me. So don't be resentful that I am so late with my answer. Be healthy, greet the gang for me, and come for a visit.

Your friend, Hanah, who waits for you with impatience

She put the letter in an envelope, wrote the address on it, laid it on the table under a newspaper, and forgot about it again—but only because the next day was Saturday. Saturdays and Sundays were the hardest days of the week for Hanah. On Saturdays she needed to get everything ready, because on Sundays the whole family was home, and there was also no shortage of guests. All day Saturday, both Primus stoves hummed away: a big buckwheat porridge would be cooking on one, and a bean and potato soup on the other. Meanwhile, a five-liter pot of compote would be cooling by the kitchen window. But the main thing that kept Hanah busy was the onion cutlets. This was a special delicacy she had invented herself, and it was extremely popular, not just with her family but with everyone. The first time Hanah shared it with Frida and Leah, they said they'd never heard of such a thing. But as soon as she gave them the recipe, the dish became part of their regular menus, too. Because not only are onion cutlets very nutritious, they are also very tasty!

"You have to cook up the onions whole, put them through the food grinder, add dried breadcrumbs, a little pepper, salt, and don't skimp on the eggs," Hanah said. "If you do everything the way I tell you, the cutlets will turn over by themselves when you fry them in the skillet, as long as the oil is hot when you put them in."

To make this delicacy for the entire family was not an easy undertaking for Hanah. She used to say:

"Everything is finished, but I'm finished, too!"

But in spite of all this hard work, no sooner had the rest of the family gone to bed than Hanah would sit down at the table to write.

* * *

One Saturday, Hanah was even more busy than usual: it was her turn to clean the "common areas." As she worked, her neighbor Mikhail Mitrofanovich stood at the kitchen table, fussing with a goose. Not only was he cleaning this goose, he was also having a lively conversation with it. The conversation was, unfortunately, one-sided, because the goose had no more to say than any other slaughtered goose. But the neighbor's eloquence did not flag: "Yes, you honked, you slapped the ground with your webbed feet, you beat your wings; but now you've fallen into Mikhail Mitrofanovich's pot!" As Hanah washed the floor, she felt as though she was about to fall over laughing. It was all she could do to keep a straight face as she threw the rag into the pail and ran out of the kitchen. As soon as she was in her own room, she exploded with laughter. Then she heard the baby crying, so she looked in on him and made sure he was all right. She rocked him, gave him a few sips of water, and then went back to the kitchen to finish washing the floor.

Her neighbor came bounding over in a fury:

"How dare you? You splashed my trousers with your rag! And who do you think you are, anyway? You think I don't know you're from the country? Kulaks are fleeing from there like rats from a sinking ship! I'll expose you for who you really are. I'm not just anybody, you know! Everybody knows I'm an activist!"

Listening to this tirade, Hanah burst out laughing again. But although her neighbor kept on ranting that he would expose her for who she really was, and insisting he was an "activist," Hanah stopped listening, because the doorbell had begun to ring urgently, over and over again. So she ran and opened the door, and saw . . .

Hayaleh Grinshteyn.

* * *

After their initial shrieks, kisses, and hugs, Hanah led Hayaleh into her room, sat her down, and showered her with questions. Hayaleh didn't know which one to answer first. To Hanah's question "When did you get here?" Hayaleh blushed and stammered:

"It's already . . . almost a . . . a year since I came to Moscow."

"A YEAR?!"

"What are you shouting about? You didn't answer my letter, so I thought you had turned your back on me and the whole commune."

"How could you think such a thing?!"

"Let me finish. You remember, I wrote to you that the commune got turned into a collective farm? And that everybody there had to get married, whether they wanted to or not, because the government would only give cows to married couples?"

"I remember, but what does that have to do with me? And why didn't you come to see me for a whole year after you moved here?"

"Just listen. Shimke from the stable—you haven't forgotten him, have you? Well, to make a long story short, we were in love. But when the commune became a collective farm and was renamed 'International Friendship,' Shimke told me he'd rather have a 'communal friendship' with me than an 'International Friendship' . . . and then, bang! Off he went to Moscow."

"Shimke is here, too?"

"Don't interrupt, just listen. Yes, Shimke is here, and Toybke and Charlie, too. You remember, I wrote you that somebody named Makar sent a letter home to his uncle in Jabahi? This Makar wrote that a huge factory was being built in Moscow, and that he was working there, living in a barracks and earning a good living. Well, his uncle started spreading the word, and pretty soon, people on the commune heard about it, too. So Shimke and Shachne and some of the other communards went off to

Moscow. Some of them even turned in their cows first. To tell you the truth, I didn't want to come, but Shimke kept bombarding me with letters. He wrote: 'You won't regret it. Here, once you finish your shift, you're as free as a bird. You want to go to the cinema?—Go! You want to go to a club?—Why not?' In short, I realized that life without Shimke was no life at all. So I followed him."

"That's wonderful! Nothing could be better!" Hanah exclaimed.

"Maybe it's wonderful, and maybe not. It's easy to make judgments about somebody else's life—just like it's easy to see a splinter in someone else's eye. It's seeing what's in your own eye that's difficult!" Hayaleh said; it was clear she was still bitter that Hanah had not answered her letter.

Hanah was about to respond, but the baby started crying, so she lifted him into her lap. Hayaleh reached out to help, but Hanah waved her away.

"Look what a little troublemaker I have. You see how he loves to eat?"

The child was, indeed, nursing with great enthusiasm. Hayaleh watched for a bit and then remarked:

"A baby has no patience: the moment it comes, he has to drink it all up. What's his name?"

"Sender, after Nehemyah's father. So you're an expert on babies now? I'm telling you, Hayaleh, caring for an infant is such a delight, a sweetness I feel in the very marrow of my bones. I love it when they're tiny like this. You know, I often think that kindness is the true source of everything. Ask yourself, how would babies grow up if their mothers didn't jump out of bed ten times a night, but just left them lying in their wetness and filth? If we didn't shower them with love, and blow every little speck of dust off of them? But of course, you can't understand any of this yet."

"Why wouldn't I understand? First of all, I'm not a child; I'm twenty-four. And second, in four months' time, I'll be holding a baby in my arms, too."

"Really? Congratulations!"

"You're the one who should be congratulated. The truth is, I didn't want this, but Shimke, whenever he sees a child, he's like a different person. When he's not working a shift, the mothers at the factory can't wait to leave their children with him. The whole barracks knows what a dependable nanny he is."

"I envy you. I can't leave Senderke alone with Nehemyah even for a minute. He's wonderful with the girls, but with a baby like Senderke, he says he's no good."

"Well, what do you expect, Hanah? He wasn't the one who carried the baby for nine months, and he isn't the one who breastfeeds him," Hayaleh remarked.

"Stay here and read a magazine," Hanah suggested, putting Senderke back in his crib. "I have to wash the floors in the corridor."

"I'll come with you. We'll make short work of it together," Hayaleh offered.

It turned out that Mikhail Mitrofanovich, the "activist," was still in the kitchen. He was no longer entertaining himself with his friend the goose; sadly, she was now lying in the broiler. Instead, he stood in the kitchen doorway, spouting nonsense:

"A guest has arrived—somebody give her a rag so she can wash the floor! From now on, whenever a guest comes to visit me, I'll do the same thing."

The two women paid no attention. Hanah wrung out the rag, Hayaleh washed the floor, and they really did finish the job very quickly.

When Nehemyah came home and discovered Hayaleh was there, he did a joyful little dance, kissed her, and then went right out again. He soon returned with a bottle of wine, and it became an afternoon of *"L'chaim!"* and endless rounds of "Do you remember . . . ?" Not until late in the evening did Hayaleh leave, promising to come back the following Saturday with Shimke.

* * *

Saturdays now became easier for Hanah. Shimke would take Senderke out for a three-hour stroll while Hayaleh helped with the housekeeping. The wife of the "activist" asked Hanah several times:

"Is she your sister?"

"More than a sister," Hanah said, to appease her neighbor's curiosity.

One Sunday, the "activist" and his wife were shocked at how many people came to visit. First Charlie arrived with Toybke, the milkmaid who could never recognize her cows on the commune. Then Makar came in with his young wife. And of course, Hayaleh and Shimke came, too. On this particular Sunday, Shimke took the three little girls to Gorky Park, while Charlie went for a walk with Senderke, Makar stood in the kitchen peeling potatoes, and his wife chatted with Hanah. When Nehemyah came home from the Institute, he exclaimed:

"Look at this! It's like a new branch of the commune!"

"Do you disapprove?" Hayaleh wanted to know.

"Why should I? You should come over more often—it will be even better!"

Nehemyah had exaggerated only slightly when he said the apartment had become an extension of the commune. Very often Hayaleh and Shimke, Charlie and Toybke arrived on Saturday morning and didn't leave until Monday morning. Both couples slept on the floor of the big room. Hanah would lay down two double mattresses for them, and until late in the evening, the little girls would jump from their cots onto Shimke and Hayaleh's mattress, and Shimke would join in the fun. No one else could entertain children the way he could.

One Saturday when Hanah and Hayaleh were alone in the apartment, Hanah showed her friend the journal with her story printed in it. Hayah read the story, looked at Hanah, and voiced her opinion:

"What can I tell you? It sounds so natural, just as though you're talking to me. Why didn't you show me this before?"

"I really wanted to show it to you, but I was embarrassed."

"I wouldn't have expected that from you. Of course, I can't give you any advice about writing, but as you know, I'm never without a book. And believe it or not, I think this is very good. So don't give up. You should keep writing whenever you have a free minute."

That's what Hayaleh thought, and that's what she said—but at the same time, she understood that for Hanah, a free minute didn't come along very often. So, in spite of the fact that she herself was well along in her pregnancy, Hayaleh now began coming over every Friday night to help Hanah however she could. This way, Hanah had a couple of hours free on Saturday mornings to sit and write.

Nehemyah teased Hayaleh:

"Look here, what are you trying to do? You're going to turn my wife into a lazybones!"

"How could I? As you know, your wife has been lazy her whole life. It would be impossible to make her any lazier."

"Oy, women, women!" Nehemyah sighed, and added, "After God created Adam, He had to rest—but ever since He created Hanah, nobody has gotten any rest!"

"On the contrary, Hanah is so spoiled, I don't even know how you can stand her!"

"A person has to be full of beans to argue with you," Nehemyah declared. "Next time, I'll eat a whole sackful before you come over!" And he winked at Hayaleh.

* * *

In the mornings, before leaving for the Institute, Nehemyah would come into the kitchen and watch Hanah work. Then he'd say:

"Hanukel, I'll be home late tonight. I'll grab a snack at the Institute buffet. Make sure Senderel doesn't roll out of his bed. Remember, he can sit up now."

* * *

And so their life went on—and, as previously noted, they should have been completely satisfied. The older children were doing well at school; Senderke was already toddling around. And Nehemyah didn't have to move heaven and earth to support them all, because Hanah was such a thrifty housekeeper. It was just as she always said: "My work is my wealth." She kept the family well fed with beet-and-potato salads, potato pancakes, big puddings made of white bread, and the famous onion cutlets. But she never bought fancy foods like those she saw on other artists' tables: cold cuts, sausages, sardines, sprats, *pirozhki,* assorted cheeses.

Every Friday she did a big load of laundry, and Hayaleh helped. Now Hanah appreciated, even more than she had on the commune, what a good friend Hayaleh was. One day, Hanah said:

"Hayaleh, why do you ignore me when I tell you not to bring me any herring, fish, or other expensive foods?"

"You're always complaining! What do you want me to do, leave the food under my bed at the barracks? Is it spoiled chopped liver I'm bringing you? You should be ashamed to turn up your nose at perfectly good food! You know, Shimke told me he wasn't sure you really wanted us to keep coming over here. And sometimes I think so too: maybe we don't belong around you, now that you've traded in your cows for a pen and paper."

Hanah turned red. She couldn't say a word. She went into the bathroom and busied herself with the laundry. A little later, Hayaleh walked in, and the two of them stood side by side and did the washing in silence. Suddenly Hanah exclaimed:

"Remember, Hayaleh, you were worried that Future Humanity would criticize you for treating the communards to extra cucumbers? Well, I have to tell you, I pity Future Humanity, because it will never know how well we treated each other."

"Why should we pity Future Humanity? Instead, let's try to avoid giving each other any grief," Hayaleh said. Then she added:

"Take those sheets out, Hanah, you're going to wear holes in them from all that scrubbing. Shimke is out in the yard with the children; he'll help you hang them up."

That was how Hayaleh showed Hanah that she took her words to heart—and how she made peace, under the pretense of talking about the laundry.

* * *

One Sunday, Makar didn't show up. Hanah asked Hayaleh if she had seen him at the factory lately.

"No, but that doesn't mean anything," Hayaleh said. "The factory isn't like your backyard, you know—it's a whole city unto itself!"

"Do you know how I met Makar?" Hanah asked her. "I worked with him at a kindergarten, right after I came here from the commune. He saved me from a false accusation." And Hanah told Hayaleh how Makar had cried out, that time in the kitchen, "Hanah Davidovna, look what that witch is doing with your purse!"

"I would never have believed it of him," Hayaleh said. "Makar is always so standoffish! It just goes to show, you should never judge a person too hastily."

* * *

There is a saying: "Something for everyone leaves nothing for anyone." Hanah understood this saying very well, because she never had any time to herself. So she made a habit of sitting down and writing every day—not until dawn, as before, but rather from ten o'clock at night until two in the morning. As previously mentioned, however, there was one thing that Hanah could not control about herself. If she forgot to put away the book she was reading before she sat down at the table, she was doomed. She didn't even realize until afterwards that she had wasted all her time reading instead of writing.

Hanah loved books so much that she often sat Hayaleh down and read aloud to her. It didn't bother her that Hayaleh used to say, "We have other things to do, you know."

"Never mind, never mind; Dickens knows better than you what people should be doing. Listen to this: 'For the poor man,' he says, 'it is much harder to be virtuous than it is for the rich one. The rich man can be a very good father, an attentive husband; his wife is also very lovely, virtuous, senses every caprice of the children. But take away from his pretty wife her silken clothes, her jewels; tousle her pretty coiffure; take the poor mother's wrinkles and lay them upon the face of the rich woman; give the rich man, that exemplary husband and father, the poor man's pennies—then you will see how genuine this extraordinary virtue is!' What do you say to that? You have to admit, Dickens knows what he's talking about!"

"What do you want me to say? May I be as rich as those people," said Hayaleh. "Now put down the book, we need to rinse the laundry."

Eventually the day came for Hayaleh's lying-in. After the baby was born, Hanah persuaded Shimke to bring Hayaleh and the child to stay with her, and they wound up living there for three months. As before, Shimke would go for a walk on the boulevard on Sundays, but now he pushed Senderke in the carriage and held his own baby girl in his arms. The mothers and grandmothers walking on the boulevard with their children would advise him:

"Comrade, if you have twins, you should order a double carriage. Holding one in your arms and pushing the other is too difficult."

Shimke would smile and say nothing.

* * *

The time crawled by; the days piled up into years. Senderke was walking; Hayaleh's little girl, Blyumkeleh, was already out of diapers. Several short stories of Hanah's were printed in the journal *Shtern,* which was published in Minsk, and she received a kind letter from the editor. Nehemyah read the stories and expressed his opinion:

"They're not bad . . . but all you ever write about is yourself!"

Hanah could not comprehend such a reaction, and she said exactly what she thought and felt:

"What else should I write about, since I don't know anybody else as well as myself? That's the first thing. Second, I'm glad you aren't talking about my writing the way you did before!"

"What do you mean? When did I talk about it before?"

"You've forgotten?" Hanah said. "But I haven't—and now I know very well that even creative people demand obedience from their loved ones, and won't tolerate anything else . . ."

Thus did Hanah finally fire her cannon, so long after she had loaded it.

* * *

There is nothing in the world that resembles quicksand like housework does. It swallows up all your time, day after day. Hanah never knew what to do first; she spent all her time running around and looking after Nehemyah. A typical day went like this:

Nehemyah is standing in front of her with an outstretched arm as she sews a button onto the cuff of his shirt. Then she runs into the kitchen. But no sooner does she get there than she hears his mild, quiet voice:

"Hanukel, where are the shoe polish and the shoe brush?"

"Ask Pereleh, she's in charge of things like that," advises Hanah, and begins rubbing a large beet against the grater.

A minute later, Nehemyah is standing near her in the kitchen. She inserts two or three spoonfuls of grated beet into his mouth and wipes his lips with the gauze she uses for straining the juice. He gives her a kiss; his black eyes twinkle; then he bids her goodbye and goes out.

Now Senderke is crying. Hanah takes him out of his cot and, holding him with one arm, she continues making the beet *rossel*. She adds seasonings: sour salt, sugar, regular salt. She tries it, decides it's not bad, and turns off the Primus. Just then, she notices that Senderke's little cheeks are covered with red blotches from the kisses of her beet-stained lips. She washes his sweet little face at the faucet and, recalling that he was crying for a drink, she pours some warm milk into a bottle and gives it to him. He immediately falls asleep.

As soon as Senderke is back in his cot, Hanah gets back to the housework. Today is Saturday, still her busiest day, especially because Hayaleh and Shimke seldom come to help her now. Dragging themselves here from the ball bearing plant isn't the easiest thing for them these days because they're so busy with little Blyumkeleh. Nevertheless, Hanah's day flies by. She can hardly wait for the children to go to bed. As soon as she sits down at the table to write, her weariness disappears.

On one such evening, she was sitting and writing as usual. She didn't know how long she had been at it, but it couldn't have been more than four hours. As she wrote, she felt a growing sense of exultation. The story was about a mother who had a great many children and an unsuccessful husband, but her biggest problem was that the hunger of one of her little boys was never satisfied, no matter how much she fed him. One day, an interfering old woman gave her some advice and helped her shut the child into the drawer of the dresser—and the child lost his craving for food and drink . . .

Wiping the tears from her eyes as she read through the story, Hanah understood that she had written something of great truth. But she didn't show it to anyone.

Meanwhile, Leyb Kvitko, the famous children's poet, had started coming to visit them, because the Children's Press had commissioned Nehemyah to illustrate a lullaby that Kvitko had written. Hanah was intrigued by Kvitko's work. One day, she overheard another well-known writer praising his poems, and she said sincerely:

"Why do you call them children's poems? Someday, people will sit down and really read what Kvitko has written, and they'll discover exquisite poems for adults."

Soon after Hanah wrote the story about the little boy who gets shut up in the drawer by his mother and the old woman, Kvitko came to visit. The story was lying in plain sight, because Hanah had forgotten to put it underneath the newspaper, where she kept all her stories and her blank writing paper. She went into the kitchen to bring her guest some tea, but before she could even take the teapot off the Primus, Kvitko strode in with some sheets of paper in his hand. He came right up and stared at Hanah, very hard and—as it seemed to her—very sternly, even angrily. In a low voice, he asked, "Did you write this?" And he waved the papers in her face.

"I probably did."

"Probably?"

"Show me, what is that?" Hanah tried to take the papers from him.

"What do you mean, show you? You don't know? 'The Parasite.' If this is your work, why don't you say so? Oy, I don't believe this! I've never seen anything like it!" And he literally ran out of the kitchen.

Hanah ran after him, back to the room. She found the poet standing across from Nehemyah, still holding the sheaf of papers and shouting:

"She didn't read it to you? You poor fellow! You have no idea who you're living with!"

Hanah rushed out of the room like the wind. Her heart ached with pity for Nehemyah. A little later, when she came back in with the teapot and poured out two glasses of tea, Leyb waved his glass away and said to her:

"I'll take the story with me and give it to Kushnirov. It will be published."

Without even noticing she was doing it, Hanah began shaking her head, even as a thrill passed through all her limbs. Leyb seemed to understand how she felt. He reassured her:

"Why are you so flustered, Hanah? Let me tell you something: I've read and heard a hundred stories about mothers who would do anything to get their children to eat more. But never have I heard or read a single story about a mother who tried to *decrease* her child's appetite! Don't be discouraged; believe me, it will be published. I'm telling you the truth."

Hanah did give Kvitko the story. A few days later, as she was tidying up the corridor, someone rang the doorbell. Hanah opened the door and saw an unfamiliar man standing there. He took off his hat and asked:

"Are you Hanah?"

"Yes—but let's talk inside."

In the apartment, the man didn't want to sit down, although Nehemyah offered him a chair several times. Standing with his hat in his hand, he introduced himself as follows:

"I am Meyer Viner. It's no accident that your story fell into my hands. There is not a drop of *Literaturartigkeit* in it."

"But I really did write it myself," Hanah stammered, blushing.

Meyer Viner began coming over frequently to tutor Hanah, and everything he taught her was a revelation. One day he took the mirror from the closet, held it in both hands with the reflective side facing the ceiling, and showed her how he had used a mirror to study Michaelangelo's paintings in the Sistine Chapel when he had visited Rome. Hanah was in awe of Meyer's many stories about his travels, and she was also fascinated by his ideas about world literature and about Jewish literature, old and new. They became such good friends that they even considered renting a summer house together in Kratovo—but fate had other ideas . . .

* * *

Since Lithuania had become Soviet, Hanah had begun receiving letters from her mother there. Her mother kept saying the same thing: while she was still alive, she wanted to see Hanah again.

On the eighteenth of June, 1941, Nehemyah accompanied Hanah and Reyzeleh, the youngest daughter, to the Moscow Belarusskaya Railway Station and helped them board the train to Kovno.

When Hanah woke up on the train on the morning of the nineteenth, she reflected that it had been almost twenty years since she had abandoned her hometown. As she drew closer and closer to the shtetl, she felt excited, agitated, even afraid. She couldn't imagine her grandmother's house without her grandparents in it. But what scared her the most was the prospect of reuniting with her mother. She remembered all too well that it had been her grandmother, not her mother, who had come to reclaim her and the baby. And it had been her grandmother who'd run after the wagon, clutching the cart rail and begging, in her Lithuanian accent, "Write, Hanke, write to us, have mercy . . ."

* * *

Meanwhile, Hanah's mother, Gitel, had already run to the Commander of the Soviet Army in Kovno several times to show him the telegram she had received from Hanah. She begged him not to bear any grudge against her daughter for her previous Zionist activities, and asked him over and over, "Are you sure the Kovno train won't be late?" She was so anxious, she couldn't rest for even a moment—or allow anyone else to rest, either. It was just as her husband, Hirshe, said:

"Ever since that telegram came, my wife has been standing on one foot, chewing with one tooth, and sleeping with one eye!"

As the day of Hanah's arrival drew near, the oven stayed lit day and night; the menu included everything from pfeffernusse to chopped liver. Already the cakes stood waiting, tall as top hats. There were babkas made with egg yolks and cream, sprinkled with chopped nuts, cinnamon, and sugar, shining as though they'd been lacquered; there were fruitcakes, fat and fluffy, with a powdered sugar frosting. Atop the golden honey cakes, Gitel had created little pictures of a goose and her goslings out of cloves. There was also a variety of *kichlach*: sugared, plain, soaked in syrup, cooked in honey. And in a big tin-plated copper kettle Gitel had boiled the bones of sheep, calves, and chickens, from which she had removed the meat; the resulting broth was so thick that the spoon stuck to the side of the bowl.

"Who can possibly consume such an ocean of broth?" Hirshe couldn't refrain from asking.

"If we don't finish it, I'll pour it out. When somebody comes to visit *you*, you can do things your way! Meanwhile, you can help me fill the kreplach: lay them on the baking sheets and smear more fat on them—don't skimp!" Gitel said as she scooped chopped liver onto a large platter, garnished it with thinly sliced green onions, sprinkled on hard-boiled egg yolks, added a little pink radish here and there, spooned up goose grease with the cracklings, and poured it over the top.

"The whole house is going to float away!" Hirshe warned.

"As long as you stay with me, that's all that matters."

"May my worst enemy have such a skillful wife," he grumbled.

"And may the wives of my best friends be spared your skills," Gitel rejoined, jabbing at the slices of veal breast with the point of a knife. Jab—she speared a clove of garlic; jab—a piece of carrot, a sprig of parsley. Then she covered the whole pan with minced angelica, poured beaten eggs over it, sprinkled on finely ground challah crumbs, doused it in poultry fat, and—into the oven . . .

* * *

Finally, everything is ready. Gitel studies the fully laden tables, the bottles of liquor standing between the deep glass bowls of preserves. The translucent gooseberries look like round amber beads; the dark red strawberries, speckled with white seeds, are bursting with juice, as though fresh from the garden.

But Gitel is no longer looking at them. Gitel is far away. In her mind's eye, she is holding Hanakeh under her little arms and Hanakeh is taking her first steps, while Gitel's mother, Grandma Pesyeh, passes a knife between Hanakeh's knitted booties and recites an incantation: "May you run like a stream, may you grow like a nettle, may you cause good people to rejoice, and your mama and papa to swell with pride . . ."

Yes, and Gitel remembers shouting, when Hanah was having her own baby girl: "May you lie in the sick house in Kovno, may your bastard's little head get stuck inside you, I want no part of it!"

Gitel's heart aches: "Hanakeh, of course, remembers that, too . . ."

* * *

The moment she heard Hanah's voice in the house, Gitel gave a start. A wild cry tore from her throat as she sprang up from the bed where she had been resting. She tripped over the threshold and saw stars; then, as though through a mist, a pair of outspread arms came toward her and embraced her . . .

"Maminke, you're as young as ever," Hanah said.

"You're only as old as you feel, my child. Sit down, let me give you a glass of chicory; have a *teigel.*"

Hanah bit into the *teigel* and lapsed into silent thought.

"What are you thinking about, my child?"

"Mama, I want to go inside Grandmother's house, but I'm afraid to. Tell me, Mama . . . how was it at the end?"

"After your grandmother came home from the public bath that Friday, she became unwell. So your grandfather, may he rest in peace, called me in. I asked her, 'Mama, can I give you a spoonful of stewed cherries?' But she said, 'Gitke, don't be a fool; light a candle.' And that was all . . ."

Hanah looked at the full tables and smiled, because people were already coming in and gathering around. No one had come empty-handed; each brought a bottle of liquor, a cake, or an elaborately braided challah. And no one needed any urging to eat.

It was Shabbes, a bright, warm morning. All the windows in Gitel's house were open, the sun was shining—and Gitel was shining, too. Her long brown muslin dress with its high handmade lace collar fitted her like a glove. Her flushed face and blue eyes glowed with pride. Every once in a while, she would cast an anxious glance at Hanah, as though to ask:

"You aren't ashamed of me, are you, my child?"

Hanah looked at her mother and thought: "Now I know what kind of mother I really have. What does it matter what happened in the past? . . ." The more she looked at her mother, the more she felt how very fortunate it was that she had come here.

In the happy commotion of their arrival, Reyzeleh had momentarily been forgotten. Hanah eventually found her sitting on Hirshe's lap.

Hirshe was stroking the child's head and handing her a piece of cake, but Reyzeleh didn't seem to know what to do with it.

Things quieted down for a little while, but then Taybeleh the Baker came in. She was the first person to arrive empty-handed. After exchanging kisses with Hanah, she walked over to Gitel and said quietly:

"Don't be offended with me, Gitel. I'm here to tell you what I have in my heart. You were born with a silver spoon in your mouth, and now your child has come back to you. I'm jealous! May she forget what happened in the past, and cherish you in spite of all the tears she shed because of you."

Still later in the evening, Gitel and Hanah found themselves alone together. Gitel's lips were moving silently, but no words came out. Finally, she voiced what she was thinking:

"Tell me, Hanakeh, why did you leave your first husband?"

"Mama, we'll have time for that later. But I can't promise I'll tell you anything. Just because it's over doesn't mean I'm ready to talk about it."

* * *

Suddenly there was a thundering sound.

"Papa, what's making that noise?"

"I think it's just a military exercise."

But by the next morning, when Hirshe drove Hanah and Reyzeleh to Dotnuva to catch the train back to Moscow, they knew it was no exercise . . .

The road to the station in Dotnuva was unreal, like something in a bad dream. When Hirshe said goodbye to Hanah and Reyzeleh, they all wept so hard and clung to one another so tightly that it seemed as though they would never let go. There was a train standing on the nearest track. Hirshe helped Hanah and Reyzeleh into a coach. It was a comfortable sleeping car, and they had it all to themselves. Hirshe stood next to the window for a little while; then, when the train started to move, he covered his face with both hands and went back out to the station.

In Kėdainiai, a station not far from Dotnuva, the train stopped. There was a sound of gunfire, and through the window Hanah could see people running with bundles and suitcases—running and, in some cases, falling to the ground and staying there . . .

Reyzeleh burrowed into Hanah's lap, shaking with violent sobs. She had, of course, seen the same thing Hanah had seen. When the train started moving again, a Jewish woman came into their car, so disheveled she looked like a madwoman. She told them:

"The Nationalists surrounded us with their automatics, and everyone ended up on the ground. My husband and my little boy, too." As she told this story, the woman began to sob and tear out her hair.

Until Radviliškis, the only people in the car were Hanah, Reyzeleh, and the woman. But as soon as they stopped at the station, a large Jewish family came in—men, women, children, and a little old grandmother, who set up a continual wailing:

"Oy, *vey iz mir*, a misery on my old head! Where are my other sons, I'm sure they must be gone! Beloved God, why didn't you protect us! Why should I drag my brittle bones on such a long journey!"

Whenever the shooting began again, the grandmother would become quiet. But if someone from her family wanted a drink of water and reached for the pitcher, the old woman would run over, wave her hands, and say urgently:

"Leave it alone, do it later. Don't bang the lid, or they'll hear!"

Before they reached Sebezh, the pitcher was empty. Now the grandmother herself wanted a drink. One of her relatives took the pitcher and headed toward the platform to refill it, but the grandmother tore the container away, handed it to Hanah, and said:

"Daughter, you go; I'm sure your child probably wants a drink too." But Reyzeleh clung to her mother, crying in terror:

"Don't go, Mama, don't go! I don't want a drink!"

So the grandmother's daughter-in-law went out for water. As soon as she left the car, the sound of shooting began. When it became quiet, the train stayed still for a long time, but the woman who had gone to fetch the water did not come back . . .

The grandmother began to wail again, the train started to move, and the family was now smaller by one person.

* * *

Reyzeleh now refused to separate herself from Hanah; she would not let go of her for even a moment. In Sebezh, the large family got off the train. Then the Station Master came and led Hanah and Reyzeleh to another train, where he put them in a car full of women whose husbands were in the military and had left for the war.

The railcar was crammed; besides the women themselves, there were piles of trunks, sewing machines, bicycles, leather suitcases, and children of all ages. Hanah seated Reyzeleh on their own small suitcase; she herself sat on the floor near a woman with a small child in her arms. The child, whose eyes were closed, lay stretched out in the woman's arms, his little yellow feet dangling down from her lap. The woman kept taking the child's bare toes in her hands, and bitter tears rolled unceasingly down her cheeks.

"Give him to me; I'll hold him like you're doing. It will be comfortable for him," Hanah offered.

"He was sick. My husband put us in the car with only the clothes on our backs. We didn't even have a chance to say goodbye . . . I don't want you to take him, it's not necessary, it's all the same to him now . . . But will you help me, when the train stops? . . ."

* * *

Late in the night, the train stopped in the middle of a field. On one side of the tracks stood the small shack used by the railway watchman. Hanah ran to the shack, found a woman there, and told her what had happened. The woman gave Hanah a shovel, took another shovel for herself, and behind the shack they dug out a small, narrow grave. Hanah went back to the train, and the mother came and lowered the child in with her own hands . . .

* * *

The train stood at the station until dawn. The whole time, the bereaved woman lay in a sort of faint. In the morning, the Chief Officer in charge of the Troop Transport came into the car. He announced that the train was going to Penza. Later, when they arrived at the Plekhanova Station in Tula, Hanah took her suitcase and woke Reyzeleh, and they got out of the car. Climbing across the tracks, Hanah and Reyzeleh came to a road that was completely deserted. The weather was magnificent, the road was surrounded by woods, and the sun was dazzlingly bright. But Hanah had no idea which way to go.

Suddenly she heard voices. She turned and saw some women walking along with empty milk cans in their hands. One of the women came over to Hanah, looked her up and down, and then shook her head sadly. That

was when Hanah realized how she must look. She did, indeed, look frightful; it was already the second of July . . .

The woman seemed to understand. She took the suitcase from Hanah's
hand and said:

"I assume you're from Moscow? Two *versts* from here there's a train
that goes to Serpukhov. You'll be home later today."

The woman took Reyzeleh by the hand, and before long, they came to
a small railway station. The woman seated Hanah on a bench and said
to her:

"Stay here, I'll bring you something to eat."

The woman brought them some food, waited with them until the train
came, and helped Hanah and Reyzeleh get into a coach. And by evening,
they were home.

* * *

When Nehemyah saw Hanah, he froze. His face turned as white as
chalk, and he couldn't utter a word. Suddenly he started to sob, but Hanah
didn't see any tears. Even if there had been tears, she wouldn't have seen
them, because at that moment she fell into a faint, and it was quite a while
before Nehemyah managed to revive her.

They didn't get a wink of sleep that night, but they spoke very little.
From time to time, Nehemyah would stare at her and marvel:

"Hanah, Hanukel, am I really seeing you, are you really here? . . ."

Reyzeleh was lost in silence; she wouldn't speak at all. In the days that
followed, she didn't play with her sisters as she had before. And several
times she asked:

"Mama, why didn't we take Grandpa and Grandma with us?"

Hanah didn't say anything in reply. She didn't know how to tell Reyzeleh that her parents had said:

"Hanaleh, you have to leave right away. Everybody here knows you
came from Soviet Russia . . ."

* * *

Moscow seemed strange now. In the evenings all the windows were
covered, and air raid sirens kept going off. The Housing Authority sent
repeated warnings that people with children should evacuate. On the fifth
of August, 1941, Nehemyah accompanied Hanah and the children to the

Kazansky Railway Station. As Hanah stood in the wide doorway of the train car with Senderke in her arms, Nehemyah ordered:

"Hanukel, protect the children; the children must be protected, do you hear?"

The Troop Transport was headed for Cheboksary, a city on the Volga. The car that Hanah and the children were to ride in was completely filled with the wives and children of Moscow artists. It was a freight car, without any steps for boarding. Before the war, it had been used to transport cattle, and a ramp had always been set up for the cattle to walk on. But now there was no ramp; the women and children had to climb into the car as best they could.

Once the car was completely crammed with people, a "civil, polite" disagreement broke out among the passengers. Each one wanted a place that wasn't next to the windows or near the wide open door. But even away from these areas, it was very difficult to find a spot that was out of the wind, because there were wide slots in the walls of the car. Hanah didn't take part in the conflict; she staked out a corner of the bench near a little window, covered the children with a blanket, and sat down next to them.

Not far from Ryazan, the train came to a halt and antiaircraft sirens began to sound. A frightful racket erupted outside the door. The Commander of the Troop Transport ran past the car and shouted: "Get out! Hurry, hurry!" Then the sirens started wailing again, drowning out the Commander's voice. The women who had no children began jumping from the car, but the drop was so far that they couldn't land on their feet; they fell onto all fours and had to crawl on the ground. The children were weeping in terror. Women were begging:

"Don't push—help me—my child, my child!"

Silent amid the shouting, Hanah, with Senderke in her arms and her three girls clinging to her dress, pushed her way to the door. As the sirens continued to wail, Hanah jumped from the car with Senderke, helped the girls jump down, led them to a safe spot, and shouted:

"Pereleh, Beylkeleh, take Senderke, and keep an eye on Reyzeleh! Don't move!"

She herself ran back to the door, stretched out her arms, and called to a woman who was holding a child:

"Jump, don't be afraid! I'll catch you!"

When the woman and her child were safely on the ground, Hanah ran back to the girls and Senderke and said something to them—she herself didn't know what. Before long, the sirens stopped. Hanah started dragging fragments of railroad ties and loose bricks to the door of the car to make it easier for everyone to climb back in. Once they were all on board, a new round of arguing started, because all the riders had lost their previous places. The woman that Hanah had helped sat down beside her and marveled unceasingly at the way Hanah had stretched out her arms and caught her. "Thank you, thank you," she kept repeating. Hanah couldn't help smiling, because she was thinking: "My dear, if you could ride a horse like me, and catch bull calves to take to the slaughterhouse, you wouldn't be so surprised—in fact, you'd be able to jump just as well as I can."

As night fell, the women fed their children and lay down in the car wherever they could. Hanah's place was at the very end of the wide bench. In addition to the slots in the wall, the little window above the bench had no glass, so it was very drafty. Hanah found two pieces of wood and used a knife to whittle some pegs; with these she hung a blanket over the window and covered some of the cracks. Then she laid the two oldest girls right against the wall, Senderke next to them, and Reyzeleh beside him. She herself lay down next to Reyzeleh. When the other women saw what Hanah had done with the blanket, they started covering the walls too. Now there was less of a draft.

Once the train started moving, everyone was gradually lulled to sleep—only to wake up again when the train came to an abrupt halt. Soon, the Commander of the Troop Transport reappeared. He gave them the "good news" that the train would be standing here for a long time. A little later came the sound of crying. Three of the children in the car were having gastric problems. Their mothers were not only the wives of artists, they were artists themselves, and members of MOSKh—highly capable professionals. But in this situation, they were unsure what to do.

But Hanah knew. She jumped out of the car, and in the blink of an eye she had made a small campfire between two stones. From one of the women she obtained some potato flour. Hanah herself had brought some sugar. Soon the sick children were eating the soothing pudding she had prepared. Hanah's fellow passengers watched in amazement as she jumped in and out of the car, tore thin twigs from the bushes next to the tracks, fashioned a broom, ordered everyone to sit on the benches, and quickly swept out the filth that had collected on the floor. Cries of "Hanah Davidovna, Hanah Davidovna" were soon heard from all sides, and she helped out however she could.

After a while, the train started moving. The woman that Hanah had helped to jump down with her child sat beside her again and murmured confidentially:

"Don't be offended, but I'd like to ask you something. Tell me, are you the woman that Nehemyah Moyseyevich brought to Moscow from some collective farm in Crimea?"

"Yes, I am. But it wasn't a collective farm. It was a commune."

"A commune?" the woman asked, fascinated. And the more Hanah told her, the more amazed the woman became, and the more she wanted to know. What were the commune's holdings, and how many Jewish communes and collective farms were there in Crimea?

"Interesting, very interesting!" The woman shook her head, and then she related:

"I remember once, I was at a party at the home of a well-known artist. A graphic designer told us that one of his friends had gone on a field assignment to a Jewish collective farm in Crimea. And he made a joke: 'Now no one dares take an assignment on a collective farm for fear he'll come back with a wife and three children!'"

Hanah listened, smiled, and said:

"I can't argue with that; he was absolutely right."

And there the conversation ended.

Hanah managed to build a campfire and cook some millet porridge for her children each morning before they woke up, because the troop train did more standing than moving. Early on the fifth day, the evacuees finally arrived in Cheboksary. The following day they reached Mar-Fasad, where some of the women were to stay. But Hanah and a dozen other women, together with a large number of children, were taken by wagon from Mar-Fasad to a nearby village called Dimyashkino. Not far from Dimyashkino was a health spa for river workers that had been requisitioned as a Children's Home for the offspring of the Moscow artists. That evening, Hanah brought Senderke and Reyzeleh to the spa and left them there with the other children. Pereleh and Beylke stayed with her.

The village of Dimyashkino, on a high bank of the Volga, was not a large place. Nevertheless, it had several boarded-up houses, the homes of kulaks who had been sent away. Andrey Pokhomich, the Chairman of the local collective farm, which was called "Sunrise," said to the evacuees:

"You cows can take whichever houses you want."

Andrey Pokhomich, the one remaining male in the village, had only one eye, and on each hand he had a tiny extra finger next to the thumb. If Andrey Pokhomich had not possessed these bizarre physical traits, Hanah would not have been placed in his service, because he wouldn't have been here—he would have been serving in the military.

Hanah organized a short, informal meeting of the evacuees in one of the boarded-up houses, and immediately afterwards, she took Pereleh and Beylke with her to the collective farm's repair shop. When they got there, the shop's doors were wide open. At first, all Hanah saw were two cutting machines without blades and several pitchforks with bent tines, but then, on a table next to the wall, she discovered some tools she could use. She took a hatchet for herself, gave a second one to Pereleh, handed a pair of pliers to Beylke, and back they went to the boarded-up houses.

Already, Hanah was not the same woman she had been before. Her rosy cheeks had become pale; the sparkle in her blue-gray eyes had dulled; the full, rounded softness of her whole body had hardened. She had been transformed into a driving force aimed like a cannon at one thing: survival.

Soon, the peace of the village was shattered by the blows of axes and the creaking of boards being pried off. By evening, two of the houses had functional doors and windows. Entering these houses, the women discovered that each consisted of a large room, which they dubbed the all-purpose room, along with two smaller ones that had probably been bedrooms, since they still contained wide wooden benches piled with straw. The walls were made of logs; the floors, windows, and doors were blanketed with dust and cobwebs. Each small kitchen was dominated by a large stove. Hanah took a look inside one and found several shallow cast-iron pots. When she pulled them out, she was shocked to see that every pot was filled to the brim with greenish-gray mold. Immediately, she understood: the householders had left their homes in such a hurry that they hadn't even had time to eat the food in the oven.

While the rest of the mothers took their children to the former resort that was now a Children's Home, Hanah got to work with Pereleh and Beylke. Soon, one of the little houses was completely renovated. When the women came back and saw how much Hanah had achieved, they couldn't believe it. Hanah did not mince words:

"Starting now, we're going to have to learn to do things we've never done before. This isn't a summer holiday, you know. When we rode here from Mar-Fasad, you all saw how hard those people were working in the fields. As soon as I got here, I sent my younger children away and went straight to work. So what are you all waiting for?"

First thing next morning, Hanah went out with her daughters. She walked over to the barn and looked inside. The cows were already out in the fields, but the barn was so filthy that she immediately went to the repair shop, took three pitchforks, and got to work cleaning it out with her daughters. Later, two boys from the village came and helped them. In a few days, the barn was an entirely different place. The rafters and the roof actually seemed higher than before because Hanah and her helpers had shoveled out all the manure. The cows' udders were now clean and dry, and the animals began to regrow the tufts on their tails. One day, Andrey Pokhomich said to Hanah:

"Great work! Anna Davidovna, you're an expert farmer."

"You're doing good work, too," Hanah replied. "Of course, you're no Jewish woman, but the cows seem to like you."

Hanah's past experience served her well here; she could do any type of work that was needed. Andrey Pokhomich soon stopped questioning her judgment; indeed, he followed all of Hanah's recommendations. As she had done on the commune, Hanah directed that the midday milking should be done outdoors, rather than bringing the cows back into the barn. She had already gotten to know several women at the local collective farm, and she began going out to the fields with them every day at noon. That summer was an unusually productive one; the grass grew so high that it touched the cows' bellies, and the well-fed animals produced plenty of milk. But the three village boys who worked as herders, and whose combined age was barely forty-five, resisted Hanah's recommendation to drive the cows down to the Volga every day for water.

"Andrey Pokhomich," Hanah advised the Chairman, "if you give the boys milk to drink, they'll be willing to drive the cows." So he did start giving them milk. After that—although their task was difficult, because the high bank where the village stood was almost like a cliff—the boys drove the herd down to the river every day.

It soon became clear that the collective farm was willing to provide flour to the evacuees, but they themselves would have to bake it into bread. Of course, this made more work for Hanah. The artists' wives wanted bread; they were capable of baking bread; they loved to eat bread—but to bake it themselves? . . .

One evening Hanah called a general meeting.

"I can and I will do the baking, but someone else has to go into the forest and gather wood."

"What are we, lumberjacks?" several women protested.

"If you don't want to do it, that's your business. Here's what I propose: Those who are willing to gather wood will receive bread. The rest of you will get only flour."

This did the trick. The next day, several women went off into the forest, and Hanah and two other women walked to the collective farm to get the flour. Hanah borrowed a baking trough from a woman named Glafira whom she'd gotten to know. And twenty-four hours later, very early, the aroma of fresh-baked bread filled not only Hanah's house but the air all around it, too.

Every morning Hanah roused the women by calling out, "The early bird gets the worm!" Most of them were now willing to weed potatoes. A few, however, had begun volunteering at the Children's Home, and from then on, nobody in Dimyashkino saw hide nor hair of them.

Once a week, Hanah went to visit Senderke and Reyzeleh, but seeing Reyzeleh used to break her heart. Reyzeleh was miserable. The caregivers told Hanah that she shouted in her sleep and ate poorly. Whenever she saw Hanah, Reyzeleh would talk about only one thing: the war. Her gray eyes would open wide, and she would quietly repeat over and over again, "Mama, you and all the other grownups should go to the war and kill all the Fascists, every last one of them!" Reyzeleh's words burned Hanah's soul like hot coals, because, of course, not a day went by that she didn't think about her parents in occupied Lithuania. She bitterly regretted that she hadn't forcibly dragged them away with her, and she was constantly thinking: "Fate has played such a cruel trick on me, it's just inconceivable! It reunited me with my loved ones, only to make me suffer all the more when I lost them again." She also understood all too well that Reyzeleh was in such a state because she, Hanah, had brought her along on her journey to Lithuania and back.

From Nehemyah, Hanah had so far received only one short letter:

My only one, my dearest, by the time you receive this brief note, I will no longer be in Moscow. I am joining the military. I am sure you understand me when I say: Protect yourself, and protect the children. We will be happy again after the war. Eternally yours.

Nehemyah

Hanah had immediately answered:

My dearest, my life, my crown! I knew it would be so, and so it must be. May you be safe, sound, and secure from all the dangers that lie in wait. You know I am with you everywhere, now and always. I would have done the same thing as you, if not for the children. Pereleh and Beylke are making me proud. They are obedient and help me as much as they can. Senderke is already quite the schoolboy; in the Children's Home they call him Professor, because he has a habit of holding his little hands behind his back and he overwhelms the teachers with his endless questions. The Children's Home is located right next to the Volga, in a big, beautiful house that was a health resort for sailors, fishermen, and buoy tenders. You'll laugh, but I often say, in the words of my grandfather: *chadesh yameinu k'kedem,* which means "renew my days as before," because I am once again working in a cattle barn. Every day I get three liters of milk to bring home. Also, in exchange for my work in the field with Pereleh and Beylke, the collective farm gives me wheat and rye meal. And on top of that, they've presented me with a two-month-old piglet. It is kept in a pen at Marusya's; we are raising it jointly. Soon we'll harvest the wheat. We've already cut some of it; Marusya taught me how. Swinging the sickle made me so sore that for a long time I could only sit bent over. I'll write more about Marusya next time. Be well, and consider yourself kissed.

Your Hanah

Just two weeks later, Hanah received another short letter from Nehemyah. As soon as she read it, she was beside herself with worry. He wrote:

My mother used to say: A person decides, and God laughs. My darling! I was assigned to a military unit, and would surely have been at the front by now, but I started suffering from stomach pains. They put me in the hospital for observation, and the doctors found that I have a hemorrhage from an ulcer in my duodenum. To make a long story short, I am still in the hospital. Please try to remain calm; we must all do our duty. There are very skilled doctors here, and they say that in a month they will discharge me. As for my going to the front, they say I should forget about it. Now I understand, my dearest, why I've so often had pains in my stomach, and it bothers me that I kept this hidden from you. Be calm, and keep the children safe.

Your Nehemyah

My dear, my dear! I was very upset by your letter. But if that is what's happening, you should be patient, and stay in the hospital however long the doctors tell you. While I wait for more reassuring news from you, I'll tell you about my new acquaintances, especially about Marusya. I don't know if you're in the mood for reading now, but I'll write about it anyway, and I hope it will cheer you up. So pay attention.

You already know that I am living in Dimyashkino, and that Dimyashkino means "smoky place" . . . but you may not know that this little village is perched atop a high mountain, with a lot of trails leading down to the Volga. The Volga is not very wide here, and not at all deep. I can walk far, far out, and the water only comes up to my knees. On the opposite bank is the Koksheyer Forest, which is lush and green. The trees seem close enough for me to reach out and touch.

In the village there are nothing but women and children. When I go out to work with them, Glafira always says: "You ladies keep your tears in your pockets, your troubles in your sleeves, and your hands on your work. A plague take the Fascists!" Not that the "ladies" are in the habit of crying. They only give a loud sigh from time to time as their bare feet sink deep into the dust of the road. But a couple of days ago when we got to the potato field, Marfa Vorobyova, who's raising five children by herself, started groaning like a rusty hinge as she yanked out the weeds. Suddenly she burst out crying, wringing her hands: "Our cottages are miserable, my children are wretched orphans, yesterday when I did the laundry, my tears filled the washtub. What good is laundry without any men's clothes? Where is my man lying dead right now?"

"Yours, mine, ours—why don't you shut up! It's bad enough without your two cents!" shouted Marusya, and her own tears started falling, drip-drop, onto the potato blossoms.

We barely managed to weed and hoe the potatoes before it was time to start cutting the wheat, because the days here are hot, the ears are bending over, and when it's windy the ripe kernels fall to the ground. I've never seen so many birds in one place as the flocks that fly over the wheat fields. They peck up so much wheat they can hardly fly. In fact, they fly so low that the boys can shoot them down with slingshots and carry whole armloads of them home to cook.

In the mornings we stand outside the collective farm office. Glafira, Marfa, Marusya, and Yufemia look very much like the women in those frescoes that you and I saw in the cathedral outside Moscow. The Chairman comes out and peers at us in silence with his one eye. Then he asks, "Is everything in order?" "Aye-aye," we answer, and off we go to the wheat field.

I walk with Marusya; she is in her third trimester. Her face is sunburned, and her eyes look out from under her white headscarf with a pained, entreating expression. Her arms, which swing as she walks along, are brown from the sun and muscular from hard work. All those who walk with us, carrying their sickles, have a noble air about them from their sorrows and their enduring womanly strength.

Arriving at the field, we all bend over and get to work. I watch how Glafira grabs up a handful of wheat ears, gives a cut with the sickle: *slash*, and done. I do exactly as she does, but for me, the roots come up with the stalks. Glafira laughs at me. Marusya snaps at her: "Glafirka, don't bray like that, or I'll chop your teeth out with my sickle." Then she comes over to me, takes my sickle hand, and guides it for a while, until I can do the task by myself. Believe me, Nehemyaleh, she's given me quite an education! When we're done cutting, I arrange the sheaves that I've cut and bound together; they remind me of big braided challahs lying there on the stubble.

You know, Nehemyaleh, I marvel that in such horrible times I can take pleasure in binding the sheaves, and even more pleasure in the fact that Pereleh and Beylke have learned how to cut and bind wheat, too. The three of us together produce up to two hundred sheaves a day. In the evening we carry them to the wagon. There are a total of five horses on the collective farm; the old nag that's hitched to the wagon stands with her head down, as though she's ashamed. The driver, a boy of thirteen, is up in the wagon bed; he's so small he practically turns a somersault whenever he hoists a sheaf into place. The nag whinnies quietly. Marusya throws a bale onto the wagon and pats the little colt that's nuzzling the mama horse. When the colt dances away, the nag twists her head, and the bridle slides down over her ears and covers her eyes so she can't see where the colt is. Her nostrils twitch, her upper lip curls back, and she gives a quiet, lonesome neigh. Marusya says to the driver: "Lyonke, you miserable boy, straighten the bridle. You have eyes;

you can see it's bothering her." Lyonke climbs down, approaches the nag's head, stands on tiptoe to fix her bridle, gives her a pat on the neck. Marusya watches him, and suddenly big, heavy tears start rolling from her eyes. They rinse the dust from her cheeks and leave damp, pale streaks down her face.

The cart is loaded, the nag is dragging the creaky wagon, the sun has set, and the air has grown cool. Over the dark, jagged ridge of the trees spreads a fiery light. I go with Marusya down to the Volga; she leads the way. She places her bare feet cautiously, but her body is turned forward and her arms swing like shapely, well-carved oars in the evening air. To me it seems as though they are steering, guiding, turning Marusya, as though she is a boat with a secret, invisible crew.

Marusya sits down at the edge of the river; she undresses, lifts her arms, wraps her thick fair braid around her head. Her neck is brown, like her arms, but upon the rest of her body the sun has had no effect. Her flesh is yellowish-white, like whipped cream . . . Those parts of her which will soon nourish her baby resemble two small, living wineskins. A dark crown encircles each nipple, as though to conceal the welling juices within. These wineskins are ready, heavy, womanly, innocent. Marusya's entire form radiates holiness. She hides the wineskins in her hands, runs into the river, stretches herself; all around her fly bright clouds of spray. Oh, Nehemyah, if you could see it, what an exquisite picture you would paint!

It is so cool by the river that my weariness begins to wane. I watch Marusya's arms wave over the water and I think about my mother, and about all the mothers and daughters who are being driven, naked and blind, to their deaths. And as I think about this, I hear Marusya calling me: "Why are you just sitting there? Come bathe!" But I can't get up. So she runs out of the river, comes up to me, and says: "Don't cry. You still have a mother somewhere, and friends. If only they could be here with us, we could share our food and shelter with them." I don't answer. Marusya doesn't go back into the river; she sits next to me and starts chanting in a loud, sing-song voice, like a professional mourner in ancient times: "What a love I had. He never drank, he didn't smoke. A year ago we got married. How many times he carried me to the river in his arms. I would swim beside him, on his right, and when we got out of the water, he used to tell me: 'Your skin is as scratchy as the sand at the bottom of the Volga.' Now my fate is sealed, I'm doomed to widowhood."

I want to shout, too. But my voice fails me. I see mothers, daughters, small children, surrounded by machine guns, and suddenly I remember that Marusya will soon be a mother. Oy, Nehemyaleh, may she never be numbered among the mothers of our people, who are being slaughtered with their children. Don't be annoyed with me for writing such a long letter. Be well, and write back soon.

Your Hanah

* * *

The next day, after the morning milking, Hanah went to Mar-Fasad. When she got to town, her first stop was the boat terminal, where she paused at the entrance and listened to the latest sad news on the radio: "Our military divisions are retreating eastward . . . The strength of the enemy's forces and weapons has greatly increased." Then she dropped the letter to Nehemyah into the mailbox and entered the terminal. But she had to watch her step, because a woman was lying on the floor just inside the door, sleeping. Looking for a place to put her feet, Hanah discovered that the whole room was filled with people lying on the floor. When she glanced back down at the sleeping woman's face, Hanah gave a start and, in a voice not her own, cried out, "Hayaleh!"

The woman opened her eyes, stared at Hanah in confusion, and, finally comprehending who was standing before her, uttered a moan—as did Hanah at the same moment. All the people around them got up off the floor and watched the unexpected reunion. When the two women had calmed down a little, Hanah said:

"Hayaleh, get your things and come with me."

"What you see on me is all I have," Hayaleh answered.

As they walked to Dimyashkino, Hayaleh related:

"Shimke volunteered right when the war started. I have no children now. My Blyumkeleh died of diphtheria. And my little boy lived only a month. That was right before the war. That's really why Shimke was so quick to put himself in the line of fire."

Hayaleh had been depressed for many long weeks, helpless and almost totally despondent.

Hanah certainly had her own share of trials and tribulations. But her work, her active nature, and the general troubles that were now inundating millions of people forced her to keep her feelings in check. For Hayaleh, however, nothing helped; she was sunk deep in her own unhappiness. If Hanah brought her along to work, Hayaleh would just sit there with her head down. Finally Hanah found a remedy. In the evenings, she sat with Hayaleh and helped her write letters to the War Offices of many different cities, trying to find information about Shimke. And very soon, a letter arrived from Shimke himself, saying that he was in a hospital in Tomsk. A few days after that, Hanah saw Hayaleh off on her journey to be with him. After Hayaleh's boat had left for Kazan, Hanah dropped in at the Mar-Fasad post office and found, to her great joy, that had she received another letter from Nehemyah.

My one and only, my dear Hanukel!

Although it is now very uncomfortable for me to be delighted, your letter delighted me. You may sometimes forget it, but I must tell you that I am very proud of you. Your letter was so diverting that by the time I checked out of the hospital, I had forgotten I had any such thing as a "duodenum." I hope you will forgive me, but I sent your description of Dimyashkino to the Jewish Antifascist Committee in Kuibyshev. I've already had an answer from Leyb Kvitko, saying he gave it the title "Our Mothers" and sent it off to the Sovinformburo to be published.

Moscow is dark at night, and the houses are unheated, although it is a very cold autumn. Here is what I hope, what I want, and what I think will happen: this winter, we'll be together again. I'm sure the Fascists are going to catch hell before they can reach Moscow!

You didn't write a word this time about the children. I am uneasy about Reyzeleh. Ever since that delightful trip to Lithuania and back, she has been very traumatized. Pay close attention to our daughters, especially to Reyzeleh. I kiss you a thousand times, my one and only, my farmer, my woman of letters.

P.S. Forgive me that I once tried to clip your wings. With loyal, eternal love.

Your Nehemyah

Hanah wanted very much to write to Nehemyah about Reyzeleh. But she didn't, because the situation was too terrible. Whenever Hanah went to visit the children and Reyzeleh saw her, she would run over and shout: "What are you doing here? Go to the war, everyone should go to the war! Not one Fascist should be left alive! You remember when we left Grandma's? How many people did the Fascists kill that time?" The doctor from the Children's Home didn't have anything comforting to tell Hanah; she said Reyzeleh should be committed to a hospital for the mentally ill. But how was such a thing possible right now? At the time, Hanah didn't understand how dangerously ill her child was. One evening, she wrote to Nehemyah:

My only one, my true one! I forgive you for sending "Our Mothers" to Kuibyshev. I don't doubt it can be published, because I worked very hard to depict with my words the great suffering here.

I have a surprising piece of news for you. Hayaleh from the commune was here with me. When times are better I will tell you how I ran into her. Right now, all I can say is that Hayaleh is a shadow of her former self. She lost both children . . . But she did manage to locate Shimke, and she recently left for Tomsk to be with him.

You shouldn't blame yourself for trying to "clip my wings." At the time, you did not yet know or understand that there are some voices that cannot be silenced . . .

Reyzeleh is sick. In future letters I will explain in more detail. Our problems, our partings can be multiplied by the millions these days. On the other hand, I often think that if it were not for the war, I would never have known that there was such a place as Dimyashkino, or that in Dimyashkino there was such a beauty as Marusya. Listen closely to how she gave birth.

I'm in the barn. Suddenly, Glafira runs in with a flushed face and yells: "Hanah Davidovna, Maruske is about to calve! Come with me, hurry!" I run over to my place, grab two bedsheets and some soap, and I'm off to Marusya's. I go in—no one is there! I run outside and see smoke coming from the bathhouse. (Everyone here has a small bathhouse. Most of them are very smoky inside. But Marusya's husband was a master innovator, so he redesigned the chimney to let the smoke out into the sky.)

What do you think was going on? I took a guess and went in. Sure enough, Marusya was lying on the bath bench and screaming loud enough to shatter the walls. Yufemia, the local midwife, turns around, pours hot water into the wooden pail, shakes her head at me, and announces: "It's showing already. A big peasant. The head is like a pumpkin . . . Hanah, get a sheet under her!"

Marusya heard the word "sheet" and became quiet. She turned her head toward me, her eyes met mine, and she said quietly, "Not now, afterwards! . . . " So I left, and wasn't present at the main event, although I did very much want to see how a person is born.

The following evening I grab the sheets again and go over to check on the new mother. I walk in—Marusya is sitting at the table, eating bread with onions. "What are you doing?" I yell. "Get back in bed, quick!" She gets up from her chair and declares: "I'm not in the hospital, you know; why should I lie down?" She leads me over to the bed so I can look at her baby boy. What can I tell you, Nehemyaleh? There on a cushion, wrapped up in a swaddling cloth, lies a tiny doll with a round, pink, plump little face, a pleasure to look at. But Marusya doesn't let me admire him for long, because— she informs me—it's bad luck to look at a newborn for very long. And as for the sheets I brought, I had to take them back with me, because Yufemia, the modern twentieth-century midwife, warned Marusya that factory-made sheets are very harmful for a new mother. Marusya told me this important information in an extremely serious voice: "Anna Davidovna, they really are very harmful; ask anyone you like."

To make a long story short, three days later, Marusya was back at work with all the other women. We were harvesting peas. Pea plants, you should know, aren't cut down at the end of the season, they are torn up by the roots. On harvesting day, there was a big black cloud in the sky, hovering right over the field. In its shadow all the women looked like ghosts. Yufemia brought Marusya's baby out to the field, and the new mama sat down with him on a heap of pea pods. The child suckled well, but his little face soon turned black with dirt. When I voiced my concern, Yufemia reassured me: "There's nothing harmful about it, he'll grow up to be a healthy collective farmer."

Everything happened just as I've told you, my dear. All that remains is for me to wish that you'll stay healthy, that you'll write back quickly, that the Fascists won't live long enough to leave Russia, but will drop dead outside Moscow, and that this bloody war will come to an end.

Your Hanah

* * *

One evening after the milking, Hanah was mucking out the barn when Andrey Pokhomich suddenly showed up and said:

"Anna Davidovna, throw away that pitchfork. Look what I've brought you!"

Hanah turned her head and saw several large bream hanging from a bent stick. She went back to shoveling manure.

"Didn't you hear what I said? Throw the pitchfork away! We'll boat over to the Koksheyer Forest and I'll cook us up a fish soup. I have onions and bay leaves. Why are you looking at me with those calf eyes? You're not like all the other stupid cows around here!"

"You're right, Andrey Pokhomich—I'm not stupid. And I want you to be smart, too, and take home those fish that you brought me, and give them to your wife."

Andrey Pokhomich was out of the barn like a shot. Hanah was very disturbed by the incident. But the next day, the Chairman acted as though it had never happened. And such a thing never occurred again.

* * *

The deep autumn set in, with its angry winds and frosty mornings. Gradually, the other artists' wives all left for one place or another, but Hanah stayed on in Dimyashkino with Pereleh and Beylke. The house they lived in was like a sieve. The walls, the windows, and the doors were falling apart, and the wind whistled through the house as fiercely as it did outside. One day Glafira said to Hanah:

"Anna Davidovna, you and your daughters are going to freeze to death in that place! Come stay with me. It will be easier to gather firewood if there are two of us."

At Glafira's, it was warm and cozy. It was also much easier for Hanah to borrow Glafira's baking pan now that they were both using the same oven. At this time of year, there wasn't much work to do in the barn, so Hanah spent long hours in the evenings writing by the light of a small lamp. One day, Glafira said to her:

"Anna Davidovna, all you ever do is write, write, write. You're going to make yourself as blind as a bat! Put that pen down for a minute and listen to what I have to tell you. You know Yufemia? Well, her son is in a hospital in Kuibyshev; they had to cut off one of his legs. Naturally, as a mother, Yufemia went to visit him. Now, he was stationed in a lot of different places before he was wounded—and he told Yufemia that wherever the Fascists have been, not a single one of your people is left alive."

Hanah stayed silent, but she decided that if there was even the slightest possibility of returning to Moscow, she would. The next day, she walked over to the Children's Home.

Reyzeleh was sitting on the floor next to the wall; her eyes were closed, her lips moving. When Hanah called to her, Reyzeleh ran over and shouted:

"Go to the war, how many times do I have to tell you, you should go to the war! You think I don't know, my father isn't fighting in the war either, I don't want you to come and visit me, I hate you!"

Hanah summoned the doctor, and with scarcely any trouble, Reyzeleh was admitted to the hospital. The next day, Hanah walked to Mar-Fasad and sent Nehemyah a telegram saying he should put in a housing claim for her and the children.

* * *

At the end of 1941, Hanah and the children returned to Moscow. Reyzeleh was admitted to a psychiatric hospital; she did not allow Hanah to visit her. In spite of her daughter's illness, or perhaps because of it, Hanah now began thinking constantly about the past. One evening she said quietly:

"Nehemyaleh, I really believe I could have prevented Reyzeleh's illness if only I had never come back from Palestine. Of course, Elkind didn't drag me here by the hair, but I believed him when he assured me that in Russia all people are like brothers and sisters. But now I know the truth. Now I've heard how my comrades from Gdud were arrested, how they were forced to walk the final leg of the journey to Vorkuta. My old friend Tager lay down in the snow, in the dreadful cold, and refused to get up even when the others hit him, even when they dragged him by the hands and feet. He could barely speak, but he begged them: 'Kill me, if you can; I can go no further. Cover me with my work jacket, pile some snow over me, and go wherever "justice" leads you.'" She added, "It's clear that Reyzeleh is never going to get well, so that's one more thing on Elkind's conscience."

"My truth," Nehemyah said, "Elkind is not to blame; he didn't intend or want any of this to happen. It's a great pity what happened to him, Hanaleh."

"You're right," Hanah conceded. "The only thing he was guilty of was having misguided and blind hopes, just like all the poor Gdudniks who followed him."

Reyzeleh continued to languish in the hospital. The doctor in charge of the ward said it would be worthwhile to try giving her insulin injections, but unfortunately, this treatment didn't help. Her condition grew worse and worse. She completely stopped eating. The nurses fed her artificially, but at the end of 1942, Reyzeleh died.

* * *

Hanah fell apart. Nehemyah had to step into her shoes and do all the housework himself, because Pereleh and Beylke were now working during the day and attending night school in the evenings. Nehemyah often scolded Hanah:

"Your talent isn't your private property. You have no right to keep it to yourself. How can you not write?"

Hanah heard his words. She gazed at him with a look of anger, wonder, and shock, but said nothing. Where had all her energy gone? Now she just sat for days at a time with idle hands and a lowered head. Her indifference was so complete that she calmly looked on as Nehemyah spent whole days taking care of Senderke and doing all the housework by himself. And after that, he would sit at his art table and draw all night, because bread was not magically going to appear on their doorstep, and the five of them needed to eat.

* * *

It sometimes happens that in the middle of the night, Nehemyah stops working, comes and sits next to Hanah, caresses her, strokes her, and speaks to her as one speaks to a child:

"Hanaleh, my truth, the worst thing that can happen to a person is for unhappiness to cut him off from the world, and especially from his loved ones."

"Nehemyaleh, stop. I have to get over this by myself. There is no other remedy." She looks at him with eyes so full of sorrow that he has to turn his head away. He continues to sit beside her for a little while, then goes back to the table. And it often happens that the pencil in his hand cannot make a single mark on the page.

* * *

Hanah had been right in saying she had to overcome her grief alone. One night, when the children were asleep and Nehemyah was, as usual, sitting at his table, Hanah called to him:

"Get some paper and come here—my grandfather has arrived!"

"Right this minute!"

"Listen, Nehemyaleh: never have I woken up so easily and eagerly as on those mornings when my grandfather used to wake me at dawn. He never pulled the covers off or acted angry. He would touch my head ever so softly, and say even more softly, 'Get up, Hanaleh, get up, my little drop of quicksilver.' I don't know for sure, but it seems to me that I always awoke instantly. His beard used to scratch my cheeks, and I could see joyful little lights dancing in his brown eyes. He would smile and order me to get dressed quickly. He poured the ritual water over my hands, then led me by the hand into the forest. But one time, instead of the forest, my grandfather went past the priest's creek and down the street where the gentiles lived, and I realized he was leading me to the rye fields. He walked in front, and every once in a while he would look back and urge me, 'Come along, come along, don't be a slowpoke!' We walked past the rye; blue flowers were blossoming among the high ears. I wanted to pick them, but my grandfather called out: 'Don't pick them now, or they'll wilt before we get home. You can pick them on the way back.'

"It was cool, damp; high above the rye ears floated a light, thin mist. The whole sky was greenish, but a yellow glow was spreading across one side of the horizon. I vividly remember a vision that came into my mind of Father Abraham leading his son Isaac to the sacrifice. First I heard the Angel's voice: 'Do no evil to thine only son, because God sees that thou art loyal and God-fearing,' and then Grandfather's voice, interrupting my thoughts: 'Don't play around, just sit here on the grass and wait.'

"As I sit down, he advances a little way by himself, unbuttons the first few buttons of his *kapoteh,* pulls down the sleeve, grasps it under the armpit, and pulls again, until he's freed his arm from the coat. Then he rolls up the white sleeve of his shirt, takes the *tefillin* from their velvet bag, and begins wrapping the leather *retsueh* around his bare arm. His arm is white, and the strap is black. His arm becomes black-and-white striped. This seems very strange to me, but even more curious is watching him tie the *shel rosh* onto his head. The *shel rosh* looks like a miniature top hat. I don't understand why my grandfather is doing all this, because we are, of course, out in a field, not inside the *bes medresh*. But what amazes me most of all is that my grandfather doesn't recite any Hebrew prayers but starts talking the way he always does—the same way he talks to my grandmother.

"He talks like this: 'God in Heaven, merciful Father! You know everyone's heart, you listen to everyone's prayer—so listen to mine. Hear what I'm asking of you, Father in Heaven. Lead and direct my children and my children's children to good deeds, so that they never, God forbid, cause anyone harm, and never, Heaven forfend, bring anyone humiliation. May they never flatter anyone, and never bow their heads before anyone. Give them strong hearts to do good deeds, and give them strong bones to perform good acts.'

"With these words, my grandfather takes the *shel rosh* off his forehead, unwraps the *retsueh,* rolls down the sleeve of his shirt, puts his arm back in the sleeve of his *kapoteh,* buttons the top buttons, looks at me, says, 'Cuckoo!' and points up at the sky. Seeing this, I understand that the sun will soon come up. In the direction where I saw the yellow glow in the sky, shining needles of light have now appeared. My grandfather starts walking ahead of me again and saying, 'Come along, come along. Your grandmother must be up by now.'

"As we walk into the house, he gives a friendly greeting: 'A good day and a good year to you, Pesinke; what sort of breakfast do you have for us?' And my grandmother says, as always, 'A good year to you, Elinke; it's almost time to take the lid off the pot and show you.' She bustles over to the table with the two-handled copper kettle, sets it down, and with the big wooden ladle she starts spooning out rye bread crumbs cooked in milk. The dark crumbs stand out against the pale milk like little pebbles. My grandfather watches as my grandmother hands him the clay bowl, and he asks, 'Pesinke, have you looked at the sky today?'

"'You need to ask?' she replies. 'Do you think, Eliyeh, that a person who gets up early enough to make breadcrumbs isn't up early enough to see the sunrise?'

"'You're a very capable person, Pesinke—may it always be so. And furthermore, I want you to know that today your cooking has all seven flavors.'"

This memory hadn't just awakened in Hanah's mind when she called out to Nehemyah; it was already fully formed before she called him. And from the time of this memory on, she was released from the agonizing pressure of her grief. She gradually began to write again. And, of course, she also took the housework back into her own hands.

* * *

After the Victory over Fascism, Pereleh, the elder daughter, got married and moved away with her husband to Minsk.

* * *

One day, Hayaleh and Shimke came to see Hanah. Although Shimke was now disabled, he was once again working at the ball bearing factory. It was from Shimke that Hanah found out that Makar and Charlie had both been killed in the war. Hanah also learned that Frida and her mother, Leah, had died of typhus in a village not far from Samarkand.

As before the war, Hayaleh and Shimke began visiting Hanah every Saturday evening and staying over until Monday morning. Now, however, the mood at Hanah's house was completely different. Seldom did any-one laugh, and only very rarely did Hanah crack a joke. As time passed, they learned more and more about the horrors carried out by the Fascists. Sometimes Hanah would vividly imagine how her parents had been driven to their deaths, and her slanted blue eyes would overflow with tears.

That Hanah was one of those people who are far from complacent, from self-indulgent, from easily satisfied—this, all her acquaintances knew. But few people realized that not a day went by when Hanah's soul did not bleed. She could not allow herself to display her grief openly, because now Nehemyah was not feeling his best . . .

In 1948 the publisher Der Emes brought out a collection of Hanah's stories and novellas.

Nehemyah was constantly by her side. His soul, his warmth, his cour-age gave her strength. Always he was near her, always she heard his brave, proud voice. And this helped her in all her hours of need. But even this could not help Hanah overcome the great sorrow of Reyzeleh's death or to stop mourning the fate of the innocent, annihilated communards.

AFTERWORD

Shira Gorshman is a modern Yiddish writer greatly admired for her stylistic versatility, commitment to social justice, feminist perspective, and wry sense of humor. Her work, which is largely autobiographical, spans almost the entire twentieth century and depicts both earthshaking events and intimate moments that would otherwise be lost to history. Gorshman was born into two closely interconnected worlds: the sociocultural world of Eastern European Jewry and the geopolitical world of Imperial Russia. During her lifetime both underwent profound changes which directly affected the trajectory of her life and the nature of her work.

* * *

Shira Grigorievna Gorshman was born on April 10, 1906, in a Lithuanian shtetl variously called Krok (in Yiddish), Krakės (in Lithuanian), or Kraki (in Polish and Russian). At the time, Lithuania was part of the Russian Empire. Prior to the annexations of the Commonwealth of Poland and Lithuania in the late eighteenth century, Jews had been forbidden to live within the borders of Russia; after these annexations, the Russian Empire found itself with a vast Jewish population. The absorption of so many Jews, with their high level of literacy and cultural cohesion and their tendency to excel in trade, manufacture, and the professions, was viewed as a threat by the Russian merchant class. In response to the merchants' 1791 petition, the government issued a decree forbidding Jews from settling in Moscow or St. Petersburg, then created the Pale of Settlement, to which the Jews were confined. With Russia's annexation of more territory over the next several decades, the Pale expanded several times. It ultimately encompassed parts of today's Latvia, Lithuania, Poland, Moldova, Belarus, Ukraine, and western Russia.

Unlike the more assimilated Jews of Western and Central Europe, most Eastern European Jews retained their ethnic distinctiveness, traditional religious culture, and Yiddish language. Nevertheless, the Jewish Enlightenment movement, or Haskalah, did make inroads into Eastern Europe; indeed, by the 1840s it was centered in Imperial Russia. The relatively liberal Tsar Alexander II (r. 1855–1881) included some concessions to the Jews in his sweeping government reforms. Among these, he permitted certain favored groups of Jews to reside outside the Pale and established Jewish schools which followed the Haskalah ethos of deemphasizing Talmudic studies in favor of secular knowledge, Russian and other modern languages, and training in productive labor. The Army Law of 1874, which granted military deferments to students and reduced military service for graduates, motivated many Jewish parents to send their children to these schools.

After the emancipation of the serfs in 1861, the economic situation worsened for Russian Jews, who were squeezed out of their previous roles and were able to get only menial jobs. To add to their woes, beginning in the 1870s there arose a new type of anti-Jewish hostility in Russia, dubbed "antisemitism," that focused on Jews' biological descent and the threat posed by their stateless, international nature. A series of antisemitism congresses was held, and various antisemitic political parties were established. After Alexander II was assassinated in 1881, there was a wave of pogroms. In 1882 the "May Laws" curtailed Jewish residence in peasant villages and reversed the pro-Jewish policies of the previous era. Later in the decade, quotas were placed on Jews working in professions and attending Russian schools and universities. Many modernized Jews responded to these existential threats in one of two ways: by embracing the egalitarian and revolutionary ideals of socialism, or by championing the idea of a Jewish national homeland.

By 1900, Russified Jews were playing a conspicuous role in all the main radical movements within the Russian Empire. Marxist socialism, which asserted that a worldwide proletarian revolution would replace capitalism with an egalitarian and just society, was especially compelling to these modernized Jews. Downtrodden Jewish workers in urban centers within the Pale began to form labor unions and mutual aid societies and to organize strikes, with pamphlets often printed in Yiddish. In 1897 the General Union of Jewish Workers in Lithuania, Poland, and Russia (commonly known as the Bund) was organized. It quickly became one of the most effective branches of the Russian left.

After the pogroms of 1881–82, Jews fled Russia in large numbers. Most emigrated to the Americas, but in an era when nationalist movements were becoming ubiquitous throughout Europe, the idea of reestablishing the ancient Jewish Land of Israel, or Zion, also took hold. Hibbat Zion (Love of Zion) societies began to proliferate. From Russia, this Jewish nationalism spread to Central Europe. In 1897 the First Zionist Congress was called by Theodor Herzl and his Hibbat Zion allies, with the platform of establishing a Jewish national homeland in Palestine (then part of the Ottoman Empire) that would be recognized by international law.

While many in the Zionist movement were idealists with no practical plans to settle the Land of Israel, the Labor Zionist movement took it upon itself to begin farming the Holy Land. In 1881, the existing *yishuv* (Jewish community in the Land of Israel) numbered around 24,000 pious traditional Jews, half of whom lived in the city of Jerusalem. In the 1880s and 1890s, the First Zionist Aliyah (literally, "ascension") resulted in twenty new agricultural settlements in Palestine. In 1904–5 the Second Aliyah brought 40,000 more Jews, mostly idealistic young members of the Marxist Poalei Zion (Workers of Zion) and the non-Marxist Ze'irei Zion (Young People of Zion) movements. During the Third Aliyah following World War I, an additional 40,000 Jews arrived from Eastern Europe and undertook projects such as building towns and roads and draining swamps in the Jezreel Valley and Hefer Plain.

Largely for the sake of survival, the so-called pioneers developed cooperative farming communities, or kibbutzim (singular, kibbutz). These settlements were organized on a pure communist model: all wealth was held in common, no member owned any individual property, and all profits were reinvested into the operation. Adults lived, worked, and ate together; children were housed and raised separately. In 1924, one of those who embarked on this utopian adventure was the teenaged Shira Gorshman, together with her romantic partner and their infant daughter.

* * *

According to her friend Leonid Shkolnik, the former editor in chief of the *Birobidzhaner Shtern,* Gorshman's father, Tsvi-Hirsh "Grigorii" Kushnir, was a religious scholar who taught at the Dotnuv yeshiva and later wrote commentaries on the Torah. A month after his wife, Gitel, gave birth to Shira, Tsvi-Hirsh divorced her, secure in the knowledge that he had fulfilled the biblical injunction to "be fruitful and multiply." He subsequently devoted himself full-time to religious study, becoming a so-called *poresh min-ha-tsibur* (literally, a "dissenter from the community," a Jew who rejects his communal obligations). Gorshman does not appear to have had any further contact with Kushnir; she often stated that she did not have a father.

Gitel remarried to a man named Hirsh, and they had four children together: a daughter, Broche, and three sons, Wulf, Gedalyeh, and Benzion. Gorshman repeatedly describes her stepfather as abusive to her. In a video interview with Boris Sandler, she relates that when she was less than eight years old, her grandfather witnessed her stepfather beating her and tore her from his hands. "He faced him and said, 'Hershel, hit me! Why are you hitting someone smaller than you? What a hideous display!'"

Thereafter, Gorshman was raised by her maternal grandparents. Her grandfather, Eliyeh, was a religious scholar and traveling mason; her grandmother, Pesyeh, although illiterate, added to the family income by dyeing cloth and selling herbs. She also had a strong sense of charity (in Yiddish, *tsedokeh,* a word closely related to *tsedek,* justice or fairness). Gorshman told Sandler that her grandmother would bake some twelve loaves of Sabbath bread every week and distribute them to her impoverished neighbors, both Jewish and non-Jewish, according to need.

Although Gorshman clearly appreciated both her grandparents, she found her grandmother a harsh, even malicious taskmistress: "My grandmother was not a kind person. When I was twelve, I would knead the heavy dough for black bread—a really hard job. She would . . . tear the dough from my hands and say that such hands should be broken and thrown to the animals." In the story "Hanakeh," she writes: "Grandmother Pesyeh was constantly overworked, so she didn't notice how well her granddaughter, Hanakeh, used to tidy up the house . . . Grandma Pesyeh used to put a kettle blackened with smoke on the freshly scrubbed table. 'Grandma, what are you doing?' Hanakeh would shout. Her grandmother would then rotate the kettle several times, leaving a black, oily ring on the table." But Gorshman also credits her grandmother with transmitting her skills and work ethic to her: "She was a real dynamo. She worked very hard, and I grew up to be quite competent under her tutelage." One skill that her grandmother taught her would later prove particularly invaluable to Gorshman: the ability to raise cows and other livestock.

In contrast to her harsh grandmother, Gorshman's grandfather is always described as kind and affectionate. He is frequently depicted waking Gorshman up in the morning with great tenderness. In "Fun vanen shtam ich?" (Where Do I Come From?"), Gorshman describes how, as a small child, she would comb her grandfather's beard for him: "Right after [the Sabbath meal] my grandfather used to take a religious text, I used to sit down on his lap, and with the wooden comb that my grandfather had made himself, I would start to comb his thick gray beard. I would comb and comb until my grandmother couldn't endure it: 'Eliyeh! *I* don't have any beard, you know . . . Eliyeh, it's time to go to afternoon prayers!'" Gorshman's grandfather taught her to read Hebrew, and she also appears to have attended a traditional Jewish primary school *(heder)*. Both opportunities were relatively rare for girls.

During World War I, when Gorshman was nine years old, the commander in chief of the Imperial Russian Army falsely claimed that the Lithuanian Jews living near the front were colluding with the Germans, and he ordered their expulsion. These expulsions began in March 1915, with as little as eight hours' notice. On May 5, 1915 (the Jewish holiday of Shavuot), 160,000 Jews were forced out of Kovno province, which included Krok. The order of expulsion limited their destinations to certain districts in the Poltava, Yekaterinoslav, and Tavrichevsky governates; Tambov and Penza were later added to the list. Many of those who arrived in Vilna remained there, living in synagogues, poorhouses, and stables, or on the streets. Others were put aboard freight cars and subjected to horrific treatment as they were carried deep into the Russian interior.

While a few biographers maintain that Gorshman and her family were exiled to Vilna, most claim that they went to Odessa. Kherson governate, where Odessa was located, was not one of the official destinations for the deportees (although by the time Russia and Germany made peace in 1920, displaced Jews were scattered throughout the Russian Empire). I have found no evidence that Gorshman ever lived in Odessa as a child, although she did reside there briefly as an adult.

Shortly before turning fourteen, Gorshman left her grandparents' home and moved to the nearby city known as Kovno (in Russian) or Kaunas (in Lithuanian). Shkolnik's biography states that she "attended the Kovno (Kaunas) boarding school where, among other subjects, she studied secular Jewish literature." Others say she lived in an orphanage; some even maintain that she was sent to an orphanage after losing both parents in World War I (although we know from her work that her mother and stepfather were still alive until at least 1941).

In Gorshman's story "Rayzene kashe" (Rice Pudding), her alter ego Hanah leaves home and takes a job at a Jewish orphanage in Kovno. The story is in the form of a letter from Hanah, not yet fourteen, to her grandparents in Krok. She begs them to understand that she did not really run away but left because there was no future for her in the shtetl. She then describes her life as a kitchen employee and student at the Kovno orphanage run by a Dr. Lehmann, where she is receiving a salary, learning standard Yiddish, and being introduced to secular Yiddish literature: "Grandfather taught me only Torah and the Book of Psalms; now I know that besides that, there is a Sholem Aleichem and a Sholem Asch."

At the orphanage, Hanah also learns about a harsh reality of urban life: "Can you believe it? At night here, they put baskets outside, and they lay pillows and blankets in the baskets, and in the morning, the kindhearted nurses go to the baskets and take small children out of them . . . One nurse, Klara, took a very small boy out of a blanket, and he didn't cry even a little. To tell you the truth, Grandma dear, I myself started crying immediately. That someone should leave such a little angel outside for a whole night! And it's so cold outside!"

Because Gorshman names the head of the orphanage in the story, it is reasonable to conclude that the institution where she lived, worked, and studied during this period was the Kovno Children's Home, founded by the German-born Jewish physician and educator Dr. Siegfried Lehmann (1892–1958), a socialist and Zionist. In 1927, Dr. Lehmann led a group of Jewish orphans from Kovno to Palestine, where he founded the Ben Shemen Youth Village, a large agricultural boarding school which still exists today.

Zinovy Beckman, a close family friend of Gorshman's, and Lev Fruchtman, her Russian translator for some thirty years, both state that after the orphanage, she lived in a camp run by HeHalutz (The Pioneer). HeHalutz was an international Zionist organization that trained Jewish youth for agricultural settlement in the Land of Israel. Both biographers also state that Gorshman studied for a short time at the Kaunas Jewish People's University. This educational institution, known in Yiddish as the Kovner Folks-Universitet, was not officially established until 1926, after Gorshman had emigrated to Palestine; it was preceded, however, by a program of college-level courses organized and taught by Esther Elyashev, chairman of the city's Society for the Dissemination of Higher Education Among the Jews.

Given her youthful associations with Dr. Lehmann and HeHalutz and the modern education she received from Elyashev, it is hardly surprising that Gorshman moved to Palestine. By the time she did so, at age sixteen, she was partnered with a man named Hayim Hatskelevich and had a daughter with him (Ruth, born in Kovno on December 25, 1923). In her writings, Gorshman consistently uses the word "husband" (Yiddish, *man*) to refer to the father of her children, but there are indications in her work that the two never officially married. Very little is known of Hatskelevich. A genealogical website lists his birth year as "circa 1900," making him about six years older than Gorshman. In a Russian documentary, Gorshman relates their meeting as follows: "I was going on fifteen years old. I met a man. He kissed me, and I was thinking: 'What wonderful people there are in the world! They kiss you.' No-one did that at home. And when he said that I should do this, and I should do that, I listened to him. And when we went to Palestine, we already had a child."

In Palestine, Gorshman and Hatskelevich joined Gdud HaAvodah (the Labor Battalion), a work corps founded in 1920 in honor of Zionist militia leader Yosef Trumpeldor, who had been killed a few months earlier in an armed conflict with Arabs at the settlement of Tel Hai. Trumpeldor had envisioned such labor legions paving the way for mass Jewish migration into Palestine. The historian Walter Laqueur states: "The legion had eighty members at first, but grew eventually to seven hundred. It existed for only six years but was the vanguard of the pioneer movement, the first to settle in the Yesreel Valley, the first to establish kibbutzim." He characterizes the legion's members, most of them male, as "graduates of the Russian revolution and the civil war, full of youth and fire, ready to burn and to be burned." The organization was divided into small groups that built roads, erected buildings, repaired vehicles, and performed other manual labor. Its economic model was one of pure communism: "Members received no wages or salaries, all their earnings disappearing into a common fund, and their basic needs were covered according the principle of full equality."

Fruchtman says that in Gdud HaAvodah "Shira was a laborer, took on everything, and, in particular, was a purchaser of provisions for a large 'plow' (detachment). Her husband, like other men, worked at a quarry, mined stones for the construction of dwellings." At some point during this period Gorshman also worked as a housekeeper in the home of the renowned Yiddish and Hebrew poet Hayim Nahman Bialik (1873–1934).

Gorshman and Hatskelevich quickly produced two more daughters, Shulamith (b. 1925) and Eliyah (b. 1926). The year Eliyah was born, a political split occurred in Gdud HaAvodah; a minority attempted to turn it into a communist organization. According to Laqueur, the group had failed to attract as many new workers as it had hoped, and by 1926 its disappointed members were becoming more radical: "Some members began to dissociate themselves from Zionism altogether. Since . . . in their scale of priorities the world revolution weighed heavier than Zionist ideals, this anti-Zionist turn seemed only consistent. In December 1926 the legion split, mainly on political lines. The larger group later joined the existing Zionist-Socialist parties, while the minority faction dissolved itself in 1928."

In this conflict, Shira sided with the communists, Hatskelevich with the anti-communists; their partnership dissolved. According to the historian Yakov Pasik, the communist faction was subjected to ostracism and persecution: "[The anti-communist faction] did not disdain anything to suppress the left opposition. 'Spies of the Comintern' were expelled from work, deprived of public housing and medical care, children were beaten in school, the water was cut off from communist settlements. In December 1926, [the communist-faction leader Mendel] Elkind and his associates were expelled from Gdud." Gorshman, with her three children in tow, followed Elkind to the Soviet Union to found a kibbutz-style farm in Crimea. Hatskelevich remained in Palestine, and then the State of Israel, until his death sometime after 1967 at the kibbutz Ein Harod.

Throughout *Hanah's Sheep and Cattle*, Mendel Elkind functions as a kind of nemesis for Hanah. Not only is she forced to resist his unwanted sexual attentions, but she also comes to blame virtually all her problems on the fact that he brought her to the Soviet Union. Indeed, Elkind becomes a kind of proxy for the Soviet Union itself: Hanah seems to hold him personally accountable for everything about Soviet life that she finds unsatisfactory.

Menachem "Mendel" Elkind was born in 1897 in Berislav, Kherson province, and grew up in Yevpatoria, Crimea, where his father was a rabbi at the city's Main Synagogue. He graduated from the Yevpatoria Gymnasium in 1916, then studied mathematics at the Yekatorinoslav Jewish Polytechnic Institute, where he developed an enthusiasm for Zionism, socialism, and communism. After leaving school, he became a follower of Joseph Trumpeldor and a member of HeHalutz. In 1920 Elkind arrived in Palestine as part of the Third Aliyah. That same year, he was among those who established the Joseph Trumpeldor Labor and Defense Battalion, more commonly known as Gdud HaAvodah.

Abraham Cahan, the editor of the New York City Yiddish daily *Der Forverts* (*The Forward*), met Elkind in 1925 and described him as follows: "When you sit and talk to him, you become increasingly exposed to his charm. Elkind is 28, tall with broad shoulders and clear eyes as guileless as a child's. He was wearing a loose shirt of the kind that all the young radicals of Tel Aviv and the settlements wear. All in all, he was dressed like a poor man, a hired laborer . . . Needless to say, he is extraordinarily intelligent, possessing excellent qualities and a keen, clear and logical mind."

In her story "Firers . . ." ("Leaders . . ."), Gorshman describes Elkind this way: "A very quiet man of middle height, his dark eyes look inward, seldom at the person with whom he is speaking. His thick curly hair is always mussed, because it can't take a comb. He keeps quiet more than he talks. Like all Gdudniks, he gets his clothes from the warehouse. His shoes are well worn. He is the Chairman of the group in Jerusalem. At the Assembly he also speaks little. But when the Gdud split into left and right [factions], he spoke more."

In 1927 Elkind traveled to the Soviet Union to visit Jewish agricultural settlements in the fertile Crimean peninsula. Jewish colonies had existed there since the nineteenth century and were now being supported by foreign Jewish charities, most notably the American Jewish Joint Distribution Committee (also known as the JDC or Joint), in cooperation with the Soviet government. Elkind successfully negotiated with Moscow to allow his "Gdudniks" to create a farming cooperative in Crimea, with the understanding that the settlers were to cut off all contact with Palestine, renounce their previous Zionist activities, and live in accordance with Soviet law. A plot of land formerly occupied by a nobleman's estate was allocated for the group in the Yevpatoria region.

The first group of Gdudniks arrived in 1928. They named their endeavor Vojo Nova, Esperanto for "New Way." (At the time, the invented language of Esperanto was considered "the Latin of the proletariat" and "the language of the world revolution.") In 1929, more former Gdud members arrived from Palestine, and local Jews also began to join. In the summer of 1929, Elkind's wife, Maria (Miriam) Elkind (1898–1969), arrived from Palestine with their two sons. According to Shira Gorshman's story "Leaders . . . ," Gorshman and her three daughters came at the end of 1929 in a group of twelve adults and ten children, their English sweaters and sandals woefully inadequate against the winter weather.

It is worth noting that this was the first time Gorshman had ever lived in the Soviet Union; Lithuania had been ruled by Imperial Russia at the time of her birth and became an independent democratic state when she was twelve. Gorshman's decision to follow Elkind to Soviet Crimea was, in effect, an abandonment of the Zionist ideal of a Jewish national homeland in favor of the communist ideal of equality and brotherhood among people of all ethnic and religious backgrounds. In "Leaders . . . ," Gorshman admits that Elkind did not coerce his followers into joining him but instead appealed to their idealism: "Of course, Elkind did not drag anybody [to the Soviet Union] by the hair. He merely said, in his quiet, penetrating voice: 'In Russia all people are sisters and brothers. The children there do not learn to pinch their pennies.'"

Elkind and his followers arrived in the Soviet Union at a time when agricultural practices were in a state of flux. Most Russian farmers were the descendants of peasants who had lived since medieval times in cooperative, self-governing farming communities, known in Russian as *obshchina* or *mir* (often translated into English as "villages" or "peasant communes"). The village *skhod,* or assembly, managed the community's finances, resources, and infrastructure. Periodically, the *skhod* would redistribute the community's main resource (usually land, but in some regions timber or fishing rights) in keeping with the needs and abilities of each household.

After the Russian Revolution, the Communist Party tried to reorganize agricultural production into a network of collective farms *(kolkhoz).* Under this model, a farm's workforce was divided into a number of "brigades." Each worker theoretically received a share of the farm's product and/or profits according to the number of days worked. But the Soviet plan encountered strong opposition from the peasants, and it was deferred. Only when Stalin forcibly collectivized farming as part of his first Five-Year Plan (1928–1932) was the regime able to make the transition, and only at great cost to the peasants, many of whom were branded "kulaks" or "enemies of the people" and sent to penal colonies or executed.

Because Vojo Nova was established by former Labor Zionists with their own agricultural and sociocultural practices, it was a unique entity in the Soviet Union. Gorshman refers to it as a "commune" (Yiddish, *komune)* and to its members as "communards" (Yiddish, *komunarn,* singular *komunar).* These terms were imported into Yiddish from the French and originally referred to the Paris Commune, a revolutionary government established in March 1871, when insurrectionist members of the Paris National Guard took over the city and managed to institute numerous progressive reforms before being suppressed by the French government two months later.

Economically and socially, Vojo Nova was modeled on a Zionist kibbutz. Unlike in a Russian peasant village, its members lived in group housing, owned no personal property, and received no wages. The children were raised collectively in a so-called Children's Home (Yiddish, *kinderheym,* a calque of the Hebrew *beit yeladim).* Yet Vojo Nova also somewhat resembled a Soviet *kolkhoz* in that its workers were divided into brigades, each with its own leader. (Gorshman became the brigadier of livestock operations.)

Initially, the Soviets do not seem to have objected to the unorthodoxy of the enterprise; it is likely that they were particularly permissive with Vojo Nova because it represented such an extraordinary propaganda tool for the regime. The historian Jonathan Dekel-Chen explains: "The Soviets claimed (with some accuracy) that dissatisfaction with the accomplishments of socialism in the Jewish community in Palestine had triggered [the Gdudniks'] return 'home' to the USSR. From the outset of the [Soviet Jewish agricultural] settlement project, the regime had hoped that these colonies would 'steal the thunder' from the Zionist undertaking in Palestine. Therefore, Voyo Nova must have seemed a godsend from the regime's point of view." Pasik likewise notes: "During its heyday (1928–31), the commune aroused great public interest as an original and important social phenomenon and as an attempt to organize a new way of life. The activities of the commune left no stone unturned [in dispelling] the myth of the inability of the Jews to [perform] physical agricultural labor. The commune was frequented by delegations of workers and collective farmers from all over the Soviet Union, who [visited in order to become] acquainted with the achievements and experience of its work."

In its first few years, Vojo Nova received additional land, livestock, and equipment from the Soviet government. By 1932 it had two hundred head of cattle, 1,300 sheep, and 1,200 breeding chickens. But by this time the honeymoon with the regime was over—and the first to pay the price was Mendel Elkind. According to Pasik, the commune was subjected to constant inspections, which revealed real and imaginary shortcomings, including "the concentration of leadership exclusively in the hands of the chairman of the commune Elkind, inefficient organization and payment of labor, errors in the staffing of the commune, national isolation, staff turnover, large debts on loans, neglect of socialist competition, etc. . . . In March of 1931, Elkind was removed from the post of chairman of the commune and a criminal case was initiated against him on suspicion of negligence and inaction."

While awaiting the outcome of the investigation, Elkind continued to do agricultural work in Crimea. In the summer of 1933, the case against him was dropped, and he and his family moved to Moscow. In 1935 Elkind began working in the planning department of the First State Bearing Plant

Kaganovich, usually referred to simply as Sharikopodshipnik (Ball Bearing). Pasik notes, "This largest industrial enterprise in the country became a refuge for many 'Palestinians' who [had] returned to the USSR [with Elkind]." The factory plays a significant role in *Hanah's Sheep and Cattle;* Gorshman, however, never draws any connection between the factory and Elkind, although he was presumably instrumental in helping his former Gdudniks obtain employment there.

Between 1936 and 1938, Soviet general secretary Joseph Stalin sought to consolidate his power through a campaign that came to be known as the Great Terror. Under his direction, the NKVD (secret police) targeted Communist Party and government officials, military leaders, peasants accused of resisting collectivization (kulaks), certain ethnic minorities, and others perceived as a threat to the regime. Such "enemies of the people" were subjected to violent interrogation, imprisonment, torture, and execution. Members and former members of Vojo Nova were among those targeted and accused of being either British spies or Zionist agents. On December 2, 1937, Mendel Elkind was accused of espionage. On February 19, 1938, he was sentenced by the Military Collegium of the Supreme Court of the USSR to capital punishment and was shot on the same day. Between May 13 and August 13, 1938, twenty-seven other current and former members of Vojo Nova were arrested for belonging to an anti-Soviet Jewish nationalist organization and sent to labor camps, where fourteen of them died.

* * *

Fortunately for Shira Gorshman, in 1931 she had married Soviet artist and illustrator Mendel Gorshman (1902–1972), who had been sent to Crimea by the government as part of a four-person team to document Jewish agricultural life. Unlike many of her fellow communards, she was never punished for her previous affiliations with Vojo Nova or Gdud HaAvodah; nevertheless, there were times during the Stalinist purges of the late 1930s when she kept her suitcase packed and remained in a constant state of readiness for arrest.

In interviews, Gorshman relates that she was initially resistant to Mendel Gorshman's advances; she disapproved of his status as a bourgeois professional and had trouble relating to his artistic career. She told Sue Fishkoff: "I believed it wasn't right for Jews to be doctors and academics and artists. I felt . . . that we should work at ordinary labor." In an interview with Fishkoff and Frieda Johles Forman, she related: "He spoke to me about love. I told him, 'You don't need this [life]. You have talent—you have an easy job, although I don't understand it, because in the shtetl my grandfather taught me Torah and the Scriptures, but didn't teach me anything about art.'" In addition, she was concerned that Mendel might have offspring from previous sexual liaisons: "You are also very young, and I don't know how you live. I suspect that your children are selling newspapers somewhere, and you don't know about them, you don't even know that you have [children]. But that is not my thing. That is your thing. So you shouldn't talk to me about love. Because I am not ready for that now." Even after she declared her love for Mendel, Shira was initially reluctant to place her children under a stepfather after her own traumatic childhood experiences, but Mendel's gentle nature eventually won her over. The couple married in 1931 and moved to Moscow with Shira's three daughters; a son, Alexander, was born in 1937. Shira ultimately declared Mendel "a better father than I was a mother."

In Moscow, where the family shared a tiny apartment with the artist Meyer Akselrod (1902–1970) and his wife, the writer, critic, translator, and Yiddish literature professor Rivke Rubin (1906–1987), Gorshman experienced profound culture shock and homesickness for the commune. She soon took a menial job at a kindergarten, while her daughters boarded at what Fruchtman describes as "the Jewish Orphanage in Malakhova." This may have been the Third International Jewish School-Camp for War Orphans in Malakhovka, funded by the JDC and well known in the 1920s for the famous Jewish intellectuals who taught there, including author Der Nister, artist Marc Chagall, and poet David Hofstein.

To get along in Moscow, it was necessary for Gorshman to gain fluency in Russian, which she did with her husband's help. Mastery of the language gave her access not only to great Russian literature but also to world literature in translation. In *Hanah's Sheep and Cattle,* we see Hanah reading a translation of Hans Christian Andersen's fairy tales not long after moving to Moscow. Within a year or so, she has advanced to Tolstoy's novella *Strider: The Story of a Horse* and to translations of Dickens and other classics. In Moscow, Gorshman was also exposed to contemporary Yiddish literature, including the work of the many well-known writers and poets in her husband's circle. After initially being ignored by these people, who were overwhelmingly male and better educated than she was, she eventually befriended some of the greatest Yiddish literary figures of the 1930s. She also began to write stories herself, and eventually aspired to a literary career of her own.

In her 1995 interview with Forman and Fishkoff, Gorshman recounts how the writer Leyb Kvitko "discovered" her:

> I had written a story . . . and I left it on the desk and I was washing the floor in the kitchen . . . Kvitko came to me with the papers, and said, "Did you write this?" And I said yes. "Good Lord," he said, "why have you kept silent? Good God. I knew that all mothers give their children the breast so they can eat. But this is the first time I've read a story about a mother who locks her son in the drawer of a dresser because he always wants to eat." The story is published, it's called "The Parasite" . . . That was my first serious story . . . and it was judged to be the kind of story Sholem Aleichem couldn't write. Not that it's better than Sholem Aleichem! But that's what the critics said . . . Leyb Kvitko . . . said, "Even if you write nothing else, with just this story you'll be recognized in our literature."

* * *

One of the many interesting features of *Hanah's Sheep and Cattle* is the diversity of writing styles employed, both by the author and by her alter ego, Hanah. Gorshman imbues sections of part 1 with the tone of a romance novel (or perhaps a serialized Yiddish novel of the *shund* genre, similar to American pulp fiction). Within the narrative, the protagonist Hanah composes an impromptu folktale to entertain a group of young children and pens another for her own enjoyment. Near the end of the novel, Hanah writes a letter describing refugee life in the Volga region in such masterly prose that her husband, who formerly forbade her to write, submits it for publication. As a whole, the book can be categorized as literary fiction, with realistic dialogue and lyrical descriptions of the natural world. Gorshman was primarily a short story writer, and the book incorporates several of her short works almost verbatim. One of the most notable examples is the section in which Hanah visits her mother in Lithuania just before the Second World War, which closely resembles Gorshman's story "Zich nisht oysgeredt di hertser" (Unspoken Hearts).

Gorshman told Forman and Fishkoff that she had begun writing in childhood: "I began to write a very long time ago! But all of it was lost. At the beginning of the war we traveled to Lithuania. I went to my mother's, and she told me that in the attic there was a box [filled] with what I had written." Her childhood writings may have been lost when her family was killed during the war. As we have seen, Gorshman was introduced to secular Yiddish literature around age fourteen as a student at the Kovno Children's Home, but there is little or no evidence that she did any more creative writing until she became part of Mendel Gorshman's literary circle in Moscow in the early 1930s.

There is ample evidence that Gorshman was a gifted oral storyteller. According to Sandler's video, members of Gdud HaAvodah nicknamed her "Shirkeh the Storyteller." She told Fishkoff that although she believed Jews should work at ordinary labor rather than being professionals or artists, "all those years, I continued telling myself stories, but I didn't write them down. I kept them in my heart." And Fruchtman describes how Gorshman dealt with Russian translations of her work that she found lacking: "Visiting the homes of her friends and acquaintances (not only Jews) as a guest, she herself retold her stories [in Russian]—quite expressively and artistically. And soon she gained popularity in Moscow, and significance in Jewish culture no less than her husband." Gorshman's oral storytelling style carries over into her prose, which is characterized by unexpected changes in tense—a common feature of Yiddish writing that derives from its origin as a language used mainly for spoken rather than written communication.

In *Hanah's Sheep and Cattle,* we get a sense of Gorshman as an omnivorous reader with many literary influences. She told Forman and Fishkoff: "Chekhov was my teacher. [But] my first teacher was Peretz! The first was Peretz! Yitzchak Leybush [Peretz]! Not Sholem Aleichem." Yitzchak Leybush Peretz (1852–1915) is considered one of the three founders of modern Yiddish literature, along with Sholem Aleichem and Mendele Mocher Sforim. According to Goldie Morgentaler, Peretz "subscribed to the notion of *doikeyt,* which translates awkwardly into English as here-ness, the belief that Jews should fight for equality in the countries where they lived." Many of his stories have a folkloric feel. Morgentaler explains: "Peretz saw folk tales as an expression of the inner life of the Jewish people . . . In the folk tales [he wrote], Peretz found a means to restore to the Jews . . . their own artistic grandeur, the revitalizing richness of their cultural life."

Another influence on Gorshman was Hans Christian Andersen, whose story "The Princess and the Pea" Hanah recounts in *Hanah's Sheep and Cattle*. According to *Britannica,* Andersen (1805–1875), one of the most famous fairy-tale writers of all time, is considered innovative in his use of spoken idioms. His work has great appeal to both children and adults because "he was not afraid of introducing feelings and ideas that were beyond a child's immediate comprehension, yet he remained in touch with the child's perspective."

A related influence on Gorshman was her mentor and champion Leyb Kvitko (1890–1952). Although Kvitko wrote for both adults and children, he was particularly famous for his children's poems, which became classics throughout the Soviet Union in Russian translation. In *Hanah's Sheep and Cattle,* Hanah dismisses the idea of limiting Kvitko's target audience to children: "Why do you call them children's poems? Someday, people will sit down and really read what Kvitko has written, and they'll discover exquisite poems for adults."

Because of Stalin's belief that Jews were likely to be disloyal to the Soviet regime, Yiddish writers became targets of repression, and a twelve-year ban was imposed on Yiddish publications. The Yiddish literary journal *Heymland* (Homeland), which published many of Gorshman's stories, shut down shortly after putting out her collection *Der koyekh fun lebn* (The Power of Life) in 1948; the Yiddish newspaper *Eynikayt* (Unity), to which she was also a contributor, folded the same year. Faith Jones states: "By mid-December 1948, Stalin's 'anti-cosmopolitan campaign,' in which up to seventy percent of the named individuals among the censured were Jewish, and a simultaneous campaign of repression against Jewish institutions and cultural figures, transformed Yiddish culture in the Soviet Union. Publishing came to a halt and was slow to pick up even following Stalin's death and Khrushchev's 1956 speech acknowledging Stalin's crimes."

Several of the writers in Gorshman's circle were killed in the Great Terror, including Leyb Kvitko. Kvitko had previously run afoul of the Communist Party in 1929, when his sharp criticism of certain literary figures had led to his being removed from the editorial board of the Yiddish journal *Di Royte Velt* (The Red World) and forced to take a job in a tractor factory. Within five years, however, his career rebounded. At the start of World War II, he joined the Jewish Antifascist Committee (JAC), helping refugee writers from Nazi-occupied countries resettle in the Soviet Union. In 1949 he was arrested for his JAC affiliation and brutally interrogated before being formally charged by the Supreme Soviet Military Court. He was executed on August 12, 1952, the so-called Night of the Murdered Poets, along with twelve other members of the JAC.

Gorshman survived the Stalinist purges—perhaps, as Jones suggests, because she had a lower profile than many of her peers. She was, however, unable to publish in the Soviet Union during the ban on Yiddish literature between the late 1940s and the early 1960s. She did publish a collection of stories, *33 Noveln* (33 Stories), in Warsaw in 1961. (Soviet writers sometimes published in Poland, which was not considered disloyal to the Soviet regime.) That same year, under Khrushchev, Yiddish publishing in the Soviet Union resumed, although the twelve-year gap caused lasting damage. Not only did many writers die in the purges or stop writing, but also "Yiddish literacy and interest in Jewish culture had been seriously undermined; the audience for Yiddish was diminished and unsure of its relative worth in the new political situation."

Nevertheless, Gorshman continued writing prolifically. Starting in the 1960s, she was one of a handful of women whose work appeared regularly in the journal *Sovetish Heymland* (Soviet Homeland) published by Sovetskii Pisatel (Soviet Writer). This publisher also brought out a new edition of Gorshman's *33 Noveln* in 1963; a new collection of her stories, *Lebn un licht* (Life and Light), in 1974, with a Russian translation in 1979; a slim book of sketches, *Ich hob lib arumforn* (I Love to Wander), in 1981; and another large collection, *Yontef in mitn vokh* (Midweek Holiday), in 1984. Yet Gorshman never received anywhere near the critical attention of many of her male counterparts. Jones suggests three possible causes for this marginalization: the unequal treatment of women in both Yiddish literary culture and Soviet ideology; Gorshman's relative lack of political victimization compared to those executed in 1952; or her choice of the short story rather than the novel as her primary genre.

Gorshman's third story collection, *Life and Light,* was published two years after the death of her husband; the book includes the sixty-nine-page novella *Hanehs shof un rinder* (Hanah's Sheep and Cattle), a lightly fictionalized retelling of the unlikely circumstances through which Shira and Mendel Gorshman met and married. According to Fruchtman, the title is a subtle critique of the Soviet system; the expression "sheep and cattle" is an ancient biblical expression denoting wealth. "The irony is hidden in the name itself: the socialist agricultural system inspired young Jews with the idea of a new public good; the heroine of the story . . . sincerely believes that these fat herds and flocks are the common property of the communards, including her[self]." Fruchtman also notes that Gorshman tends to downplay the hardships suffered by the communards due to Soviet censorship. "To circumvent censorship, the writer had to soften the pictures of the everyday life of the Communards, their desperate attempts to overcome hunger and discomfort, crop failures, illness, etc."

This earliest version of the story makes no mention of Gdud HaAvodah or Palestine. Gorshman's first story collection, *The Power of Life*, published in 1948, had included some stories set in Palestine; but later that year the Soviet Union ended its brief alliance with the newly formed State of Israel and resumed its long-standing mistrust of Zionism. Gorshman was only too familiar with the fate of Soviet Jews accused of "anti-nationalism." Thereafter, for as long as she remained in the Soviet Union, she set all her pastoral stories in Crimea—even those based on events that had occurred in Palestine.

In 1984, *Hanah's Sheep and Cattle* reappeared in the Gorshman anthology *Midweek Holiday*. This time, instead of being buried late in the book, the novella is placed right up front. It has also been greatly expanded: it is now 148 pages long and extends from Hanah's first meeting with Nehemyah in 1930 to the publication of her first book in 1948. The story now includes Hanah's visit to her mother in Soviet-occupied Lithuania (or, as Gorshman phrases it in deference to the censors, a Lithuania "liberated" by the Soviet army) on the eve of World War II with her youngest daughter, Reyzeleh; her removal to the Volga region with her children to work on a collective farm during the war; and Reyzeleh's death in a psychiatric hospital in 1942. As in the 1974 edition, however, there is no mention of Hanah's having previously lived and worked in Palestine.

At the end of 1989, Gorshman took advantage of Gorbachev's new policy allowing emigration to Israel. Within three years of relocating, she had published a new, standalone Yiddish edition of *Hanah's Sheep and Cattle*. This 199-page novel is quite similar to the novella published in the Soviet Union in 1984, but there are some notable changes. For the first time, Gorshman references Palestine and individuals from Gdud HaAvodah. Early in the book, Hanah expresses anxiety about the Soviet secret police; later she grieves the loss of friends (although their absence is not explicitly linked to Stalin). In the Israeli edition, Lithuania has not been "liberated" by the Soviet army; it has merely "become Soviet." Perhaps most significantly, the 1993 edition gives the previously anonymous chairman of the commune his real-life name—Mendel Elkind—and, in a brand-new opening paragraph, alludes to the political rift between him and David Ben-Gurion, who headed the anti-communist wing of the Poale Zion party in the 1920s.

By this time, as Jones points out, Elkind's name cannot have been significant to many people other than Gorshman herself. Jones also finds Hanah's newly expressed longing for Palestine somewhat implausible: Gorshman and her comrades came close to starving there. This nostalgia for Palestine, Jones suggests, may have been a way for Gorshman to ingratiate herself with her new Israeli audience, "to repudiate Soviet life in ways acceptable in her new surroundings." Even if Gorshman's enthusiasm for Palestine in this final version of *Hanah's Sheep and Cattle* is somewhat exaggerated, there can be little doubt that when Gorshman moved to Israel, she felt genuinely relieved to be able to write about her years in Palestine openly, without fear of reprisal. The publication of this third and final version of the book, free of Soviet censorship, was clearly a personal triumph.

* * *

According to Fruchtman, Gorshman's emigration to Israel in 1989 began as a trip to visit friends. Her decision to stay was dramatically and publicly announced while she was giving a reading at the Yiddish Lovers Club in Rehovot. When asked what impression Israel made on her as a pioneer of the 1920s and how long she would be staying, "Shira suddenly became so excited that she almost shouted out: 'But I'm not going anywhere from here. I finally came home. I'm staying with you, my dear readers, *mayne Yidishe leyener!*'" By the time Gorshman resettled in the land that had played such a significant role in her early life, she was almost eighty-four years old. While most writers become less productive at such an advanced age, Gorshman's output increased. From the time of her arrival in Israel until her death in April 2001, she produced five books: *Oysdoyer: Dertseylunden, noveln, zichroynes* (Perseverance: Stories, Novellas, Memories), 1992; *Hanehs shof un rinder: Roman* (Hanah's

Sheep and Cattle: Novel), 1993; *Vi tsum ershtn mol: Novele, dertseylungen, skitsn* (Like the First Time: Novella, Stories, Sketches), 1995; *On a gal: Dertseylungen, skitsn, zichroynes* (Without Malice: Stories, Sketches, Memoirs), 1996; and *In di shpurn fun Gdud HaAvodah* (In the Footsteps of the Labor Brigade), 1998.

In Israel, Gorshman also found a new life partner: Daniel Ben-Nahum (formerly known as Daniel Prokhovnik Pirchiyahu), a Kovno-born poet, writer, essayist, literary critic, editor, and translator, who had immigrated to Israel in 1933 and joined the kibbutz Beit Zera. Fruchtman reports that Ben-Nahum made two proposals to Gorshman: first, that he should translate *Hanah's Sheep and Cattle* into Hebrew, and second, that the two of them should spend the rest of their days together. Gorshman agreed to both proposals, and Ben-Nahum duly translated the book and prepared it for publication. He also flew to Moscow to meet her family, "and with the pride and directness of a true kibbutznik he said: 'I am your Papa from now on!'"

Unfortunately, the relationship was short-lived. Neither Ben-Nahum's adult children nor the administrators of Beit Zera, the kibbutz where he lived, approved of the union. Instead of living with Ben-Nahum, Gorshman obtained a room in a hostel in Ashkelon. Her oldest daughter, Ruth, emigrated to Israel and moved into the hostel to care for her. Ben-Nahum came to Ashkelon often to visit Gorshman and to work with her on the Hebrew translation of the novel, which he completed before his sudden death in 1992. It was published in 1997 but had such a small print run that it is now considered a bibliographic rarity.

* * *

Shira Gorshman died on April 4, 2001, just six days before her ninety-fifth birthday. Although she made the State of Israel her home for the last eleven years of her life, she recognized that it was a very different place from the Palestine she had left behind in 1929. Among other things, the socialist idealism of the past had been replaced by an affinity for American-style capitalism. Zinovy Beckman, her longtime friend in both the Soviet Union and Israel, relates this anecdote. "Once I asked her if she could tell me the difference between the Jews who lived in Palestine [in the 1920s] and those who now live in the State of Israel (I meant the recent demographic changes due to the law of return). She smirked, slyly.

'Previously, JEWS lived in Palestine, and now in Israel—SHEKEL-MEN.'"
In her 1995 interview with Sue Fishkoff for the *Jerusalem Post,* Gorshman
describes a speech she made when accepting a literary prize from the Far-
band Hamlin House in Tel Aviv: "I told them . . . [i]t's nice to have paved
roads and nice cars, and happy, successful people sitting in those cars, but
you're forgetting the majority of the people, in Israel and the world, who
don't have such nice cars. There are children starving everywhere." At this
point during the interview, Gorshman points to a multistory apartment
complex going up across the street and adds, "The American Jews spend
millions on these nice white apartments, but will they open the door to a
mother and child without a roof?"

Gorshman spoke and read Russian fluently, and there is little doubt
that while living in the Soviet Union she could have chosen Russian as her
literary language. Instead, she chose to write solely in Yiddish, despite Stalin's persecution of Yiddish writers, the twelve-year ban on Yiddish publications, and the subsequent decline in the use of the language. Similarly,
when she relocated to Israel, she was still fluent in modern Hebrew, the
language developed by Zionists in the late nineteenth and early twentieth
centuries, which she had spoken in British Mandate Palestine sixty years
earlier. Her facility with modern Hebrew is evident in a video documentary made in Israel in 1989 to celebrate her return. It is quite possible that
she would have been able to begin writing in Hebrew to reach the largest
possible Israeli audience. Instead, she continued writing in Yiddish until
the end of her life.

Small numbers of Yiddish speakers had been settling in the Holy Land
since the fifteenth century, but for Zionists intent on establishing a homeland safe from increasingly intense waves of Russian pogroms, Yiddish
represented "diaspora and feebleness." The revival of the Hebrew language, representing a "wild, strong, muscular and independent" self-
image, became a core element of Zionism. During Israel's pre-statehood
period, Hebrew-language extremists used propaganda, intimidation, and
even violence to delegitimize the use of Yiddish. New immigrants were
required to stop using it in public meetings within two years of arrival.
A year after independence, the government banned Yiddish theater and
periodicals under a law controlling the use of "foreign languages." The
state began to take a more tolerant attitude toward Yiddish in the 1950s,
and a large influx of speakers from the Soviet Union in the 1980s had a

further salutary effect. Nevertheless, the language in which Shira Gorshman wrote was never widely embraced in modern Israel.

In the *Jerusalem Post* interview with Fishkoff, Gorshman states, "Yiddish is the real holy tongue of the Jewish people." This comment is characteristic of her personal ethos. Traditionally, Hebrew was the liturgical language of Judaism, but it was not the language that Eastern European Jews used in their everyday lives. Gorshman does not seem to have been religiously observant, but she did internalize and act upon the Jewish cultural values of pursuing justice and helping the less fortunate. These values were shared by the Jewish socialists who strove to make Eastern Europe a place where Jews could enjoy the same rights as non-Jews. The preferred language of these proponents of "here-ness" was Yiddish, the millennium-old vernacular of the Ashkenazi people. Gorshman remained an idealist throughout her long and extraordinary life, and it is only fitting that when she expressed her ideals through her writing, she did so in Yiddish.

by Edith Otchin McCrea

ACKNOWLEDGMENTS

I would like to express my deepest gratitude to the following people and groups for their help and support on this project: my good friend, first Yiddish teacher, and *landsman* David Forman; the YIVO and Workers Circle Yiddish teachers with whom I have studied, including (but not limited to) Miriam Trinh, Vera Szabó, and Anna Fishman Gonshor; translator Faith Jones, who provided me with many valuable resources on Shira Gorshman as well as much-appreciated encouragement; the Yiddish Book Center 2022–23 Translation Fellowship Program, including academic director Mindl Cohen, Translation and Education Program manager Margaret Frothingham, and workshop leaders Daniel Hahn, Aviya Kushner, and Julia Sanches; my extraordinarily helpful, supportive, and enthusiastic YBC Translation Fellowship mentor Ellen Cassedy; my cohort of YBC Translation Fellows, viz., Alona Bach, David Brenner, Ada Hetko, Vardit Lightstone, Jonah Lubin, Devin Naar, Roberta Newman, Jacob Romm, and Julia Zarankin; the late Frieda Johles Forman, who graciously shared her knowledge of Shira Gorshman with me by telephone and through the mail; Yelena Shmuelson, who generously acted as an intermediary between me and Gorshman's granddaughter in Russia; the international scholars of the online research group Yidforsh, who are always willing to share their remarkable and diverse expertise; the ever-patient Amy Farranto, acquisitions editor at Northern Illinois University Press; and my friend and longtime neighbor Slava Paperno, who was kind enough to give me his feedback. Finally, I thank my husband, Larry McCrea, for all his encouragement, suggestions, and technical support.

Edith Otchin McCrea

GLOSSARY

akkreditiv Russian for "letter of credit." In the Soviet Union there were no personal checks. An *akkreditiv* could be purchased at any bank or savings institution. The buyer made it out to a particular recipient, who could cash it only upon presentation of an internal passport.

Akselrod, Zelik The poet Zelik Akselrod (1904–1941) was born in Molodechno, Belarus, and was the younger brother of artist Meyer Akselrod (the model for the "blond artist" in the novel). He was one of several Belorussian writers at the First All-Union Congress of Soviet Writers in 1934; all the rest were killed in the purges of 1937–38. He was arrested in May 1941 for "Jewish nationalism" and executed by the secret police on June 26, 1941.

aliyah Hebrew for "ascension." Denotes the modern immigration of Jews into Palestine/Israel.

aveyres Sins, transgressions.

babka A sweetened bread, often braided and containing raisins or cinnamon.

Babruysk A city in central Belarus.

Ben-Gurion David Ben-Gurion (1886–1973) was a leader in the Poale Zion Party in Ottoman-occupied Palestine. After World War I, he headed the right (anti-communist) faction of the party. He oversaw the successful struggle for Israeli independence and led the new country during the 1948 Arab–Israeli war. He served as prime minister and/or minister of defense almost continuously until 1963.

bes medresh Prayer house, religious study house, or small synagogue.

Borech Yiddish name derived from the Hebrew word *baruch,* meaning "blessed."

bream In Yiddish, Russian, and Polish, *leshtch.* A European freshwater fish.

calves' foot jelly A traditional Ashkenazi delicacy of aspic made from calves' hooves.

chadesh yameinu k'kedem Hebrew, "renew our days as of old." From Lamentations 5:21: "Take us back, O Lord, to Yourself,/And let us come back;/Renew our days as of old!"

challah Egg bread, often braided, traditionally served on the Sabbath and on holidays and other festive occasions.

Cheboksary Port city on the Volga River between Nizhny Novgorod and Kazan. Capital of Chuvashia, the home of the Turkic-speaking Chuvash people. Part of Russia since 1551.

Chebotarka Agricultural Institute Also referred to as the Chebotarka Jewish Agricultural Institute, this school, established in the 1930s, was located in the village of Chebotarka, near Saki, Crimea. In 1956 it merged with the Pribezhnoye Agricultural College near Yevpatoria, and the Chebotarka location was abandoned.

chuppah Traditional canopy used in the Jewish marriage ceremony.

collective farm Russian *kolkhoz,* acronym for *kollektivnoye khozyastvo* (collective farm). In the Soviet Union, a village of farmers living in separate family homes but working the land collectively according to socialist principles.

commercial store Beginning in 1929, the Soviet government ran stores that functioned outside the national rationing system. The goods in these "commercial stores" were higher in quality and price than those sold at the "closed distribution stores" that workers could access through their jobs.

communard; commune In Yiddish, *komunar* and *komune,* respectively. The terms were imported into Yiddish from the French and originally referred to the Paris Commune, a short-lived revolutionary government established in March 1871 by an uprising of the Paris National Guard. In the novel, Gorshman uses the term *komune* primarily for the farm in Soviet Crimea where Hanah works. This enterprise features collective housing, shared property, and equally divided profits. (When referring to a typical Soviet collective farm on which workers live in family units and receive wages from the state, Gorshman uses the word *kolkhoz.*)

Der Emes Yiddish for "The Truth." A Yiddish publishing house in Moscow which published Shira Gorshman's first story collection, *Der koyech fun lebn* (The Power of Life), in 1948. In November of that year, it was shut down, along with all other Yiddish publishers and Jewish cultural institutions in the Soviet Union. (*Der Emes* was also the name of a Yiddish daily newspaper published in the Soviet Union between 1918 and 1938.)

"devil's skin" Gorshman uses the Russian *chortova kozha* (demon's/devil's skin). This appears to be a borrowing from the French *peau de diable,* another name for moleskin, a heavy cotton fabric used in cold-weather outerwear.

Dimyashkino An apparently fictitious place-name.

Divine Presence Yiddish *shchineh,* Hebrew *shechinah,* "dwelling" or "presence," usually referring to the presence of God in the world. Can also refer to the divine feminine aspect of God.

"Dizzy with Success" An article by Joseph Stalin that appeared in *Pravda* on March 2, 1930. It called for a temporary halt to forced agricultural collectivization, which had been occurring on a massive scale since the fall of 1929.

Dobrushin Yechezkel Dobrushin (1883–1953) was a Soviet Jewish poet, playwright, literary critic, and scholar. In the late 1920s he visited a number of Jewish agricultural settlements in Crimea, collecting material for theatrical sketches and plays.

dreidel Four-sided spinning top with a different Hebrew letter on each side, used in a game of chance traditionally played during the festival of Hanukah.

Eighth of March On International Women's Day, March 8 (Gregorian calendar) or February 24 (Julian calendar) of 1917, women textile workers in Petrograd began a demonstration that launched the February Revolution. A week later, Tsar Nicholas II abdicated and the provisional government granted women the vote. The Soviets (who adopted the Gregorian calendar) declared the date a national holiday. It is still celebrated in post-Soviet Russia.

Elkind, Mendel Menachem "Mendel" Elkind (1894–1938) was a founding member of the Zionist labor brigade Gdud HaAvodah in British Mandate Palestine. Elkind became the leader of the communist faction within Gdud, which was expelled in 1926. In 1927 he led his supporters to Soviet Crimea, where they founded the Jewish agricultural commune Vojo Nova. He was the commune's first chairman but was removed and later executed by Stalin's regime. He was posthumously rehabilitated in 1958.

everlasting flowers Flowers of the genus *Helichrysum,* comprising about six hundred species in the sunflower family. Several species are popular as dried flowers because they maintain their original color and shape when dried young.

"factotum" Gorshman uses the word *yednitse* in quotation marks. This seems to be an invented word, a feminine noun possibly based on *yederer* (everybody, anybody) or *yedneral* (general).

Father Goriot Lead character in *Père Goriot,* a French novel by Honoré de Balzac published in 1835. It was translated into Russian by Fyodor Dostoyevsky.

Gdudniks Members of Gdud HaAvodah (the Work Brigade), a Zionist labor brigade in 1920s British Mandate Palestine, officially called the Joseph Trumpeldor Labor and Defense Battalion.

Gemara A collection of Hebrew writings on the Mishnah (ancient compilation of Jewish oral traditions).

Gorky Park A large public park near the center of Moscow, officially called the Gorky Central Park of Culture and Leisure.

government wedding palace Gorshman uses the term *zags-palats* (ZAGS palace). ZAGS is a Russian acronym for "Civil Recording Hall." Early Soviet weddings were drab affairs; in response to public dissatisfaction, the government repurposed former palaces and manor houses into wedding halls.

groschen Colloquial term for small-denomination coins used in various European countries.

Gurshteyn Aron Gurshteyn (1895–1941) was a journalist, editor, professor, and critic. He served in the Red Army during the Revolution of 1917, and rejoined immediately after the German attack on the Soviet Union in June 1941. He was killed in action in the fall of that year.

Halkin Shmuel Halkin (1897–1960) wrote lyric poetry and plays and translated many writers (including Shakespeare) into Yiddish. During World War II, he was a member of the Jewish Antifascist Committee, thirteen of whose leaders were executed in 1952. Halkin, however, suffered a heart attack after his arrest and thus (ironically) avoided execution.

halvah Confection of sweetened sesame paste originating in the Middle East.

hare sorrel One of several common names for *Oxalis acetosella*, a flowering plant widespread in parts of Asia and Europe.

hectare A unit of area used mainly for measuring land. One hectare contains slightly less than 2.5 acres.

Hofshteyn Dovid Hofshteyn (1889–1952), a poet, prose writer, and playwright, was born near Kiev and began publishing Yiddish poems in 1917. He worked in Moscow from 1920 to 1924 as an editor and chair of the Sholem Aleichem Theatre Group. An activist in the Jewish Antifascist Committee, he was the first of its leaders to be imprisoned for "anti-Soviet activities" in 1948 and was among those executed on August 12, 1952. He was posthumously rehabilitated in 1958, and a collection of his poems was published in Russian translation the same year.

hospodi! Russian equivalent of "good Lord!" The first letter is a "g" but is often pronounced more like an "h."

Institute of Art The Moscow State Academic Art Institute. Mendel Gorshman taught there as a lecturer between 1937 and 1941.

Jabahi Seemingly a fictitious place-name.

Jacob and Laban In Genesis 29, Laban agrees to marry off his younger daughter, Rachel, to his nephew Jacob in exchange for seven years of work. Jacob does the work, but Laban tricks him into marrying his elder daughter, Leah, instead. Jacob then marries Rachel in exchange for another seven years of work.

Jankoy and Freidorf Jankoy (also transliterated as Dzhankoy or Dzhankoye) is a city in northern Crimea that had a large Jewish population prior to World War II. A nearby Jewish collective farm of the same name was the subject of a popular Yiddish song, "Hey, Dzhankoye!" Freidorf was a Soviet Jewish autonomous region in Crimea established at the beginning of 1931.

Jewish Antifascist Committee (JAC) An organization of Jewish labor leaders and cultural figures established by the Soviet government after the Nazi invasion in 1941. It raised millions of dollars for the war effort from the international Jewish community. After the war, it aided Holocaust survivors and documented fascist atrocities. Shortly after the establishment of the State of Israel in 1948, its members were arrested and, in some cases, tortured. Thirteen were executed on August 12, 1952 (the so-called Night of the Murdered Poets); all were posthumously rehabilitated after Stalin's death.

kapoteh A long coat traditionally worn by Jewish men.

Karahurt This village name appears to be fictitious; there is, however, a village near Odessa (not on the Crimean peninsula) called Karakurt.

Kazansky Railway Station Railway station in Moscow with lines heading east along the Trans-Siberian Railway to Kazan, Yekaterinburg, and points beyond, and southeast to Ryazan.

Kerch A city on the far eastern side of the Crimean peninsula, 268.8 km (167 miles) east of Saki.

Kharik Izi Kharik (1898–1937) was one of the most important Soviet Yiddish writers of his era. Born in Zembin, Belarus, he began publishing Yiddish poetry as a teenager. After moving to Moscow, he became an official Soviet writer and editor and received high acclaim. In 1937, at the peak of his career, he was arrested and later killed in the Stalinist purges. He was posthumously rehabilitated after Stalin's death.

khudozhnik Russian for "artist."

kichlach Plural of Yiddish *kichel,* a cookie or sweet biscuit.

Koksheyer Forest This name appears to be fictitious.

kolkhoz See **collective farm.**

kopek A monetary unit of Imperial Russia and, later, Soviet Russia and some other Soviet countries, worth one hundredth of a ruble.

Kostroma Russian city located 322 km (about 200 miles) northeast of Moscow.

Kovno Russian name for the city now known as Kaunas in south-central Lithuania. Gorshman grew up in the shtetl of Krok (Lithuanian, Krakės), 95 kilometers (59 miles) north of the city.

kreplach Plural of Yiddish *krepel,* a filled dumpling.

Kratovo A district with many summer homes (dachas) located 40 km (25 miles) southeast of central Moscow.

Kuibyshev City in southwest Russia, renamed by the Soviets for a prominent Bolshevik, Valerian Vladimirovich Kuibyshev. In 1991 it reverted to its previous name, Samara.

kulak Russian for "fist" or "tightfisted." Originally an Imperial Russian colloquial word for landowning former serfs. In the Soviet Union, it initially referred to peasants who were reluctant to provide grain to the Bolsheviks during the Revolution. Eventually, any peasant perceived as wealthy or anti-nationalist was branded a kulak. Stalin's first Five-Year Plan included a program of "dekulakization," under which millions of farmers were deported or imprisoned and their lands seized.

Kuprianov, Nikolai Nikolaevich Kuprianov (1894–1933), a modernist painter and printmaker, was born in Włocławek (then a part of Prussia) but moved to St. Petersburg at age seven. At eighteen he graduated from the St. Petersburg workshop school of artist and philanthropist Maria Klavdievna Tenisheva (1858–1928). From 1918 to 1920 he taught at the Higher Institute of Photography and Phototechnique in Petrograd. He then worked in Kostroma until 1922, when he moved to Moscow and taught at Vkhutemas until 1930. He died in a swimming accident in 1933.

Kursk Railway Station Railway terminal in Moscow with a line that goes to Crimea.

kushat! Russian for "eat!"

Kushnirov Arn (Aaron) Kushnirov (1890–1949) was a prolific writer of Yiddish poetry and prose and an editor of numerous Yiddish periodicals. From 1934 to 1941, he co-edited the literary almanac *Sovetish: Literarisher Almanakh* (In the Soviet Manner: Literary Almanac).

Kvitko, Leyb Born to humble beginnings in Holoskiv, Ukraine, Leyb Kvito (ca. 1890–1952) was renowned for his Yiddish and Russian children's poetry. He became Gorshman's literary mentor in the 1930s. At the start of World War II, he joined the Jewish Antifascist Committee; this affiliation led to his arrest in 1949. He was brutally treated for three years before being formally charged, and was executed with twelve other JAC members on August 12, 1952. He was rehabilitated in 1955.

lapti Traditional northeast European footwear made of woven bast fibers.

l'chaim! Hebrew for "to life!" A common Jewish toast.

Literaturartigkeit A German compound word meaning "literariness" or "literary merit." In the context of the novel, Meyer Viner seems to be implying that Hanah's writing lacks literary polish.

Lyublino A district in southeastern Moscow.

mamaloshen A term of endearment for the Yiddish language. Significantly, the first part of the compound word is Germanic, while the second is Hebrew-derived.

Madame Rothschild The Jewish Rothschild family rose to prominence in banking in eighteenth-century Germany. By the nineteenth century, they had the largest private fortune in the world and their surname was synonymous with "wealthy Jew."

Mar-Fasad Mar-Fasad appears to be a fictitious place-name. During World War II, however, Gorshman and her family were evacuated to Mariinsky Posad, a town on the right bank of the Volga River in Chuvashia.

Maryina Roshcha Russian for "Mary's Grove." A district in north-central Moscow. A two-story wooden synagogue was built there in 1927. It housed a seminary, a kosher kitchen, a school, a study center, and other community institutions.

Maslovka Street Possibly Lower Maslovka Street (Russian: Ulitsa Nizhnyaya Maslovka), located in northwest Moscow near the Maryina Roshcha district.

model school In 1931, as part of a major restructuring of education, the Soviet government established "model schools" as showcases of achievement. There were ten in Moscow, of which the most famous was Model School 25, whose students included Stalin's daughter. In 1937 a campaign against school elitism resulted in the closure of all model schools.

Moscow Belarusskaya Railway Station A railway station in central Moscow with lines running west to Smolensk and Minsk in Belarus.

MOSKh Russian acronym for the Moscow Association of Soviet Artists.

Moyshe Rabeynu "Moses, Our Teacher," an honorific name for the prophet Moses, who led the children of Israel across the desert to the Promised Land.

"night patrol" The Soviet police enlisted civilians to help prevent crime. Strategies included neighborhood constables, citizens' "night patrols," and voluntary "police helper societies."

nikudah A dot or other small mark below, above, or beside a Hebrew consonant, indicating a vowel sound.

no Evil Eye A part-Yiddish, part-Hebrew expression, *keyn ayin hara*, often shortened to *kinehora*. Traditional formula to ward off the bad luck caused by saying something positive, similar to the English "knock on wood."

November holidays On October 25, 1917, by the Julian calendar, the Bolsheviks seized power, initiating the October Revolution. In 1918, the Soviet government adopted the Gregorian calendar, resulting in a "loss" of thirteen days. Thereafter, the anniversary of the Revolution was celebrated on November 7th. The holiday was later expanded to include November 8th as well.

Ozet (also OZET) Russian acronym for "Society for Settling Toiling Jews on the Land," a Soviet agency that helped Jews transition from living in shtetls and cities to becoming agricultural workers.

passport In 1932, the Soviet Union established a unified passport system consisting of an internal travel visa that also identified the bearer's place of residence. The system was used to remove "persons not engaged in socially useful work" from towns and cities and to "cleanse" those areas of "hiding kulaks, criminals, and other antisocial elements."

Penza City located 625 km (388 miles) southeast of Moscow.

Perlovka A neighborhood about 18 km (11 miles) northeast of central Moscow.

pfeffernusse German, "peppernuts," a kind of cookie containing pepper and other spices. Gorshman uses the Yiddish, *feferne kichlach* (pepper cookies).

pirezhke; pirozhki The Ukrainian and Russian names, respectively, for a baked or fried bun with a filling such as meat, vegetables, eggs, or jam. Gorshman uses the Ukrainian term when Hanah is riding the train through Ukraine and the Russian term when she is living in Moscow.

prelest Russian for "charming" or "delightful."

Primus stove A portable stove that burns pressurized kerosene.

professional mourner in ancient times The practice of hiring professional mourners has been documented in the ancient Middle East, Egypt, Greece, Rome, and China.

"Renew my days as before" Lamentations 5:21, "Take us back, O Lord, to Yourself,/ And let us come back;/Renew our days as of old!"

rest day In 1929, to improve efficiency and discourage religious worship, the Soviet government eliminated the traditional Christian Sunday rest day and instituted a "continuous workweek," with workers randomly assigned to staggered five-day shifts. Because of widespread dissatisfaction, in 1931 the government established a universal rest day every six days. In 1940, the seven-day calendar was reinstated.

retsueh Leather strap traditionally wrapped around the arm by a pious male Jew during prayer, attached to a small leather box containing Torah verses.

ritual water Jewish law dictates that upon waking, a person must pour water on his or her hands and recite the Netilat Yadayim (Hebrew, "taking up of the hands") prayer. In Yiddish this ritual is referred to as "fingernail water" *(negel vaser)*.

Rogozheska Possibly a reference to Rogozhsky Street, also called Rogozhsky Val Street, located approximately 4.5 km (about 2.8 miles) southeast of the Kremlin.

rossel A sour fermented beet broth used in borscht.

Ryazan A city located 196 km (122 miles) southeast of Moscow.

Sabantoy Road Sabantoy (or Sabantuy) means Feast of the Plough in Tatar and is the name of a Tatar holiday celebrating the coming of spring.

Saki The village of Saki in western Crimea is situated on Lake Saki, whose mud is rich in salts, minerals, lipids, and amino acids. Since the 1820s, the town has been internationally known as a mud therapy health resort. Saki is located about 15 km

(9.3 miles) south of the former Vojo Nova commune, where Gorshman lived in the 1930s.

sarafan Traditional Russian pinafore-style dress.

schlimazel From Yiddish *shlecht mazel,* "bad luck." A chronically unlucky person.

Secret Police Gorshman uses the Russian acronym OGPU (Joint State Political Directorate). In 1923 this organization succeeded the GPU (State Political Directorate) as the Soviet secret police force. It played an important role in Stalin's forced collectivization program, including sending millions of peasants to forced labor camps.

Serpukhov City 99 km (62 miles) south of Moscow. The Moscow–Tula Railway passes through the city.

seven flavors Possibly a reference to the "seven species" in Deuteronomy 8:8, which describes the Holy Land as "a land of wheat, barley, grapes, figs, and pomegranates; a land of oil-yielding olives and honey."

Shabbes The Yiddish pronunciation of the Hebrew word Shabbat (day of rest), from which the English word "Sabbath" derives. The Jewish Sabbath begins at sundown on Friday and ends at sundown on Saturday.

shel rosh Small leather box containing a parchment scroll inscribed with Torah verses that a male Jew traditionally wears on his forehead during prayers.

Short Friday The Friday before the winter solstice is the shortest one of the year, giving the traditional Jewish housewife the least possible amount of time to prepare for the Sabbath.

Shtern Shtern (Stars) was a Yiddish literary, artistic, and sociopolitical journal published in Minsk between 1925 and 1941. Izi Kharik (the model for the novel's "curly-haired poet") was its editor in chief from around 1926 until his death in 1937.

shtetl Diminutive for the Yiddish word *shtot* (city, town). Formerly, a small town in Eastern Europe with a predominantly Ashkenazi Jewish population. This way of life was destroyed by the Nazi genocide of European Jews in the 1930s and 1940s.

Simferopol City in south-central Crimea; the second-largest city on the peninsula.

smiches Authorization to perform the functions of a rabbi.

sour salt Yiddish, *zoyerzalts.* Another name for citric acid.

Sovinfomburo Abbreviation for the Soviet Information Bureau, a news organization established in 1941 to report on international events, military developments, and day-to-day Soviet life.

stolovaya Russian for "dining room," "dining hall," or "mess hall." (Gorshman renders it in Yiddish as *stolova.*)

Strider: The Story of a Horse Leo Tolstoy started writing the novella *Strider* (Russian, *Kholstmer*) in 1863 but left it unfinished until 1886, when he reworked it and published it as *Strider: The Story of a Horse.* It recounts the life of an altruistic gelding who belongs to several owners and suffers various types of mistreatment. In the end, the old horse is slaughtered and its corpse is left to be eaten by wild animals.

tefillin General term for the small leather boxes containing Torah verses and the leather straps attached to them, worn on the forehead and arm by Jewish men during prayers.

teigel (plural, *teiglach*) Small knots of dough boiled in honey syrup, often served on Rosh HaShanah, the Jewish New Year.

Tevye the Dairyman Protagonist in a series of Yiddish stories by Sholem Aleichem. The stories were the basis for the American musical *Fiddler on the Roof*.

thousand-leaf Russian name for the yarrow plant *(Achillea millefolium)*.

Tomsk A city in Siberia, almost 3,000 km (over 1,800 miles) from Mariinsky Posad, Chuvashia, where Gorshman and her family lived during the war.

Tsaritsino A district of southern Moscow.

tubeteyke Central Asian–style skullcap that was extremely popular throughout the Soviet Union between the 1930s and the 1960s.

Tula City located 193 km (120 miles) south of Moscow.

Tulchyn A city in Vinnytsia Oblast (province) in central Ukraine.

Turandot An opera by Giacomo Puccini, posthumously completed in 1926 by Franco Alfano. It premiered in Milan in 1926 and was first performed in Moscow in 1931 at the Bolshoi Theatre.

Udelnaya A suburb of Moscow 31 km (about 20 miles) southeast of the city's center.

Uman City in Cherkasy Oblast (province), Ukraine, east of Vinnytsia Oblast.

ventilation pane Yiddish, *fortke*, Russian, *forotchka*. A small window in the top part of a larger window that opens independently to provide ventilation in cold weather. Sometimes called a "Russian window" or "ventilation window."

verst A traditional Russian unit of distance equal to approximately 0.66 miles, 3,500 feet, or 1.1 km.

vey iz mir Yiddish for "woe is me."

Victory over Fascism On May 9, 1945, the second German Instrument of Surrender was signed in Britain at the insistence of the Soviet government. May 9 was celebrated as Victory Day throughout the Soviet Union and is still celebrated in post-Soviet Russia.

Viner, Meyer (1893–1941). Born in Kraków, he moved with his family to Austria and attended college in Switzerland. As an editor in Berlin, he met Leyb Kvitko and several other prominent Yiddish writers. Soon after, he began writing in Yiddish, joined the Communist Party, and moved to the Soviet Union, where he worked as a writer, folklorist, and educator. When the Germans attacked, he enlisted in the Moscow Writers Battalion and was killed in action.

Vinnytsia Name of an oblast (province) in central Ukraine, as well as a city that is the administrative center of that oblast.

Vkhutemas Russian acronym for Higher Art and Technical Studios, a Moscow state school founded in 1920 to replace the Moscow Svomas (State Free Art Studios).

Vojo Nova Esperanto for "New Way." The kibbutz-style Jewish commune in western Crimea where Shira Gorshman lived and worked as head of livestock operations between 1929 and 1931.

Volkhonka A street near the center of Moscow that has existed under various names throughout the city's history. The name Volkhonka, probably after a nearby stream, has been in use only since the twentieth century.

White Russia In Yiddish, Vaysrusland. The Yiddish name for Belarus.

"The Woman Mrs. Hanah" In Hebrew, "HaIsha Marat Hanah." A story by Y. L. Peretz published in 1896 about a widow who is cheated out of her inheritance by her ruthless brother-in-law thanks to the Russian Empire's unfair inheritance laws.

yarmulke Skullcap traditionally worn by Jewish men.

Yevpatoria A city in western Crimea located about 22 km (13.7 miles) southwest of the former Vojo Nova commune. First settled by the Greeks around 500 BCE, it was a settlement of the Khazars between the seventh and tenth centuries, was held by various Central Asian peoples, and was an important center of the Crimean Khanate (1441–1783). In 1783 it was captured by the Russian Empire along with the rest of Crimea.

Zay Greyt! In Yiddish, *Be Ready!* A Yiddish-language Soviet journal for children published in Kharkov. It was edited from 1926 to 1929 by Gorshman's mentor, Leyb Kvitko.

Zhmerynka City in Vinnytsia Oblast (province), central Ukraine.

NOTES

Part I

4   *"Tsiperke Bril"* Tsiporah Bril, who was born in 1907 in Podolia Gubernia, was one of the founders of the Vojo Nova commune. She was one of twenty-seven members and former members of Vojo Nova arrested in 1938 as part of an "operation to eliminate the counterrevolutionary spy underground of the [Jewish] Diaspora colony." She was sentenced to five years in a prison camp and was rehabilitated in 1956. Mikhail Mitsel, "The Final Chapter: Agro-Joint Workers—Victims of the Great Terror," *East European Jewish Affairs* 39, no. 1 (April 2009): 79–99, https://doi.org/10.1080/13501670902750303.

4   *"Internationalism"* "Internationalism" was a concept central to Soviet ideology. Under Stalin, it denoted solidarity among the various groups in the Soviet Union's multiethnic states. By contrast, "Jewish nationalism" connoted loyalty to a Jewish state and, hence, disloyalty to the Soviet Union. Gleb J. Albert, "International Solidarity With(out) World Revolution: The Transformation of 'Internationalism' in Early Soviet Society," *Monde(s)* 2016/2, no. 10 (2016): 33–50, https://shs.cairn.info/journal-mondes-2016-2-page-33?lang=en&tab=texte-integral.

5   *Another good reason to consider him her contemporary* Gorshman never follows up on this statement.

13   *"Go live in Vinnytsia"* Vinnytsia, a city in central Ukraine, was in the Pale of Settlement, the region to which most Russian Jews were confined between 1793 and 1917. By suggesting that the two cowherds go back to the former Pale and take up a traditional Jewish occupation, Hanah is implying that they are unqualified to be included among the "new Soviet Jews" working in agriculture.

14 *"Future Humanity"* The Soviet Union promoted the archetype of the New Soviet Man, who was (among other positive traits) ready to sacrifice himself for society and future generations. Maja Soboleva, "The Concept of the 'New Soviet Man' and Its Short History," *Canadian-American Slavic Studies* 51 (2017): 64–85, https://brill.com/view/journals/css/51/1/article-p64_4.xml.

23 *"sat on a low chair"* The granny in the story may sit on a low chair because she is in mourning for her sheep. In Judaism, during the weeklong period following the death of a close relative, mourners are required to sit on low stools or on the floor.

26 *Fyodor Petrovich* In Russian, addressing a person by his or her first name and patronymic indicates formality. This form of address is not typically used in Yiddish. When Gorshman uses first names and patronymics in the novel, it may indicate that the characters in question are conversing in Russian rather than Yiddish, and/or have a relatively formal relationship.

28 *"From then on I lived with my grandparents"* For information on Shira Gorshman's early childhood, see the Afterword.

30 *"Atop the attic sleeps"* "Atop the Attic Sleeps the Roof" ("Oyfn boydem shloft der dach") is a Yiddish song with words by Berl Shafir (1876–1922) and music by Perets Hirshbein (1880–1948). An early version was featured in Shafir's play *Avreml der shuster* (Abraham the Shoemaker) in 1910. A later version was published by M. Kipnis in 1918. "Oyfn boydem shloft der dakh," the Yosl and Chana Mlotek Yiddish Song Collection, accessed September 19, 2024, https://yiddishsongs.org/oyfn-boydem-shloft-der-dakh.

31 *"how many bears just dropped dead"* Yiddish, Ukrainian, Polish, and possibly other Eastern European languages share the expression "A bear/animal just died in the forest," used in reaction to an unexpected piece of good news or to someone doing something uncharacteristically good. My deepest thanks to David Shafir, David Braun, Karolina Szymaniak, and Yuri Zakon of the online Yiddish research forum Yidforsh for making me aware of this expression.

31 *the familiar du* I added this sentence, and the one a few lines later ("She was still addressing him as *ir"*), both of which are obviously unnecessary in Yiddish. The rest of Hanah and Nehemyah's conversation about the use of the informal *du* is a direct translation from the Yiddish.

33 *giant baking trough* Silos are used to ferment and store grain. In order for the grain to ferment without spoiling, the silos must be packed completely full and airtight. Auguste Goffart, *The Ensilage of Maize and Other Green Fodder Crops,* trans. J. B. Brown (New York: J. B. Brown, 1879), 23–35, https://archive.org/details/ensilageofmaizeo00goff/mode/2up.

35 *"discover you're a father"* In Yiddish, "Nisht getracht, nisht gedacht, far a taten dich gemacht" (roughly, "Unthinkable, it shouldn't happen, that someone has made you a father"). I have not been able to find any other examples of this saying.

38 *"peasants"* The Yiddish word *poyerim* (singular, *poyer),* meaning "peasant" or "farmer," often has a negative connotation. Here, however, Hanah seems to be using it in a complimentary way to refer to Jews in well-established Crimean agricultural colonies like Jankoy and Freidorf.

39 *"Never stand up when you can sit down"* The saying "Never stand up when you can sit down" seems to be from Winston Churchill: "[I attribute my success to] [e]conomy of effort. Never stand up when you can sit down, and never sit down when you can lie down." British journalist Paul Johnson dates the quote to 1946 (sixteen years after Elkind utters it here). Jonathan Foreman, "Winston Churchill, Distilled," International Churchill Society, December 11, 2009, https://winstonchurchill.org/resources/in-the-media/churchill-in-the-news/winston-churchill-distilled/.

40 *"three different women"* Mendel Elkind was married to Maria (Miriam) Elkind (1898–1969) and had three sons with her (Uri, Eli, and Boris). He apparently also had at least one child out of wedlock, with a woman named Miriam Kleiman. Their daughter, Dina Kleiman, was killed at age thirteen in March 1942 by Nazi "punishers," along with seven other children and two women who had remained at Vojo Nova after it was evacuated. Yakov Pasik, "Commune 'Vojo Nova': New Way" [in Russian], Jewish Agricultural Colonies of the South of Ukraine and Crimea, accessed March 3, 2023, https://evkol.ucoz.com/vojo_nova.htm.

41 *"two in a cage cost double"* In Yiddish, "Beser eyn foygel oyfn tsvaygel, eyder tsvey in shtaygel" (literally, "Better one bird on the branch than two in a cage"). Gorshman uses this rhyming couplet twice in the novel, but I have not been able to identify it as a traditional Yiddish proverb.

Part II

46 *in the fall of 1930* In the original, Gorshman writes, "One night in the summer of 1930," but the novel opens in late summer, and Elkind's removal occurs at least several weeks later. According to historian Yakov Pasik, Elkind was removed as chairman in March 1931, and a criminal case was initiated against him on suspicion of "negligence and inaction." Yakov Pasik, "Commune 'Vojo Nova': New Way" [in Russian], Jewish Agricultural Colonies of the South of Ukraine and Crimea, accessed March 3, 2023, https://evkol.ucoz.com/vojo_nova.htm.

47 *"Get down!"* Gorshman uses the Russian imperatives for "Halt!" *(Stoi!)* and "Get down!" *(Slezay!)*.

48 *"put salt on his tail"* A joking reference to the folk belief, once common throughout much of Europe and North America, that sprinkling salt on a bird's tail will render it flightless.

52 *another man* Gorshman does not name the man who replaced Mendel Elkind as chairman of Vojo Nova. A document reproduced by Pasik, however, reads in part, "Signed by the chairman, Vulf Sheveleyevich Pushinsky (born 1888, home educat[ed], main profession—hatmaker, party member since 1919 . . . , who headed the commune [Vojo Nova] in the summer of 1931)." Pasik, "Commune Vojo Nova'."

58 *Zagatzerno Grain Elevator* Gorshman does not use the term "grain elevator" here; she merely says "Zagatzerno." From the context, it appears she is describing a grain elevator (a storage facility for grain, usually located near a railway line). There was a Zagatzerno Grain Elevator in Soviet Kazakhstan, but I have not found one by that name in Crimea. Dana Salpina, "Management of Industrial Brownfields in the Context of the Post-Socialist Reality: The Case Study of Kostanay" (master's thesis, University of Padua, 2015–16).

61 *"mosquito netting"* Here Gorshman writes (somewhat cryptically): "Vu hostu genumen akrikhin far der marlieh?" (Where did you get Akrikhin for the netting?) Akrikhin is the name of a Moscow-based pharmaceutical company founded in 1936. It is also the name of the malaria drug that was the company's first product. "Our History," Akrikhin, https://akrikhin.com/about/history.php.

63 *"run off to my Uncle Hirshe"* This seems to be an allusion to Gorshman's short story "Hanakeh," in which nine-year-old Hanah quarrels with her grandmother, runs off to visit her uncle Hirshe (not to be confused with Hanah's stepfather Hirshe in the novel) and aunt Malke at their mill, swims in the river with her cousin Blyumke, and eats lunch with the family. Shira Gorshman, "Hanakeh" [in Yiddish], in *Oysdoyer* (Tel Aviv: Farlag Yisroel-Bukh, 1992), 17–22.

66   *"on this ni-i-ight"* This seems to be a parody of the Four Questions traditionally recited at the Passover seder.

66   *"the hungry shall be satisfied"* Possibly an allusion to Psalm 107:19, "For He satisfies the thirsty and fills the hungry with good things."

67   *"I Go Out on My Balcony"* "I Go Out on My Balcony" ("Ikh gey aroys oyfn ganikl") is a traditional Yiddish song, also called "Oyfn ganikl" (On the Balcony) or "A lid fun a feygele" (A Song of a Little Bird). It was published in 1912 by the St. Petersburg Society for Jewish Music. "Little Star, Little Star, Herald of Blue" ("Shterndel, shterndel, bloyer shtafeteleh") is a song by Vilna-born poet Moyshe Kulbak (1896–1937), published by M. Kipnis in 1912. The Yosl and Chana Mlotek Yiddish Song Collection at the Workers Circle, https://yiddishsongs.org; University of Pennsylvania Library's Robert and Molly Freedman Jewish Sound Archive, https://www.library.upenn.edu/collections/notable/freedman.

72   *Pereleh* This is the first time one of Hanah's daughters is mentioned by name. Gorshman clearly states here that Pereleh is the eldest. Early in part 3, the middle daughter is identified as Beylke or Beylkeleh, and the youngest as Reyzeleh. Later in the book, Gorshman inadvertently switches the names of the eldest and second-eldest daughters. For the sake of consistency, I always refer to the eldest daughter as Pereleh and the second as Beylke or Beylkeleh.

73   *lay down to sleep* Readers may notice some inconsistencies between the end of part 2 and the beginning of part 3. In the previous (1984) edition of *Hanah's Sheep and Cattle,* part 2 ends as follows: "When the children had finished drinking their tea, Nehemyah spread some newspapers on the floor. On the newspapers he threw some old overcoats. Hanah laid down the little pillows that she had brought, and she also spread a bedsheet over the coats. The children fell asleep, as it seemed to her, before their little heads touched the pillows. Nehemyah made another sleeping place on a worn-out sofa. But even if the sofa had been soft and the springs had not bounced, Hanah would not have been able to sleep. Nehemyah, however, did indeed fall asleep, and deeply asleep." Shira Gorshman, *Hanahs shof un rinder* [in Yiddish], in *Yomtev in mitn vokh* (Moscow: Soviet Pisatel, 1984), 73.

Part III

77   *Arbat Street* Arbat Street in central Moscow has existed since at least the fifteenth century. In the early twentieth century it was inhabited mainly by artists, academics, and other middle-class residents. At the western end, on the site of today's Smolenskaya Square, was a large market called Smolensky Rynok. Jessica Carattiero, "Arbat: Moscow's Cultural Heart," Liden & Denz Intercultural Institute of Languages, updated March 17, 2015, https://lidenz.com/arbat-moscows-cultural-heart.

78   *"Nye prokhaditye mimo"* A more literal translation of the Russian would be "Don't pass by! Molds for pastries, you'll lick your fingers!"

86   *curly hair* The curly-haired poet is Izi Kharik (1898–1937), who is mentioned by name a little later in part 3. The blond artist's brother is Zelik Akselrod (1904–1941); the blond artist himself is modeled on Meyer Akselrod (1902–1970).

88   *"I've never been"* In the 1993 edition (but not the earlier editions), Gorshman follows Makar's paradoxical statement with this cryptic passage: "She immediately remembered how, when Borech Goldstein and Tsalik had come to the 'Via Nova' commune, she had asked them if they would need a place to stay, and they had answered in unison: 'The place we'll be staying is the place we came from.'" I have omitted this passage because no characters named Borech Goldstein or Tsalik appear elsewhere in the book, and

I have been unable to identify them. (Interestingly, this passage is the only place in the novel where Gorshman refers to Vojo Nova by name.)

100   *"postareven"* Postaraven is a Yiddishized infinitive of the Russian *postaret'* (to try). *Kvartir* is close to the Russian word *kvartira* (apartment). I have left these words untranslated, and added "I mean, I'll try to find an apartment," to convey how flustered Nehemyah seems to be here.

101   *an angel flicks an infant* According to the Talmud (Niddah 30b, verses 21–25), a child learns the entire Torah while inside its mother's womb. At the moment of birth, an angel appears, makes the child promise to live a righteous life, and then slaps the youngster on the mouth, causing it to forget all it has learned. In Ashkenazi folk tradition, the angel instead gives the child a flick on the nose, which is said to explain the existence of the philtrum, or furrow, under the human nose. Here, Gorshman seems to be reinterpreting the tradition so that the angel's flick confers good luck upon those who receive it. "The William Davidson Talmud (Koren-Steinsaltz)," Sefaria, accessed September 11, 2024, https://www.sefaria.org/Niddah.30b?lang=bi; "What is the source for the tradition that the philtrum is formed by an angel before birth?," Mi Yodea, modified October 30, 2016, https://judaism.stackexchange.com/questions/29673/what-is-the-source-for-the-tradition-that-the-philtrum-is-formed-by-an-angel-bef.

101   *a bread card* Stalin's drastic economic reforms, including "dekulakization," mass collectivization, and increases in grain exports, led to serious food shortages and distribution problems, and eventually to the worst famine in Soviet history (1931–1933). The government was forced to ration bread, sugar, butter, and other staples. Harry Sherrin, "Why Did the Soviet Union Suffer Chronic Food Shortages?," HistoryHit, updated March 22, 2022, https://www.historyhit.com/why-did-the-soviet-union-suffer-chronic-food-shortages.

105   *a mere six days* Here Gorshman implies that Hanah now comes home only on Sundays, which would mean that she has accepted Yelizaveta Abramovna's invitation to stay with her during the workweek.

116   *"Shimke the Groom married Mineh"* Although Hayaleh reports here that Shimke has married Mineh from the Children's Home, in part 4 we learn that Shimke is now the partner of Hayaleh herself.

118   *"lies in eternal rest"* Gorshman's quotation from chapter 2 of Dickens's *David Copperfield* is significantly shorter that the English original. Presumably Hanah reads the book in translation. A Russian translation of *David Copperfield* by I. I. Vvedensky, who took great liberties with the text, came out in the 1880s, and a "free" Yiddish translation was published in Vilna in 1894. Maurice Friedberg, *Literary Translation in Russia: A Cultural History* (University Park: Pennsylvania State University Press, 1997); Melanie J. Meyers, "'Tsarles Dikens' in the Collections," Center for Jewish History, updated February 12, 2012, https://blog.cjh.org/index.php/2012/02/07/title-page-from-an-1894-version-of-david/.

Part IV

120   *"years of abundance"* The phrases "four lean years" and "seven years of abundance" (in Yiddish, *knapeh fir yorn* and *zibn guteh yorn*, respectively) may be an allusion to Genesis 41, in which Joseph interprets Pharaoh's dreams to mean there will be seven years of abundance followed by seven years of famine. (My deepest gratitude to my husband, Larry McCrea, for suggesting this reading.) There was a severe famine in the Soviet Union between 1930 and 1933, which is generally considered to be the result of disastrous economic policies. Here, however, Gorshman seems to be alluding to the Stalinist purges of 1936–1938.

120 *"full of tears"* In Yiddish, "Vos toyg mir der goldener becher ven er iz ful mit trern?" Gorshman quotes only the first half of this traditional saying.

122 *attended the early shift* In 1930, universal primary school education was introduced in the Soviet Union. Because of the large influx of new students, school days had to be divided into shifts. The youngest pupils started class at 8 a.m. and finished at noon. Alexey Timofeychev, "Here's Why Education in the USSR was Among the Best in the World," *Russia Beyond*, updated July 9, 2018, https://www.rbth.com/history/328721-education-in-the-ussr-the-best.

126 *"International   Friendship"*   The   National   Holocaust   Remembrance   Center states: "In 1935 the commune [Vojo Nova] was transformed into a kolkhoz and renamed 'Druzhba narodov' (Fraternity of Nations)." Yad Vashem, "Voyo Nova," accessed September 18, 2024, https://collections.yadvashem.org/en/untold-stories/community/14621880-voyo-nova.

127 *"splinter in someone else's eye"* A reference to Matthew 7:3 and Luke 6:41: "Why do you see the splinter in your brother's eye, but not notice the log in your own eye?"

132 *"extraordinary virtue"* This quote is a shortened paraphrase of a passage from Dickens's *American Notes* (1842). Presumably Hanah reads it in a Russian translation. "The Haves . . . and the Have Nots: Charles Dickens Describes the Burden of Poor Families," *Charles Dickens Page*, updated June 11, 2022, https://www.charlesdickens.com/haves-havenots.html.

135 *"It will be published"* Gorshman's mentor, Leyb Kvitko, helped her publish her early story "Der mit-eser" ("The Co-Eater"). Gorshman included the story in at least two collections, *33 Noveln* (Warsaw, 1961) and *Oysdoyer* (Tel Aviv, 1992). Faith Jones has translated the story into English under the title "The Parasite." Faith Jones, "Borrowed Shoes," in *Women Writers of Yiddish Literature: Critical Essays,* ed. Rosemary Horowitz (Jefferson, NC: McFarland and Company, 2015), 73; Frieda Johles Forman, "Shira Gorshman," Jewish Women's Archive, accessed September 25, 2024, https://jwa.org/encyclopedia/article/gorshman-shira.

139 *it was no exercise* On June 22, 1941, the Germans invaded Soviet-occupied Lithuania. Lithuanian nationalists immediately launched a rebellion against the Soviets, proclaiming independence on June 23rd and defeating the Soviets by the 27th. Meanwhile, on June 24th, the Germans entered Kovno and Vilna without resistance, and within a week they had taken control of the country. Aided by Lithuanian collaborators, the Germans quickly undertook the mass killing of Jews. Of the approximately 250,000 Jews in Lithuania at that time, only about 40,000 remained alive by the end of the year. They were confined to ghettos and later deported to concentration camps. Arvydas Anušaukas, *Lietuva, 1940–1990* [in Lithuanian] (Vilnius: Lietuvos gyventojų genocido ir rezistencijos centras, 2015); Lorraine Murray, "75th Anniversary of the Lithuanian Holocaust," *Britannica*, accessed September 25, 2024, https://britannica.com/story/75th-anniversary-of-the-lithuanian-holocaust.

149 *"A person decides"* Gorshman renders this Yiddish proverb gender-neutral by phrasing it "A mensch tracht, un got lacht" (A person thinks, and God laughs). It is more commonly phrased "Man tracht, un got lacht" (Man thinks, and God laughs).

158 *"My old friend Tager"* Born in Austro-Hungary, Yoysef Tager (1889–1940?) became a member of Gdud HaAvodah and, later, one of the founders of Vojo Nova. In her short story "Firers . . ." (Leaders . . .), Gorshman counts him among the best workers in Gdud and describes him as "the nearsighted, darkly handsome Yoysef Tager, who saw, with his thick glasses, better than any of the farsighted." Tager was arrested on February 4, 1938. On July 2, 1940, he was sentenced to eight years in prison for participating in an

anti-Soviet nationalist organization. He may have died on a forced march to the notorious Vorkutlag labor camp in the Russian Arctic. (I have added the words "to Vorkuta" to my translation following Gorshman's account in "Leaders . . .") Tager was rehabilitated in 1956. Shira Gorshman, "Firers . . . ," in *Oysdoyer: Dertseylungen, noveln, zikhroynes* (Tel Aviv: Farlag Yisroel-Bukh, 1992); Mikhail Mitsel, "The Final Chapter: Agro-Joint Workers—Victims of the Great Terror," *East European Jewish Affairs* 39, no. 1 (April 2009): 79–99.

158   *Reyzeleh died* In the 1984 version of *Hanah's Sheep and Cattle,* this scene is recounted in slightly more detail: "The doctor from the ward where Reyzeleh was staying said it would be worthwhile to give her an insulin injection, for which a great deal of sugar would be needed. But the hospital had no sugar. Hanah bought some sugar, and the insulin injection was given. Unfortunately, it didn't help Reyzeleh. She grew worse and worse. She completely stopped eating. They fed her artificially, but this didn't help either. At the end of 1942, Reyzeleh died." Shira Gorshman, "Hanahs shof un rinder," in *Yomtev in mitn vokh* (Moscow: Soviet Pisatel, 1984), 151.

Afterword

164   *vast Jewish population* "Modern Jewish History: The Pale of Settlement," Jewish Virtual Library, accessed July 26, 2024, https://www.jewishvirtuallibrary.org/the-pale-of-settlement.

164   *Pale of Settlement* Geoffrey Hosking, *Russia and the Russians: A History* (Cambridge: Belknap Press of Harvard University Press, 2001), 258.

164   *Haskalah* Robert M. Seltzer, *Jewish People, Jewish Thought: The Jewish Experience in History* (New York: Macmillan, 1980), 534, 569, 539–41.

164   *"antisemitism"* Seltzer, *Jewish People, Jewish Thought,* 543, 628–30.

165   *modernized Jews* Seltzer, *Jewish People, Jewish Thought,* 635, 638–39.

165   *First Zionist Congress* Seltzer, *Jewish People, Jewish Thought,* 635–38.

165   *Second Aliyah* Seltzer, *Jewish People, Jewish Thought,* 641.

165   *Third Aliyah* "Immigration to Israel: The Third Aliyah (1919–1923)," Jewish Virtual Library, accessed July 26, 2024, https://www.jewishvirtuallibrary.org/the-third-aliyah-1919-1923.

166   *raised separately* "Kibbutz," *Britannica,* updated July 22, 2024, https://www.britannica.com/topic/kibbutz.

166   *Tsvi-Hirsh "Grigorii" Kushnir* Leonid Shkolnik, "Shira Gorshman" [in Russian], *Yevreysky Zhurnal,* April 10, 2007, www.photokonkurs.com/liebkind/statyi/Ozhen 20.htm.

166   *poresh min-ha-tsibur* Faith Jones, "From Comrade to Scribe," unpublished manuscript, shared with the author on August 5, 2021.

166   *four children together* Shkolnik, "Shira Gorshman."

166   *"hideous display"* Boris Sandler, *Shira Gorshman: Yiddish Writer of Women as Folk Heroes* [in Yiddish], video, 6:22, https://www.youtube.com/watch?v=3oD_WotU04s.

166   *twelve loaves of Sabbath bread* Sandler, *Shira Gorshman,* 10:49.

167   *"thrown to the animals"* Sandler, *Shira Gorshman,* 16:35.

167   *ring on the table* Shira Gorshman, "Hanakeh," in *Oysdoyer: Dertseylungen, noveln, zichroynes* (Tel Aviv: Farlag Yisroel-Buch, 1992), 17.

167   *"under her tutelage"* Sandler, *Shira Gorshman,* 17:55.

167   *"afternoon prayers"* Shira Gorshman, "Fun vanen shtam ich?," in *Oysdoyer,* 8.

168   *subjected to horrific treatment* Louis Stein, "The Exile of the Lithuanian Jews in the Conflagration of the First World War (1914–1918)," in *Lithuania,* ed. Mendel

Sudarksy et al., trans. Judie Goldstein (New York: Jewish Cultural Society, 1951), 89–119, https://jewishgen.org/yizkor/lita/Lit0089.html.

168 *"Jewish literature"* Shkolnik, "Shira Gorshman."

168 *"Grandfather taught me"* Shira Gorshman, "Reyzene kashe," in *Oysdoyer,* 88.

168 *"so cold outside"* Gorshman, "Reyzene kashe," 86–87.

169 *still exists today* David Tidhar, "Dr. Siegfried Lehmann," in vol. 10 of *Encyclopedia of the Founders and Builders of Israel,* 3499–3502, https://www-tidhar-tourolib-org.translate. goog/tidhar/view/10/3499?_x_tr_sl=auto&_x_tr_tl=en&_x_tr_hl=en.

169 *college-level courses* Julijana Andriejauskienė, abstract of "Esther Elyashev and the Idea of the Jewish People's University in Interwar Kaunas," *Lieutovos istorijos metraštis* [Yearbook of Lithuanian History] 2020, no. 2 (2020): 113–23, https://lituanisttika.lt/ content/95503.

169 *father of her children* "Shira Grigorievna Gorshman (Kushnir)," Geni.com, updated April 29, 2022, https://www.geni.com/people/Shira-Gorshman/6000000004006500001.

169 *"already had a child"* P. Mostvoy, *One of the Wandering Stars* [in Russian, trans. Yelena Shmuelson], video (Moscow: CSDF, 1990), https://www.net-film.ru/en/film-9900/.

170 *"full equality"* Walter Laqueur, *A History of Zionism from the French Revolution to the Establishment of the State of Israel* (Toronto: Schocken Books, 2003), 295–97.

170 *"construction of dwellings"* Lev Fruchtman, "Shira Gorshman's Fortune" [in Russian], *Isrageo,* November 18, 2015, https://www.isrageo.com/2015/11/18/Fortu121.

170 *Hayim Nahman Bialik* Sandra Bark, ed., *Beautiful as the Moon, Radiant as the Stars: Jewish Women in Yiddish Stories* (New York: Warner Books, 2003), 290.

170 *"dissolved itself in 1928"* Laqueur, *A History of Zionism,* 296–97.

171 *"expelled from Gdud"* Yakov Pasik, "Commune Vojo Nova': New Way" [in Russian], Jewish Agricultural Colonies of the South of Ukraine and Crimea website, accessed March 3, 2023, https://evkol.ucoz.com/vojo_nova.htm.

171 *Hatskelevich remained in Palestine* "Shira Grigorievna Gorshman (Kushnir)."

171 *Gdud HaAvodah* Pasik, "Commune 'Vojo Nova.'"

171 *"logical mind"* Quoted in Yaacov N. Goldstein, *Jewish Socialists in the United States: The Cahan Debate, 1925–1926* (Brighton: Sussex Academic Press, 1998), 104.

172 *"he spoke more"* Shira Gorshman, "Firers . . . ," in *Oysdoyer,* 104.

172 *with their two sons* Pasik, "Commune 'Vojo Nova.'"

172 *at the end of 1929* Gorshman, "Firers . . . ," 105.

172 *"pinch their pennies"* Gorshman, "Firers . . . ," 104.

173 *each household* Hosking, *Russia and the Russians,* 15–16.

173 *theoretically received* Fedor Belov, *The History of a Soviet Collective Farm* (New York: Frederick A. Prager for Research Program on the USSR, 1955), 82.

173 *it was deferred* Hosking, *Russia and the Russians,* 399.

173 *Paris Commune* "Commune of Paris, 1871," *Britannica,* updated June 28, 2024, https:// www.britannica.com/event/Commune-of-Paris-1871.

174 *"regime's point of view"* Jonathan Dekel-Chen, "New Jews of the Agricultural Kind: A Case of Soviet Interwar Propaganda," *Russian Review* 66, no. 3 (July 2007): 424–50.

174 *"experience of its work"* Pasik, "Commune 'Vojo Nova.'"

174 *"negligence and inaction"* Pasik, "Commune 'Vojo Nova.'"

175 *"returned to the USSR"* Pasik, "Commune 'Vojo Nova.'"

175 *fourteen of them died* Pasik, "Commune 'Vojo Nova.'"

175 *readiness for arrest* Zinovy Beckman, "Shira Gorshman—Mother-in-Law of Inno-kenty Smoktunovsky" [in Russian], June 30, 2012, Proza/ru, https://proza.ru/2012/ 06/30/1477.

176 *"ordinary labor"* Sue Fishkoff, "A Female Perspective on Shtetl, Kibbutz Life," *Jerusalem Post*, January 20, 1995.

176 *"He spoke to me about love"* Frieda Johles Forman and Sue Fishkoff, unpublished audio interview with Shira Gorshman [in Yiddish, Russian, and English], Ashkelon, Israel, 1995.

176 *"Jewish Orphanage in Malakhova"* Fruchtman, "Shira Gorshman's Fortune."

176 *Third International Jewish School-Camp for War Orphans* "Artist Marc Chagall with other teachers and children in a JDC-funded school and camp for war orphans, Photographer unknown 1921/22," Google Arts & Culture, accessed July 29, 2024, https://artsandculture.google.com/asset/artist-marc-chagall-with-other-teachers-and-children-at-a-jdc-funded-school-and-camp-for-war-orphans-photographer-unknown-qAGCS2mc0I-a_g?hl=en.

177 *"recognized in our literature"* Forman and Fishkoff, audio interview.

178 *"what I had written"* Forman and Fishkoff, audio interview.

178 *"Shirkeh the Storyteller"* Sandler, *Shira Gorshman*, 0:36.

178 *"I kept them in my heart"* Fishkoff, "A Female Perspective on Shtetl, Kibbutz Life."

178 *"retold her stories"* Fruchtman, "Shira Gorshman's Fortune."

178 *"Chekhov was my teacher"* Forman and Fishkoff, audio interview.

178 *"richness of their cultural life"* Goldie Morgentaler, "I. L. Peretz's Saints and Sinners," *Tablet*, June 14, 2022, https://www.tabletmag.com/sections/arts-letters/articles/il-peretz-saints-sinners.

179 *"child's perspective"* "Hans Christian Andersen: Danish Author," *Britannica*, updated May 9, 2024, https://www.britannica.com/biography/Hans-Christian-Andersen-Danish-Author.

179 *"exquisite poems for adults"* Shira Gorshman, *Hanabs shof un rinder* (Tel Aviv: Farlag Yisroel-Bukh, 1993), 167.

179 *"Publishing came to a halt"* Faith Jones, "Borrowed Shoes," in *Women Writers of Yiddish Literature: Critical Essays*, ed. Rosemary Horowitz (Jefferson, NC: McFarland & Company, 2015), 76.

179 *removed from the editorial board* "Leyb Kvitko," *Leksikon fun der Nayer Yidisher Literatur*, Congress for Jewish Culture, accessed July 30, 2024, https://congressforjewishculture.org/people/144/Kvitko-Leyb-November-11-1890-August-12-1952.

180 *Supreme Soviet Military Court* Joshua Rubenstein and Vladimir P. Naumov, eds., *Stalin's Secret Pogrom: The Postwar Inquisition of the Jewish Anti-Fascist Committee* (New Haven: Yale University Press, 2001), 50.

180 *disloyal to the Soviet regime* Jones, "From Comrade to Scribe."

180 *"new political situation"* Jones, "Borrowed Shoes," 76.

180 *three possible causes* Jones, "Borrowed Shoes," 79.

181 *"To circumvent censorship"* Fruchtman, "Shira Gorshman's Fortune."

181 *set all her pastoral stories in Crimea* Jones, "From Comrade to Scribe."

182 *"her new surroundings"* Jones, "From Comrade to Scribe."

182 *"mayne Yidishe leyener"* Fruchtman, "Shira Gorshman's Fortune."

183 *"I am your Papa from now on"* Fruchtman, "Shira Gorshman's Fortune."

183 *bibliographic rarity* Fruchtman, "Shira Gorshman's Fortune."

184 *"SHEKEL-MEN"* Beckman, "Shira Gorshman—Mother-in-Law of Innokenty Smoktunovsky."

184 *"a mother and child without a roof"* Fishkoff, "A Female Perspective on Shtetl, Kibbutz Life."

184 *video documentary* Neely Atslan (camera), Danny Matalon (recording), *Derech hadashah: Shira Gorshman hozeret legedud h'avodah* (A New Path: Shira Gorshman

Returns to the Labor Battalion) [in Hebrew], video (Tel Yosef, Israel: Trumpeldor House, 1989), https://youtube.com/watch?v=hmGB8mFkfrE.

185 *never widely embraced in modern Israel* Zach Golden, "How Yiddish Became a 'Foreign Language' in Israel Despite Being Spoken There Since the 1400s," *Forward,* September 11, 2023, https://forward.com/forverts-in-english/560390/how-yiddish-became-foreign-language-israel.

185 *"the real holy tongue of the Jewish people"* Fishkoff, "A Female Perspective on Shtetl, Kibbutz Life."

www.ingramcontent.com/pod-product-compliance
Lightning Source LLC
Chambersburg PA
CBHW031101020726
47495CB00007B/1989